Also by Carolyn Brown

Dear Readers,

About twenty years ago, I wrote a contemporary novel, *Trouble in Paradise*, and ever since then, folks have been asking me about the seven little girls who were in that book. What did the future hold for them? Did they stay around the Paradise, which started out as a brothel during the cattle run days right after the Civil War? I listened, and *Paradise for Christmas* is the first story in the Sisters of Paradise trilogy.

As I write THE END to Ursula and Luna's story, it's not easy to leave the Paradise. I've had so much fun revisiting the old brothel, catching up with everyone, and getting to know Aunt Bernie. They have all taken up a place in my heart, and I've loved having them whispering in my ear for the past several weeks. But I've hugged Ursula and Luna goodbye for now, and Ophelia and Tertia are waiting patiently for their turn to tell me their stories in a few months. That means I will see Ursula and Luna again...maybe at a wedding?

In reality, Spanish Fort is a little ghost town right on the Red River in north central Texas. There isn't a winery or a convenience store, but in my mind, the Paradise is very real, as is the little winery that's been started south of there and the convenience store that Shane and Luna are building. Who knows? Life could come back to the community in the future if folks decide to start moving there.

I hope you all enjoy going back to Spanish Fort, Texas, and to the Paradise as much as I did.

Until next time,

Carolyn Brown

Paradise for

Christmas

CAROLYN BROWN

sourcebooks
casablanca

Published by Sourcebooks Casablanca, an imprint of Sourcebooks
P.O. Box 4410, Naperville, Illinois 60567-4410
(630) 961-3900
sourcebooks.com

Cataloging-in-Publication Data is on file with the Library of Congress.

Printed and bound in Canada.
MBP 10 9 8 7 6 5 4 3 2 1

To all my granddaughters,
Sisters: Patrisha, Isabella, Destiny, Lilybet, Hope.
Sisters: Brandy, Sarah, Kara, Makela, Bethany.
Sisters: Graycyn & Madacyn.

Chapter 1

"Holy…" Ursula was struck so speechless that she couldn't remember what to say next, but she was sure it had to be one of those four-letter words and had nothing to do with angels.

There was Great-Aunt Bernie, sitting on the porch with a cup of coffee in one hand and the leash to her yappy little Chihuahua dog, Pepper, in the other.

"What," Ursula muttered, "the…"

There was no mistaking her elderly aunt with all that curly hair the color of a fire engine. Even just sitting there, she seemed to exude sass and opinions. Ursula was frozen in the driver's seat, and her hands seemed to be glued to the steering wheel. Bernie was supposed to be in Ratliff City, Oklahoma, minding her own little dive bar. She only closed it on Christmas and Easter—never on Thanksgiving—so what was she doing in Spanish Fort, Texas, at the Paradise?

Aunt Bernie waved at her, and Pepper started barking. Ursula raised her hand and waved back, then opened the vehicle door. The Thanksgiving holiday had just taken a hard left turn. The old gal did not have a filter on her mouth, and she was always, always ready to give advice—whether Ursula or any of her six sisters wanted it or not.

"It's about dang time you got here. I been sittin' out here on this porch all morning waitin' on you," Bernie yelled as she pushed herself up from one of a half-dozen rocking chairs lined up across the front porch.

"Dang?" Ursula asked and managed a weak smile.

"Mary Jane says if I'm going to live here, I have to give up swearing, smoking cigars, and drinking bourbon before breakfast," Bernie said with a sigh. "But I figure it's a small price to pay. I eat chocolates instead of smokin' my Swisher Sweets, and I have a little kick of Jameson in my coffee in the afternoon."

She was barely five feet tall with bright red hair and blue eyes set in a bed of wrinkles. Ursula could still smell a faint whiff of Swisher Sweets cigars on her jacket, which meant she hadn't been in Spanish Fort for long. *Bernie's Place*, the name of her bar, was embroidered on her T-shirt, and her cowboy boots looked like they'd spent a good many years drawing up beer and pouring double shots of whiskey behind the bar.

"Live here!" Ursula muttered.

Bernie looped the end of Pepper's leash on the back of the rocking chair, and with her arms open, she met Ursula at the bottom of the steps leading up to the porch that wrapped around three sides of the house.

"Don't go getting your panties in a twist," Bernie said as Ursula walked into her arms and bent down to hug her. "I didn't take your room away from you, and I'm glad you have come home. It's time for you to get married and have some grandbabies for your mother."

Thoughts were running through Ursula's mind like screaming kids on a merry-go-round. Did that mean Bernie had moved into one of the other sisters' rooms and Ursula would have to share her bedroom with one of them? Why did Bernie decide to move to Spanish Fort? And the biggest one was why did Ursula's mother, Mary Jane, consent to such a crazy idea?

"Speak up, girl!" Bernie demanded. "You are more like me than any of your other sisters, and we speak our minds. Turn them squirrels loose that's runnin' around in your head right now."

Ursula chuckled. "Whose room did you take, and why are you living here?"

Before Bernie could answer, Ursula's stepfather, Joe Clay, and their longtime neighbor Remy Baxter came from around the house, each with a couple of boxes in their hands. Neither of them could wave, but Joe Clay's bright smile told Ursula that he was welcoming her home. Her heart skipped a beat and then raced ahead. Ursula had heard that Remy had come back to Spanish Fort to live on the small ranch next door to the Paradise, but she hadn't seen him in years.

Joe Clay wrapped her up in a fierce hug. "Glad you made it home and that you don't have to leave again. I hope the rest of your sisters do the same thing before long." He was looking sixty right in the eye, but he was still strong as an ox, as the old adage went. His dark hair had a few gray streaks and was a little longer than it had been when he first came around to remodel the Paradise, the old brothel, but back then, he'd just gotten out of the service.

She looked up into his blue eyes and smiled. "Me too, Daddy."

"Ursula, you remember Remy Baxter, don't you?" Joe Clay smiled at them both. "He and Shane O'Toole have agreed to help me with the decorations this year. Remy was our next-door neighbor until he went off to college in Gainesville and then got himself a job at his college. Smart boy here. Shane has taken over his grandparents' fishing business down on the river."

"Remy and I graduated together," she said and then glanced over at Remy. "I remember you, very well." She felt a bit of heat traveling from her neck to her cheeks. Evidently, the crush she had had on Remy when she was in high school was still there. Surely, though, he was married by now or at the very least had a girlfriend.

When she shifted her gaze over to Bernie, the woman was smiling like a Cheshire cat. Her eyes were all aglitter, and it didn't take a psychic to know what had her mind spinning, not after that crack about babies that she'd just come off with.

"I remember you too," Remy said.

"So how have you been?" she asked as she looked up at his face again.

"I'm doing great. I've moved back into the house next door, and I love being back over here. I didn't realize how much I'd missed it. Living in a walk-up apartment just isn't the same as living in the country," Remy answered.

In high school, he had been handsome, but he was also shy and a little awkward—maybe because he was so tall. He had measured more than six feet when they were freshmen and didn't top out until they were seniors when he reached six feet four inches. Since those days, he had muscled up and he seemed very comfortable in his body.

"That's great. It's right nice to have a sexy guy living right next door." Bernie grinned and nudged Ursula. "Y'all can get reacquainted now that you are home for good, Ursula, but for now, Joe Clay, you and Remy here can take all Ursula's stuff upstairs and put it in her room."

Remy nodded. "Yes, ma'am. I'm more than glad to help."

"Another of my baby girls is home for good!" Mary Jane yelled as she came through the door. "Come on up here and give your mama a hug."

Ursula's arm brushed against Remy's when she headed toward the porch. The touch was brief, and they were both wearing jackets, but the feeling was the same as when their hands had touched back in high school. They had been assigned lockers right next to each other their senior year— back in the days when he would barely even look her in the eyes. A few times when they had been closing their locker doors, their hands had touched, and sparks had danced up and down the halls like tiny little bursts of brilliant light.

Ursula jogged up to the porch and hugged her mother. Sassy, the big orange cat, came from around the house and began to rub around Ursula's legs and purr loudly. "She's glad to see me," Ursula said. "I thought maybe she would have forgotten me."

Pepper had crawled back under the rocking chair, lain down on his belly, and was growling at Sassy. The cat acted like Pepper was nothing more than a peasant and she was the reigning queen of Sheba.

"That evil critter ain't glad to see anyone," Bernie said. "She torments my poor Pepper. He just wants to be friends, and she spits and hisses at him like a demon. I think the madam of this place put her spirit in Sassy."

Mary Jane picked the cat up and carried her toward the door. "She's almost as independent as you are, Ursula, but not as much as that first cat we had right after we moved here. Miz Raven was the boss here at the Paradise. Sometimes I thought that the madam of this place left her spirit behind in that cat for sure." Mary Jane opened the door, set the cat down, and then held the door for Ursula and Bernie to go in ahead of her.

Ursula remembered the day that Joe Clay had brought the first cat into the house after they had all moved to Spanish Fort and into the old brothel known as the Paradise. She and all her sisters were elated to finally have a mama cat and a litter of kittens. Their biological father would never allow them to have so much as a goldfish or a hamster, but Joe Clay had toted a laundry basket full of babies into the house. That was probably the day that Ursula had decided Joe Clay was daddy material.

The smell of cinnamon and freshly baked bread met them when she stepped inside the foyer. The aroma overpowered the whiff of cigar smoke that Ursula had gotten when Bernie hugged her earlier. Ursula wouldn't be a bit surprised if that half-full coffee mug out there on the porch really did have a splash of Jameson in it, even though it wasn't five o'clock anywhere in Texas.

"I'm damn"—Bernie slapped a hand over her mouth—"dang sure glad you are here. The cinnamon rolls are ready and Mary Jane wouldn't let us touch them until you got home."

"I'm happy that you decided to follow your heart and give yourself a year to write," Mary Jane said as she sat down at the table. "We've missed having you girls in and out all the time. I even thought about fostering some kids, but Joe Clay keeps telling me to give it some time."

"Time for what?" Ursula asked.

"Time for you to come home, fall in love with the boy next door, and make a bunch of babies so Mary Jane can have children rompin' and playin' in this big old house," Bernie said as she removed her jacket. "Maybe they'll even slide down that banister over there"—she pointed to her right—"and laughter will fill this place up."

"Bernie!" Ursula scolded and hoped that Remy didn't hear what she had said.

"Joe Clay swears that you'll *all* get tired of living so far away and that someday, you'll realize where your roots are and come home. You're the third one to fly back to the nest,"

Mary Jane answered as she led them into the kitchen. "I hated what Endora had to go through, what with the breakup with her fiancé and all. I was so glad when she and Luna both came home and took jobs at the Prairie Valley school."

"And that's why I bought a travel trailer just big enough for me and Pepper to live in," Bernie said. "We dragged it up here behind my truck, and Joe Clay got us hooked up for water and all that stuff so we're right comfortable out there in the backyard. I'm going to go finish off my coffee and put Pepper in my house." Bernie spun around, put her jacket back on, and started back through the foyer.

"What have you done, Mama?" Ursula whispered as soon as she heard the front door close. "Why didn't you tell me you'd let Bernie move here?"

"She's a handful for sure." Mary Jane chuckled as she set plates out on the table for the cinnamon rolls. "Assisted living places wouldn't allow pets, especially not Pepper, and she was my support system when your father left us. She called every day and cussed him with all kinds of words that I won't repeat. At the time, I needed her, and now she needs me." She stopped long enough to make a pot of coffee. "You can get down the mugs and put the milk on the table. I don't know which one Joe Clay will want. And the reason I didn't tell you she was here is because I was afraid that if you knew, you wouldn't quit your job and come on home where you belong. If you are going to be a writer, then you need peace and quiet, and you can't get that in a noisy apartment in a city."

"And I'm going to find it in a house with a whiny sister named Endora who still believes Fate hates her and her twin, Luna, who is walking on eggshells because she doesn't want to hurt Endora's feelings," Ursula said with a sigh, "and then add Bernie to that! I can't imagine her letting me have hours and hours to write a novel without popping in with Pepper to visit with me." Ursula set mugs and glasses both on the counter. "Has she straightened Endora out yet?"

"She's working on it," Mary Jane answered. "Joe Clay loves her sass and banter. Endora doesn't roll her eyes as much as she did a week ago when Bernie arrived, so I think we're making progress. It takes a while to get over a breakup like she had, and I'm speaking from experience. To have all the excitement of being engaged and starting to plan a wedding, only to find out that her fiancé was sleeping with her best friend, was devastating."

"Yep, but it's time for my youngest sister to pull herself up out of the mud and move on," Ursula declared.

"Spoken just like Bernie," Mary Jane said with a nod. "As long as you are alive, that woman will never be dead. She didn't have kids, but she sure passed her genes right on down to you."

"That's what I get for saying that I wanted to grow up and be just like her," Ursula said. "Remember how Grandmother Marsh almost had a cardiac arrest when I was eight years old and told her that I was going to grow up and work for Bernie in her bar?"

Mary Jane rolled her eyes toward the ceiling. "Yep, and

your father fussed about it for weeks and weeks. He was so embarrassed that he threatened to send you to live with his strict mother with hopes that she would straighten you out. I told him that wasn't going to happen. If you went anywhere, I'd send you to live with Bernie."

"I bet that shut him up."

"It did until you did something else that was just like her," Mary Jane said.

"I'm back," Bernie said as she came through the back door. "Pepper is sleeping soundly, and Sassy is taking a sun nap on the back porch steps, so maybe she won't go wandering down to my trailer and pester him through the door." She removed her jacket and hung it on the back of a dining room chair. "Now, let's make a plan to get Remy to ask you out on a date. If he don't, then you can ask him out. I just love this new world when women don't have to sit back and worry about getting a phone call. If it had been like that back when I was your age and younger, I would have been out with a different man every night."

"From what I hear, you were anyway," Mary Jane said.

"Yep, but I was considered wild. No mama wanted her son to get serious about me," Bernie said. "Not that I cared. No, sirree! My sister—that would be your grandma, Ursula—got all the good genes and saved the ornery ones for me. And, honey," she said as she winked at Ursula, "I ain't never had a regret in my whole life about the way I lived. Now about Remy?"

"Shh…" Ursula cocked her head to one side and gave Bernie a dose of evil eye. "Remy might hear you."

Bernie had to reach up to shake her finger under Ursula's nose, but she did it without a bit of effort. "Don't you shush me. I saw the sparks between y'all. At least fix it so you sit beside him at the table when we have our snack. I'll keep a close watch and tell you if there's what you kids call vibes between y'all, and then we can start our strategizing."

Mary Jane gave Bernie a sideways hug. "Let's give them until after Thanksgiving before we go meddling."

Bernie sucked in a lungful of air and almost snorted when she let it out in a whoosh. "All right," she said with a shrug and a long sigh. "I guess that Luna is going to beat you to the altar. It don't seem right since she and Endora are the youngest in the family, and you are the oldest. I guess she just got tired of waiting for *you* to quit lollygagging around."

The sound of boots on the foyer's hardwood floor as well as Joe Clay's and Remy's deep Texas drawls floated into the kitchen.

"You can sit beside Remy," Mary Jane whispered. "He doesn't bite."

"Are you sure about that?" Ursula asked.

"All done," Joe Clay said as he and Remy arrived in the kitchen. He crossed the room and gave Mary Jane a kiss on the forehead. "I would have unloaded twice that much for a midmorning snack like this. Don't be bashful, Remy. Have a seat."

Remy pulled a chair out for Ursula. "When it comes to home cooking, I'm pretty brave."

"Thank you." Ursula sat down and then reached for the

coffeepot and filled her mug in an attempt to take her mind off the way Remy still affected her after all these years, but it didn't work. "So you went over to Gainesville to college?"

"Yep, it's amazing how much that college helped my self-esteem."

"You had trouble with self-esteem?" Ursula almost dropped the coffeepot. "I thought you were..." she stammered.

Remy held up a hand. "Egotistical?" he asked.

"No, just shy," she said.

"You win the prize for being right," Remy said. "I was very shy, but I got over it when I left Spanish Fort and got out in the world."

For some of us, getting out of this area worked the exact opposite, Ursula thought as she remembered her first days at college. Coming from a ghost town, she was totally overwhelmed by the campus in Tyler, Texas, and was intimidated by so many professors and students. There were more people in her dorm than lived in the whole community of Spanish Fort.

She blinked and popped back into the conversation to hear the other three talking about the Christmas decorations they would begin to put up on Friday.

"I remember," she said with a smile, "our first Christmas here at the Paradise. All of us sisters were so excited about getting our new rooms."

"Do you remember what you and your sisters asked for?" Joe Clay asked.

"We wanted to make our house the prettiest one in the whole county."

Joe Clay cut five large cinnamon rolls from the pan, put each one on a saucer, and passed them around. "Yes, you did, and I did my best to make that wish come true for all of you, and seeing your faces when we lit up the place was priceless. Just wait until you see what all new stuff your mama bought for us to put up this year."

"I found a big ninety-percent-off sale at the end of January," Mary Jane explained.

"I'm going to miss decorating my bar," Bernie said with another sigh. "I always put up a big tree over in the corner and decorated it with empty whiskey bottles. This year, Pepper and I will put lights all around our trailer and maybe have a little bitty tree on the coffee table. I'll have to have something to put his presents under or he'll pout."

"Do you have pictures of that tree with the whiskey bottles on it?" Ursula asked.

"Yep," Bernie answered. "Sometime when you"—she shot a couple of winks across the table at Ursula—"take time away from your writing and other projects that we've talked about, you can come out to my tiny house and see them."

Ursula wasn't sure she wanted to be cooped up in a small trailer with Pepper or if she wanted to endure an hour or two of Bernie's matchmaking ideas while she was there. But maybe she would try to make time to go out there in the next few days.

"Did you make these cinnamon rolls, or did the angels in heaven make them, Miz Mary Jane?" Remy asked.

"Mary Jane *is* an angel, some of the time," Joe Clay answered. "She just hides her wings and halo from most people."

Mary Jane cocked her head over to one side. "Some of the time?"

"Hey, I remember a sassy woman who knocked on my motel room and insisted I come out here and look at this old place to remodel it." Joe Clay's eyes glittered. "And that same woman called me a chicken when I started to leave that afternoon."

"Well," Ursula dragged the word out, "you *were* afraid of seven little girls."

"You got that right." Joe Clay chuckled.

"It's too bad Ursula didn't inherit that angel attitude," Bernie said. "I guess that I just loved her so much when she was born that I gave her a double dose of sass." Another sly wink came across the table, and then she shifted her gaze over to Remy. "How long have you known this family, Remy?"

"I was fourteen when Miz Mary Jane and the girls moved into this house, but I can't say I knew the family back then. I was too shy to even come over here and make their acquaintance, but I used to sit on the fence that separates our properties and enjoy all the lights and decorations at Christmas. I thought it really was the prettiest house I'd ever seen," he answered.

"Where is your mother these days?" Ursula asked, trying

to get away from Bernie's very blatant winks. "Is she still working at the school cafeteria?"

"No, she moved to Wyoming at the end of summer. She married Alan Thomas, who had been the high school principal for five years. He had to work through July to fulfill his contract, and then they packed up and left," he answered. "I moved into the house just before school started in August."

"Texas to Wyoming?" Ursula asked. "That would be a cultural shock."

Remy finished off the last bite of his cinnamon roll. "Alan inherited a ranch up there, and they both love their little log cabin that sits down in a valley between two mountains. Mama sends pictures almost every day. They've already got lots of snow. Herds of deer wander right up in their yard almost daily so they put food out for them."

"Are you going to visit her during the holidays?" Ursula asked.

"Nope," he answered. "Two reasons. I've bought a small herd of cattle that I need to take care of, and snow is already making travel up in that area tough if not impossible, so I'll spend the holidays here. It'll be my first time to have Christmas without her, so it'll be lonely."

"Then you will just have to plan on having the holiday meals with us," Bernie said.

Lord, please make her stop meddling. I've only just gotten home. I want to spend time writing another novel. I don't have time for romance. Ursula sent up the prayer, but evidently it didn't go past the ceiling because Bernie shot another wink and a slight nod over at Ursula.

"That would be great," Remy said. "Just tell me when to be here and what I can bring to help out."

"We always eat at noon on Thanksgiving," Joe Clay said, "and you don't need to bring a thing. You and Shane will be earning your dinner with all the help you are giving me."

"Well then, thank you again," Remy said.

"So you run cattle and teach over in Gainesville," Bernie said. "Do you have a girlfriend or maybe a fiancée?"

"Yes to the first question. No to both of the others." He took a sip of his coffee. "I teach American history classes at North Texas State College. That's where I went to college and got both of my degrees."

Joe Clay finished his first cinnamon roll, cut himself another one, and poured a second glass of milk. "Ursula, you left to go back to Tyler one day last August, and Remy moved in the next."

"We have sure enjoyed having him and Shane both close by," Mary Jane said. "I feel bad that we didn't make a bigger effort to get to know his family after we moved here."

"It's okay," Remy assured her. "We know each other now."

"How long has your family been living in Spanish Fort?" Ursula asked.

"More than a hundred and thirty years," Remy said. "The first record we have is of a mail-order bride who came to marry my several-times-great-grandpa. Her name was Daisy

Clayborne. She even kept a diary that's in the bookcase over at the house. Mama didn't read much of it, but Grandma said that Daisy was a spitfire."

"Where is everyone?" Luna's voice floated through the foyer and back to the kitchen. "I smell cinnamon. Please, don't tell me that Ursula has eaten all the sweet rolls." She and her identical twin, Endora, walked into the kitchen together, gave their oldest sister a quick sideways hug, and immediately sat down in a couple of empty chairs around the table.

Only a few people could tell them apart. They both had long blond hair, blue eyes, and a flawless complexion, but these days, Endora was a few pounds heavier than her sister—probably from doing too much depression eating.

Ursula took a deep breath and let it out slowly. She was tired from the drive from the northeastern part of the state, plus all the emotional pros and cons she'd gone through for a solid month about moving back to the Paradise—even though she dearly loved the old brothel that her mother had bought almost twenty years ago and had remodeled into a home to raise her seven daughters in. Plus, it didn't help that her old crush was sitting right beside her, and she didn't want to hear a bunch of teasing about him from her two youngest sisters.

"It's a good thing you got here now, or we *might* have eaten every one of them," Ursula joked.

"I even got a middle one, because I'm the oldest, and that makes me special, but they're still warm for you."

"Keep thinking that," Luna shot back at her. "Hello, Remy. Are you out of school for the whole week?"

"Yep, and then I go back for finals, and I'm done until my new classes start after New Year's," he answered. "Y'all should think about teaching on a college level."

"Not me," Endora said. "Dealing with college students would be way too rough for me. I barely make it through the day trying to teach second graders." She pushed her long, blond hair over her shoulder. The sparkle and pure orneriness that she'd had in her blue eyes ever since she was a child had disappeared. Now, thanks to Kevin, her fiancé of only a few weeks, and Krystal, her best friend, having an affair and breaking her heart, they were dull and sad.

How on earth someone with the spunk Endora had always had could let a man drag her down to this level was a complete mystery. She had always been a spitfire, and at one time, she would have gone toe-to-toe with Krystal and then had plenty of red-hot anger left over to unleash on Kevin. Being betrayed by both of them had put what seemed to be a never-melting icicle inside her heart and soul.

"Since the *old* sister is home to stay, and since she's so *special*, does this mean we get after-school treats every day, Mama?" Luna asked.

"Only if you make them," Mary Jane answered. "I'm taking Thanksgiving week off from my writing, but my publisher is screaming at me to finish the book I'm working on now before Christmas. That means I'm in my office from right after breakfast until time to make supper. And"—she

raised an eyebrow and glanced over at Luna and Endora—
"your sister might be the firstborn in this family, but she's
not old, and she will be working the same hours on her new
writing project."

"What did I do?" Endora protested. "This is Luna and
Ursula's argument. I'm just sitting here eating my sweet roll
and being nice."

"Mama is still just as bossy as ever," Luna whispered to
Ursula.

"But not as bad as Bernie," Ursula said out the corner
of her mouth. "And remind me later to fuss at you for not
telling me that she had moved to the Paradise."

"Mama threatened me and Endora both," Luna said.

"It's bad manners to whisper at the table," Bernie
snapped.

"Yes, ma'am," Luna said. "We were talking about what
we're going to get you for Christmas."

Bernie waved a hand in their direction. "Then whisper
away, my sweet girls."

"I still have really good hearing, and I *am* bossy. It would
bode all of you sisters well to never forget that," Mary Jane
said as she pushed back her chair.

"She got that from me," Bernie announced proudly.
"Her angel wings and halo came from my twin sister who
was her grandmother, but the bossy stuff is what I passed
down to her."

"That's right," Mary Jane said with a smile. "And to live
up to my name, Endora, you and Luna can clean up the

kitchen when you are done. Remy and Joe Clay have more boxes of Christmas decorations to bring in so the whole bunch of us will be ready to start decorating on Friday. Ursula has to get upstairs and get unpacked so that, come Monday morning, she's ready to start writing."

Endora glared at her twin. "You got us in trouble."

"It's just payback for all the times when we were kids and I got blamed for what you did," Luna told her.

Ursula finished off the last sip of her coffee and stood up. "Great talking to you, Remy." She pointed at her two younger sisters. "Y'all could come help me when you get done here."

"We could…" Luna said.

"If you promise to be nice to us for a whole year," Endora finished the sentence.

Luna flashed a bright smile. "And not to play the big-sister card all year."

"With answers like that, I wouldn't hold my breath for any help from the twin section of the family," Remy said with a chuckle.

"What can I say?" Ursula said with a shrug. "They're the babies of the family and we all spoiled them."

"Did not!" Endora and Luna protested at the same time.

"Yes, we did," Joe Clay told her as he stood up. "If you don't want to help your sister, Remy and I could use some extra hands bringing in Christmas boxes from the workshop."

"Looks like we'll be working no matter what," Luna said, groaning.

"If we take our time finishing our cinnamon rolls, maybe they'll have the Christmas stuff all hauled up here from the barn, and Ursula will be unpacked," Endora said.

Ursula patted Endora on the back as she passed by. "You haven't lost all your sass, darlin'."

"I've still got it," Endora snapped. "I just packed it away for a while."

Ursula let her have the last word and headed out of the kitchen with Bernie right behind her. She expected her great-aunt to say that she was going to help her unpack, but Bernie just nudged her at the bottom of the stairs and said, "I told Mary Jane you coming home would be the best thing ever."

"How's that?" Ursula asked.

"Endora," Bernie said with a shrug. "Twins have this thing about them. When one hurts, the other hurts, so Luna can't help Endora come up out of the funk she's in. But honey, just add a third one into the mix and the whole dynamic changes. You are going to help by just being here. Now, go on and get unpacked. We've still got to draw up battle plans for the romance between you and Remy." She waved as she left by the front door.

Ursula didn't have the heart to burst her bubble by telling her that the only thing she planned on fighting in the next few months was keeping her muse awake long enough to get a bestselling historical book written. Writing in the day had always been a problem with her day job at the university, so she had vowed to write three thousand words every night. Lately, she had paced the floor, cursed the computer, and eaten way too much junk food. Evidently her muse didn't care that she was wearing out the carpet and blistering the paint off the walls with her swearing or even the fact that her clothes were getting too tight. Writer's block was the worst. She'd experienced it a few times before but never as bad as this. This time, it seemed like she'd never snap out of it.

She made a new vow as she walked up the stairs. "After Thanksgiving, I will write a thousand words before breakfast, and when Endora and Luna go to school each day, I will write three thousand while things are quiet."

She might have to hang a Do Not Disturb sign on her door to keep Bernie out.

Boxes and suitcases were stacked up in the hallway outside her bedroom door. When she eased the door open, she found a pumpkin-scented candle burning brightly on the dresser and a candy dish filled with her favorite miniature dark chocolates on the nightstand. Fresh air billowed the lacy curtains out from the window that had been opened a few inches, and the whole room smelled like Thanksgiving. Maybe, just maybe, she really would write a bestseller right there at Paradise. Until then, she might be spending long hours in her room staring at a blank computer screen and shaking her muse until the critter came to life.

———

Late that night after everyone had gone to bed, Ursula slipped on her jacket and turned the collar up. She shook her long, dark hair out of its ponytail, then tiptoed downstairs and out the back door.

She wanted to know more about Daisy. Research could easily uncover facts about the days when the new mail-order bride came to Spanish Fort. But feelings and emotions were a different thing. Had Miz Daisy been appalled to be living next door to a brothel? Would she have talked to the women over the fence at some time, or would she have turned up her nose and shunned them? Ursula would bet dollars to fresh meadow muffins that there was a lot of information in that diary. Remy hadn't said much about it but enough to get Ursula's writer's curiosity going.

Hoping to get into Daisy's mindset, Ursula wandered out to the rail fence that separated the Paradise property from the acreage next door where Remy lived. She backed up against it and hooked the heel of her boot onto the bottom rail. She and her sisters had been teased a few times about living in an old brothel, but it didn't take long to put the bullies in their place. Not many people wanted to mess with seven Simmons sisters at once, and they had been taught to stand together if they were ever threatened. Did the ladies who worked at the Paradise back then feel like sisters who took up for each other against the other women in Spanish Fort?

A quarter moon hung in the sky, seemingly holding court for millions of stars and giving enough light that she could see a dozen or so cows in the pasture between the fence and Remy's house. A brisk November breeze rattled what dead leaves were left on the scrub oak trees, and a coyote sang a lonesome song off in the distance. Did Daisy ever hear the same sounds way back then? Did she feel out of her element and alone with only one close neighbor who ran a brothel?

Bernie's voice popped into Ursula's head. *You sure don't get anything like this in downtown Tyler in a third-story walk-up apartment.*

"Well, you didn't get anything like this living in an apartment in the back of your bar either, did you?" Ursula fired back. "And I'm not out here to think about the countryside. I'm trying to get inside Daisy's head."

"Since I don't see anyone around, I assume you are talking to yourself." Remy's voice so close behind her startled her and jacked up her pulse a few notches.

"I'm arguing with Bernie," she admitted.

Remy chuckled. "I guess the fight is in your head since I don't see her anywhere either."

"Do you ever hear voices?" Ursula asked.

"Oh yes, I do," Remy answered. "Most of the time, it's my grandpa who comes around to say a word or two. It's usually just when I need it. Do you need something tonight that your Bernie is giving you advice about?"

"What I need is for my muse to keep talking to me and tell me about this new character I want to write about," she answered. "I haven't written a word in months, and I need to have a book ready by spring."

He came over to stand beside her but stayed on the other side of the fence. He propped his elbows on the top rung and rested his chin on his hands. "When I look at this land,

I think about what all it could tell us if it could talk. My ancestors settled here more than a hundred years ago, right about the time that the cattle drives were going through here. Back then, Spanish Fort was an up-and-coming place. From what my grandpa told me, it was a rowdy town with plenty of bars and the Paradise was not the only brothel. But according to what Grandpa knew, it was the fanciest and most prosperous one."

Ursula turned around, hopped up to sit on the top rail, and rested her feet on the middle one. "Are all those stories what got you interested in history?"

"We've got all kinds of family lore and the diary that Daisy wrote way back when. I've never been interested enough in it to even open the cover. Grandma said that she came to Texas from somewhere back East as a mail-order bride." Remy chuckled.

Ursula could swear that her muse perked up a little more.

"I would rather talk about you than history," he said. "Did you know that I had a very big crush on you when we were in school?"

"I had no idea," she answered. "Why didn't you say something?"

Remy shrugged. "You were so smart, and you were popular, and your mama was famous. I wasn't the kind of guy that a girl like you would go out with. You lived—still live—in the biggest house in the whole area, and I was just a farm boy who was too shy to even say hello to you most days."

"I wish you would have let me know," Ursula whispered

and wondered what path her life might have taken if she'd known that Remy liked her back then.

You didn't say anything either, the annoying voice that still sounded like Bernie's reminded her.

"Most boys have an inborn fear of rejection," Remy answered. "But after a couple of sleepless nights, I did get up enough nerve to ask you to go to the prom with me."

"No, you didn't," Ursula frowned.

"I had the nerve, but just about the time I was going to open my mouth and ask you, Derrick Marlow walked up to your locker and got ahead of me," Remy said.

"Some date that turned out to be," Ursula said with a long sigh. "I ended up calling Daddy to come get me when Derrick tried to talk me into the back seat of his car. He said I owed him for taking me to the prom."

"I'm not a bit surprised. He's still known for leaving a string of broken hearts behind him," Remy growled. "Karma got him, though. He flunked out of college and is working on construction for his father in Nocona. Being a great basketball star at Nocona High School fifteen years ago didn't do much for him in the long run."

"I guess it didn't," Ursula said. "I heard he didn't finish school, but I had no idea what he was doing these days."

"Seems like Madam Karma did a lot for you, though," Remy said. "Mary Jane tells me you've published a couple of novels and feel like writing is *your* calling."

"I haven't earned out on a single one of them, but I keep hoping the next one will do better," she said with a long sigh.

"Earned out?" Remy asked.

"That means I haven't earned any more than the advance they gave me," Ursula said as she hopped off the fence. She wanted to hear more about Daisy but wasn't quite sure how to approach the subject without it seeming like that was the only reason she was eager to spend time with Remy.

"Maybe you just need a change of scenery," Remy said.

"That's what Mama keeps telling me. She said that coming to Spanish Fort was the best thing that ever happened to our family and her career," Ursula told him. "Want to jump back over the fence, come up to the house, and sit on the back porch? We've got sweet tea and beer, and it's a lot more comfortable there."

"Not tonight. Thanks for the offer, though. Maybe another evening when it's not so late," Remy answered. "I've got to get up early in the morning for chores. If you get bored, you can always come on over to the Baxter Ranch and help me feed cattle. Good hard work may make that muse of yours decide that writing is easier than hoisting bales of hay."

"Never thought of that," Ursula said with a wide grin.

"It could make the muse change its attitude," Remy suggested.

"I would feed cows before daylight every morning if it would help me get into the writing groove," she said, "but for now, I should get back to the house."

"Good night, Ursula," he said and disappeared down the path through a mesquite thicket.

"Good night," she said and then started back toward the house. "Come on, Daisy. Talk to me," she muttered.

As if on cue, a voice popped into her head. *"At first, I hated living next door to a brothel and was pretty upset at my new husband for not telling me about my neighbors before we went to the justice of the peace and got married."*

With that single sentence, Daisy became a real person with emotions and feelings. Ursula wondered if Daisy's new husband wanted a wife to take care of his house or if children were involved and he needed a mother for them. Did they slowly fall in love even though he had not told her about the Paradise or that Spanish Fort was a rowdy place to live?

Ursula eased the back door open, did not turn on any lights, and started up the stairs on her tiptoes. She came close to losing her balance and tumbling backward when Bernie spoke to her.

"Did you and Remy have a good talk? Give me details," Bernie whispered and then patted the top step where she was sitting in the dark.

Ursula could hear Daisy giggling as she sat down beside Bernie. "I went for a walk. He went for a walk. Just a coincidence that we ended up at the fence. We talked about old classmates and his great-great-grandma, Daisy."

Bernie gave her a quick sideways hug. "I don't believe in coincidences. I took Pepper out for an evening walk and saw y'all talking over the fence. What's the chance of all three of us being out at the same time? I'll tell you what they are—slim to none. Fate is helping us along in our plan. Our

Christmas present next year may be a baby in this place." She stood up and crossed her fingers close to Ursula's face. "Go get some rest. You need to be even more beautiful than you are every day so Remy will fall in love with you."

There is no peace for the wicked, Ursula thought.

"But I haven't been wicked," she whispered as she made her way to her bedroom.

She shook Bernie out of her mind, grabbed a pencil, and opened a notebook to begin outlining the first chapter of the book. With each sentence, Daisy became more real in her mind. Those were the days of the cattle runs from all over to Texas up into Kansas—not long after the Civil War ended—back when Madam Raven ran the brothel.

She finally laid the notebook to the side and opened her laptop to research mail-order brides in Daisy's time. She started a file for each link that she found so she could come back to them at a later date. When her neck began to ache, she stood up, opened the balcony doors, and went outside for a breath of brisk night air. But then her work called her back, and she was ready to outline the first chapter.

Should she start it with the scene at the train station when Daisy put her feet on Texas soil and met... She needed a name for the man who had sent for Daisy to be his new bride but couldn't think of one. She decided to call him Fred until she figured out a better name. She didn't realize how long she had been working until she heard the rattling of pans in the kitchen and noticed the first sliver of a bright-orange sun rising up over the eastern horizon.

"Halle-damn-lujah!" She did a fist pump. She was writing again, even if it was just dozens of haphazard notes in a spiral-back notebook and one page about Daisy and Fred at a justice of the peace's office in Nocona, Texas.

She left her room, splashed cold water on her face, and went downstairs. "Good mornin', Mama. Where is everyone?"

"Mornin' to you," Mary Jane answered as she cracked eggs into a bowl. "Bernie doesn't make it in for breakfast. For the past sixty years, she has worked in her bar from six in the evening until two in the morning. Her internal clock lets her sleep until sometime between ten and noon. That and after everyone goes to bed could be your most productive time to write. Your sisters will be down any minute. They still have to go to school today, but they'll be out tomorrow when everyone else starts coming in. You've got bags under your eyes. Were you up late?"

Ursula got down a stack of plates and began to set the table. "I pulled the first all-nighter I've done since college. I couldn't sleep, so I walked out to the edge of the yard and sat on the fence. Remy showed up and he told me a little about one of his ancestors who was a mail-order bride. Can you imagine some prim and proper little lady coming from back East to live right next to a brothel? That woke up my muse, and she kept me up all night."

"I never thought about how the neighbors would have felt about the Paradise when I was writing my series. That's a great idea you've got there. Run with it," Mary Jane said.

"Do you remember when you were trying to record your story, and I stole your recorder to tell my own story?" Ursula asked.

"Oh yeah, I do," Mary Jane answered. "With seven little girls underfoot all the time, I was writing when y'all took naps and even when I was cooking meals for all y'all. Those were the days of twenty- or thirty-minute sprints. I've written lots of sex scenes with a set of twins, or sometimes two sets, having a tea party under the desk."

"Is that why you got the recorder?" Ursula asked.

Mary Jane nodded. "I figured I could use it to remember descriptions or maybe eventually to record whole books and then pay someone to type them up for me. That didn't work so well since it seems my brain is powered through my fingers, not by speaking."

"And then I borrowed it to record my own story about six little kittens whose daddy had run away and left them," Ursula said.

"That's when I realized your father leaving us had caused you a lot of pain and that someday you would be a novelist," Mary Jane told her. "And I bought you a cheap little recorder of your very own. Do you remember what happened after that?"

Ursula giggled and then gave her mother a sideways hug. "I got yours instead of mine and dropped it in the bathtub."

"Just before you did that, I had sent the tape with the first chapter of my story to my agent to see what she thought of the idea of learning to tell the story that way. I had accidentally gotten yours instead of mine. My story was serious, not funny, but she laughed so hard when she called me that I figured out what I'd done before she ever said a word."

"And that was the end of us using a recorder to write, wasn't it?" Ursula said. "But, Mama, I've always wondered what caused you to write about those seven prostitutes."

"My muse told me to," Mary Jane answered with a big smile. "The truth is, I don't even know if there is such a thing as a muse. Maybe we are just waiting for the right idea to come along. Back when we were remodeling, Joe Clay found the old journals the madam had left, and I couldn't get the story out of my head. I called my agent, told her what I wanted to do, and she told me to put the contemporary I was working on to the side and get started on that seven-book series. She said she could hear the excitement in my voice—the same thing I'm hearing in yours. Her advice was the best thing for my career. I have written historical romance ever since, and I love every aspect of it—from the research to the stories about strong women in times when they didn't have the voice we have in today's world."

"I want to write about Daisy, Remy's great-however-many-times-grandmother, or about a woman loosely based on her," Ursula said. "I can change her name if Remy isn't comfortable with the idea of using a real person's name in my story. I spent the whole night doing research on mail-order brides from Daisy's time period."

Mary Jane poured the eggs into a skillet and then turned around to hug Ursula. "If you can't get that woman out of your mind, you should call Norma and tell her what's going on. Then send her a synopsis and the first chapter. If she doesn't want you to write it, do it anyway, or you will never, ever be at peace. Daisy is expecting you to tell her story. Don't disappoint her."

"Thank you, Mama," Ursula said with a long sigh. "If there is such a thing as a muse, I think it's finally coming out of hibernation."

"Sounds to me like it's helped along by a man with dark hair and brown eyes named Remington Baxter."

Chapter 2

Ursula's muse might be the Paradise instead of a person or critter. Her mind was so full of ideas that she could hardly get them written down or typed into her computer fast enough. She finally realized that she had to take a breath and stretch a bit, or she was going to freeze with her hands on the keyboard. She stood up and raised her arms, then touched her toes. After she repeated that five times, she looked around at all the familiar things in her bedroom. Over there in the rocking chair beside the balcony doors was where she recorded the story of the sad little kittens whose father left them. The desk, now cluttered with her laptop and papers and with sticky notes on the wall in front of it, had been where she wrote book reports and term papers—her favorite part of school. Maybe she just needed to be right there in her bedroom to really get in the writing zone. She opened the doors out onto the balcony and looked across the fence where she and Remy had talked. She could see part of Bernie's trailer over to the right, and to the left was the lane leading out to the road.

"Rae and Tertia are here!" Bernie's excited voice floated up the stairs and startled Ursula.

Ursula hurried back into her room, stepped over to the desk, and saved the last three pages of research she'd been working on. She closed her computer and hurried down to the foyer. She hoped the whole time she practically jogged down the stairs that Bernie would turn her attention to Rae and Tertia now that they were home. Endora and Luna were ahead of her, and as soon as they were all on the porch, a hugging fest took place with Mary Jane and Bernie right in the middle of all of it.

"I'm so glad y'all are home. There's a perfectly good bachelor living not a stone's throw away over that rail fence." Bernie pointed out across the yard. "He's sexier than Scott Eastwood or even Elvis Presley, and your oldest sister is dragging her feet about asking him out on a date. You'd think this was the Dark Ages, the way she's acting. Y'all need to either give her a talkin'-to, or else one of you latch on to Remy Baxter."

So much for hoping that Bernie would forget about any kind of romance between me and Remy, Ursula thought with a long sigh.

"Bernie!" Mary Jane scolded.

Bernie tipped up her chin in a defiant gesture and glared at Mary Jane. "I'm just tellin' it like it is. Seems a shame that one of these girls don't see what's right in front of their eyes. Remember that old song Blake Shelton sang called 'Delilah.' It was one of the most played songs on the jukebox in my bar. The words talk about not seeing the love that's right there beside a person."

"Looks like there's not going to be a dull moment here this holiday," Rae said.

Tertia tucked an errant strand of curly light-brown hair up into the messy bun on top of her head. "Five down. Two to go," she said with a yawn.

"What?" Ursula asked as she gave her sister another hug.

"Five sisters are here. We just need Ophelia and Bo to arrive, and then we're all home," Tertia explained as she rolled her suitcase into the house, hung her coat on the hall tree.

Ursula followed her and raised an eyebrow. "Did Mama tell you that Bernie had moved here?"

"She did *not!*" Tertia groaned. "Has she taken over my room for the week? I hate the idea of sharing a room with Rae. She snores."

"Oh, no, sweet sister," Ursula said. "She's moved a little trailer out in the backyard. She's here to stay until eternity."

Tertia's eyes got so wide that Ursula imagined them popping out of her head and rolling around on the hallway floor like marbles.

"What was Mama thinkin'?" Tertia whispered.

"From what I can understand, Mama is hoping that Bernie would light a fire under us all to get busy with marriage plans and making babies," Ursula said. "If our aunt had her way, I would already be looking at three-tiered cakes and planning a Christmas wedding."

"And Remington Baxter would be the groom?" Tertia asked.

"Yep," Ursula answered just before the rest of the group

made their way into the house. "He is a marked man for sure. Bernie is determined that one of us six sisters will be a Baxter before long."

"Six?" Tertia whispered. "Have you forgotten how to count? There's seven of us."

"Seems Luna already has a feller picked out so she's out of the market," Ursula said and then whipped around to face Rae, who was headed toward the door to her bedroom. "You look tired. Did you have a lot of traffic on the trip?"

"She wouldn't know," Tertia answered. "She slept the whole seven hours, but come Sunday, she's driving all the way back to the Panhandle and I'm going to sleep."

Ursula picked up Tertia's suitcase and then set it back down. "What have you got in there, bricks? It'll take a forklift to get it up to your room."

"She thinks she has to bring everything she owns even when she goes on a short trip like this," Rae said.

"Just because you are on the police force doesn't give you the right to boss me around," Tertia fussed at her sister. "Besides, I'm older than you are."

Ursula laughed out loud as she followed them upstairs. Some things never changed. Sisters argued, but Lord help anyone who tried to get between the two of them.

"What's so funny?" Tertia asked.

"Y'all are, and I'm happy to have you here," Ursula said and headed back down the stairs.

When she was on the bottom step, Joe Clay slung open the door. "I see that more of you girls made it in time for supper. Bo just texted that she's about an hour away, and Ophelia's plane has landed in Dallas."

"Happy times," Bernie said and threw one of her famous winks toward Ursula, "but they'll be even happier in another year. I can feel it in my bones."

All you can feel in your bones is whiskey and cigar smoke that's settled into the marrow, Ursula thought. *If you are waiting for me to lead the parade to the altar, then you had better order up an extra dose of patience.*

Ursula could feel Remy's presence a full minute before she realized that he was standing right behind Joe Clay. Her gaze shifted from her sisters, who were all talking at once, to Remy, and one of those delicious little shivers tiptoed down her spine.

Lord, girl! Just make the first move already, the voice in her head said.

"Ursula, darlin'," Mary Jane said and motioned with her hand. "Come on into the kitchen and help me get the rest of supper ready."

Ursula headed toward the kitchen with Bernie right behind her.

"I could actually see the sparks between y'all," Bernie whispered. "Just imagine those delicious muscled-up arms holding you. If I was thirty years younger, I'd give you a run for your money. I bet he's..."

"Shh." Ursula gave Bernie a dirty look.

"Don't shush me," Bernie growled. "I've been around men my whole life. I know them, and that one likes you. If he was sitting at my bar, he would be shooting you all kinds of pickup lines."

"You'd have to be more like fifty years younger to date Remy," Ursula scolded.

Bernie's forefinger snapped up like a pistol, and for a split second, Ursula thought the finger was going right up her nose. "Girl, I know more about how to please a man than you'll know in a lifetime."

Ursula grabbed her finger. "Then after supper, we'll go to your trailer, and you can give me detailed instructions on what you know."

"With that smart-ass attitude, you can learn for yourself," Bernie said and marched into the kitchen with her head held high.

Mary Jane looked up from the counter where she was cutting up a salad. "Looks to me she's right about Remy. That crush that I figured he had on you in high school is still there."

"How did you know that... Are you..." Ursula stammered. "Who told you that?"

"Honey, we all knew," Mary Jane said. "Only a girl that he was interested in could make him sit on that fence and stare over this way. I used that scene in my last book about the girls of the Paradise, only that guy finally got the girl to leave the Paradise and marry him."

"Remy was staring at the Christmas decorations," Ursula said.

"Yeah, right," Bernie said.

Remy's deep drawl floated from the foyer into the kitchen. "Joe Clay, I'll unload the sleigh from the flatbed and then go load the trailer up with more boxes. You can visit with your daughters."

Ursula was tired of the spotlight being on her, so she marched out of the kitchen and heard the door close before she made it to the foyer. "Daddy, I'll go outside and help Remy. Tertia and Rae will be downstairs in a little bit, and they can help Mama and tell y'all about their trip."

Joe Clay handed Ursula a jacket from the hall tree. "Honey, I overheard a little of what's been said, and Remy wasn't looking at the lights in March or in the middle of summer. I didn't know then which girl he was pining after, but it's pretty evident now."

"Why didn't you say something?"

"He was a nerd, and you never would have gone out with him, even if he had asked," Joe Clay answered.

"I had a big crush on him too," Ursula admitted. "Mama says he's my muse now for the book I'm planning to write. I think maybe the Paradise is my muse, not a person or a critter of any kind, but evidently she was right about me needing to be back here for my creative juices to start flowing again. I've already got this wonderful idea for a historical novel."

"Just like that!" Joe Clay chuckled. "You come home, and suddenly your writer's block disappears?"

"Seems that way," Ursula answered.

"I heard that last part, and that's great news." Remy poked his head in the door. "What are you going to write?

Oh, and I just wanted to ask… Is there an order to the way I need to bring the boxes up to the house, Joe Clay?"

"Nope, just haul 'em up here anyway you can stack 'em," Joe Clay said.

"You gave me the idea when you told me about Daisy," Ursula told Remy as she followed him outside. "I want to write a story about what living next door to the Paradise was like for a new mail-order bride. Can we talk more about it later?"

"Sure thing," Remy said with a grin.

What if he's not one of my muses, or if he's a one-trick pony, and I fall back into writer's block when I finish this book? she wondered as she guided the full-sized sleigh off the back of the trailer.

Girl, that feller looks like he's got more than one trick up his sleeve, Bernie's voice came through loud and clear in her head. *I can practically feel the heat between you two. Methinks the crush is alive and well twenty years later.*

"Oh, hush!" Ursula muttered.

Remy set a load of boxes on the porch and turned around. "Did you say something?"

"Just fussin' with the voices in my head again," she said, but she couldn't help but wonder why it took her so long to realize that Spanish Fort was where she belonged and to ask herself why she didn't open her eyes years ago.

━━━━━━

The house buzzed with the energy of all the sisters being home for the holiday the rest of the day, especially when

Ophelia and Bo arrived. Dark clouds rolled in from the southwest, and a cold wind whipped down from the north, making it entirely too chilly that evening to sit out on the screened porch Joe Clay had built onto the back of the house. So they all gathered up in the living room.

"I'm going to build a fire, and we can visit until the rooster crows at dawn," Joe Clay told the girls.

Ursula figured that sneaking out of the house for a walk to think about all the research she had done or simply going up to her room to work would be rude. But she was antsy to either get back to her story or get away from everyone talking at once so that she could have some peace and quiet and plot out the rest of the synopsis for her Daisy book. The woman was so real in her mind that Ursula could actually feel Daisy's heart beating, but she still had to learn more about the culture of that day, more about the cattle drives, and more about the women's rights movements.

Mary Jane had handed over the notebooks she had filled with what she had gleaned from the Paradise madam Miz Raven's journals. Thank goodness they covered the days when the brothel was first in business, back when Daisy first came to Texas.

Ophelia, the only red-haired sister in the group, was telling a story about something that had happened the last week on her military base in Atlanta when the house phone rang. Ursula grabbed the receiver and answered it without even looking at the caller ID.

"Paradise," she answered just like she'd been taught to do as a child.

"Is this Ursula?" Remy asked.

His deep Texas drawl left no doubt in Ursula's mind as to who *she* was talking to. "That all depends on which one of the Simmons sisters you want to talk to."

"I'd like to ask Ursula if she would like to ride down to Nocona with me for an ice cream cone," he said. "I'll bring Daisy's diary if she will."

She held her hand over the speaker and said, "Mama, Remy wants to know if I can go to Nocona for ice cream."

"Your sisters…" Mary Jane started.

"He's going to let me look at Daisy's diary." Ursula felt like she was a teenager begging to go on a date. Her heart pounded, and her pulse jacked up several notches. She wasn't sure if it was because she would be spending time with Remy or if it was because she was going to peek inside that diary.

Rae interrupted before she could finish. "All in favor of our oldest sister going on a date, raise your hand." Her hand shot up immediately, and all the others but Endora's followed.

"I vote no because that's being rude," Endora protested. "We don't get many days to be all together so you shouldn't go running off with Remy—or with any other man, for that matter."

"Don't go judging all men by the one bad apple that you picked out of the barrel," Bernie scolded.

Endora shot an ugly look across the room at her. "Men, other than Daddy, aren't trustworthy."

"Well, thank you, darlin'," Joe Clay said and then grinned.

"Of course you can go with Remy," Mary Jane said. "You need to spend time with your muse if you're going to get your next book written, and I remember how excited I was when I found Madam Raven's journals." She turned to face Endora. "This isn't a relationship as in a real date. It's just a business meeting. Endora, you have nothing to worry about."

Ursula took her hand away from the phone receiver. "Sorry it took so long, but the sisters had to vote on the issue."

"You *are* thirty-three years old, aren't you?" Remy asked with a chuckle.

"Yep, but when I come home, I'm only sixteen," she answered. "Shall I drive to your house?"

"No, I'm in my truck now. I'll be in your front yard in five minutes. Will I get shot if I just honk?" he teased.

Ursula stood up. "No need to test that idea. Mama says this is a business meeting, not a date. I'll be waiting on the porch." She ended the call and then turned back toward the living room. "Just so you all know..." She looked right into Bernie's eyes. "This is not a date. Like Mama said, it's a business meeting. He's bringing an old diary written by the woman whose story I'm excited about telling."

"If he kisses you good night, it's a date," Bernie called out.

Ursula had blushed more since coming back to the Paradise than she had in at least five years. Imagining Remy's lips on hers and her body pressed up against his... Well, there was no way that wouldn't make any woman's face turn scarlet.

"Even a holy woman would get a little heated at that

idea," she whispered as she slipped into a jacket and picked up her purse. When she stepped out onto the porch, the headlights of Remy's truck were already lighting up the limbs on the bare pecan trees. He hopped out of his vehicle, rounded the front end, and had the door open for her by the time she was off the porch. Maybe this was a date after all.

"Thank you," she said as she slid into the passenger seat.

"You are very welcome," he answered, closed the door, and then whistled "We Wish You a Merry Christmas" all the way around the truck.

The cab, right along with the seat, was toasty warm, and the aroma of his aftershave—something woodsy with a hint of vanilla—filled the whole truck. He got inside, put the vehicle in gear, and turned around in the driveway.

"It's not Christmas until Thanksgiving is over," she reminded him.

Remy made a right turn from the lane to the highway leading south to Nocona. "I'm only a day early, and I love the holidays."

"It's my favorite time of the year too," she admitted. "The family is all together. There's the fun of decorating and all the wonderful food. You'll have to try Tertia's brown-sugar fudge. She'll have to go back to her job, but she'll be back home for Christmas, and she gets to stay until right after the New Year, and she always makes at least one batch while she's here."

"When do the rest of the sisters come home for Christmas?" he asked.

"They all manage to get here on Christmas Eve at the latest, and they stay as long as they can," she answered. "Daddy picks them up at the Dallas airport because Mama doesn't like for them to drive at that time of year. I can see by your expression you've got another question."

"I guess my poker face isn't working so well," he grinned. "Why do you call Joe Clay 'daddy'? Have you always done that?"

"Nope," she replied. "Endora started it, and we kind of fell in behind her, but he *is o*ur daddy. He's the one who took care of us. Helped us with homework, dried our tears when we scraped our knees. He even helped us have a funeral for our cat when she died. Her name was Raven like the first madam at the Paradise. Those are things that daddies do for their kids."

"What about your real dad?" Remy asked.

"That would be Martin Simmons, and we call him 'Father,'" she answered. "His wife insisted on that from the time they got married. We used to see him for a day or two at Christmas, but these days, he might manage to arrange a dinner date with us once a year."

Remy's jaw visibly tightened. "If I ever have children, I will always be a part of their lives."

"That's because you are a good man," Ursula told him. "Mama and Father grew apart instead of together. He wanted a son and instead he got seven daughters. That had to be a big disappointment. The two sets of twins are just over a year apart, so Mama had her hands full for many years, before and after the divorce. Looking back, I don't know how she managed to write novels and raise all of us girls at the same time. Then add the time when she bought the Paradise and had it remodeled into the chaos. In my eyes, she's even better than a superhero. Speaking of that, I've started researching"—she paused—"and…" She sighed.

"You want more information about Daisy and all that?" he finished for her.

"Yes, but I also need your permission to write a fictional story about Daisy and the man who sent for her," she answered.

"I asked my mother if you could use Daisy's writings," Remy said. "She said you could have it as long as you need it, but you have to give her a signed copy of the novel when it is published, and maybe if it's ever made into a movie, she'll expect tickets to the premiere."

"She will have both for sure." Ursula couldn't believe her good luck in having an actual day-by-day journal to read about the woman's life. "Daisy has already taken up a spot in my heart and mind."

"I can't wait to read the book," Remy said. "I've got the diary in the back seat, and you can take it home with you."

"It's going to be a historical *romance*," she told him.

"There's our old alma mater over there on the right. It hasn't changed much in fifteen years." He pointed to the school as they passed by it. "And, honey, for your information, or FYI, I've read all your books and your mother's. I'm interested in seeing all of Daisy's story and how she felt about the twists and turns that life handed her."

Ursula liked the endearment *honey* and the way it made her feel all warm and cozy, but she wondered if it was just a slip of the tongue. "How do you feel about what life has handed *you*?"

Remy turned toward her and raised a dark brow. "I'll show you mine if you show me *yours*."

"You go first," she said.

He shifted his gaze back to the deserted road. "Some of the paths I've traveled have been rough and full of potholes, but looking back, I can see that every experience taught me a lesson, so I'm okay with the choices I've made. They've all brought me to this evening, and I can't complain."

Was he flirting with her? Ursula wondered. Did he still have feelings for her like he had had in high school—like she had had for him back then?

"I haven't had too many rough places in my path," she said. "The ride was a little mundane. Life after we moved here was more of an adjustment for me than my sisters. At least I feel like it was since I was the oldest. Don't get me wrong. There were good times when we were growing up, especially after Joe Clay came into our family as a daddy. Did you know that he didn't like kids when Mama hired him to fix up the house for us?"

"Had no idea." Remy sounded surprised. "He talks about you girls all the time."

"We kind of hoodwinked him into changing his mind about kids," she said with a grin as she remembered the plans that she and her sisters had made the first week Joe Clay was in the house. They'd had a secret meeting in one of the bedrooms—she couldn't remember which one at the time—and decided that Joe Clay was a nice guy and that Mary Jane should go out with him. Would there be something like that in Daisy's story if her betrothed already had children?

"I don't imagine he had much of a chance with seven of you working on him," Remy said with a chuckle.

"Nope, he sure didn't," she said.

"And after you graduated from high school?" he asked.

"University in Tyler. I was a small-town… No, that's not right. I was a *ghost town* girl tossed into a city the size of Tyler, and I was more than a little intimidated," she answered. "I didn't do the sorority thing, and I didn't have enough confidence to go to parties, so I studied. That served me well after I got my master's, because the administration hired me to teach English, Comp 101, and creative writing, but nothing much changed other than that I worked on my novels when I had time."

"'Two roads diverged…'" Remy said as he drove into Nocona.

"And which one should we take, but that could mean a lot of things," Ursula said.

"Yes, it could," he agreed with a nod. "I've got a question that has nothing to do with where we've been or where we're going. Why do all you girls have such unusual names?"

"Mama named each of us after a character in the book that she was writing at the time," Ursula answered. "Their names kind of marked Bo and Rae. Rae grew up to be a policewoman, just like the character in Mama's book, and Bo has been in Nashville for years, trying to get a toe in the country-music door, just like the character in the book with her name."

Remy made a left-hand turn into the Dairy Queen parking lot. "And you? Did you turn out like your character?"

"No, I'm not a thing like her. She was a superhero kind of woman," Ursula answered. From what she could see in the windows, the Dairy Queen was crowded that evening. "Looks like we better hustle if we're going to get a booth, and I do believe that a Peanut Buster parfait is calling my name, right along with that journal you promised me a peek into."

"Like I said, you are welcome to take the journal and keep it as long as you want," Remy offered as he got out of his truck and jogged around the front end to open the door for her.

She slid off the seat and took a couple of steps to the right so he could close the door. "I've been calling the man in the story 'Fred.' Do you know what his name was?"

"Yep," Remy said. "Daisy was my mother's great-great-grandmother. Her husband's name was Jack Dulaney." He stopped talking long enough to hold the door into the Dairy Queen open for her. "The story has it that she was a spitfire Irish woman with a temper to match her fiery-red hair."

"Which fits right in with my idea of what she would look like," Ursula said with a smile. Jack seemed to go with Daisy so much better than Fred. "I can't believe that you are trusting me with something as precious as the journal. It belongs in a museum."

"Probably," Remy agreed, "but Mama loves romance books, and she can't wait to see what you do with the story."

"No pressure there," Ursula said with a sigh. "You said that your mother read the journal?"

"My grandmother did. My mother read the first couple of pages, and a lot of that was about what she cooked that day or how many shirts she hung on the line. Mama said Daisy had tight handwriting, and she wrote very small. Probably to keep from using so much paper. I just hope you aren't disappointed in what she wrote and that you get some ideas from it."

"I'm sure I will." Ursula thought of the journals that Joe Clay found when they were remodeling the Paradise about the seven ladies who worked there. Her mother's books based on them were instant bestsellers, and then a television series based on the series was made and went through six seasons.

"Hello, Mr. Baxter." A young lady behind the counter smiled at him. "What can I get y'all this evening?"

"Two Peanut Buster parfaits and a couple of cups of coffee," he said as he pulled out his wallet and put a bill on the counter. "Keep the change."

"Thanks a lot," she said.

"Are you still working toward an English degree?" he asked.

"Just got one more year, and then I'll be looking for a teaching job," the young lady answered as she rang up the sale and put the tip in her pocket. "You want to give me a recommendation?"

"Any time," he nodded and then guided Ursula through an archway to the left.

"Hey, Ursula! Is that really you? I haven't seen you since we graduated." Derrick Marlow waved from the first booth they passed. "What are you doing back in town?"

"I live here now," she answered without stopping. A vision popped into her head of the cocky expression on his face when he told her that she was lucky to be at the prom with him, so she could get in the back seat of his car and show him how much she appreciated him for asking her. Even after all the years that had passed, she had no intention of even carrying on a polite conversation with the man. She could be forgiving—some of the time—but not today.

With his hand on her back, Remy guided her to an empty booth at the very back of the room and waited for her to slide in before he took a seat across from her. She missed the sheer warmth of his touch and wished he had chosen to sit right beside her.

"How often have you run into Derrick since prom night?" Remy asked.

"This is the first," Ursula answered. "I hope it won't happen very often. That will be one of the benefits of being a hermit, living in Spanish Fort and writing full-time this next year. I get to spend more time with characters and less time with people like him."

"You don't think you'll miss mingling with people?" Remy asked.

"Not one bit," she answered without hesitation. "How about you? If you could be a full-time rancher, would you want to teach?"

"Yes, I would." He smiled. "I love teaching. I do like the hours and the calendar too. I have time off in the summer and during holidays and breaks. It's like having the best of two jobs."

"I counted holidays as an opportunity to buckle down and meet a novel deadline, and I loved being able to work in my pajamas," Ursula told him.

A different waitress than the one who had taken the order brought their ice cream. "Here you go. Enjoy! Are you one of the Simmons girls, maybe Ursula? My daughter, Cynthia, went to school with you. She's married now and has three kids."

"Yes, ma'am, I'm Ursula," she answered. "I remember Cynthia. Tell her hello for me."

She was so glad that her aunt Bernie didn't hear that comment about someone her age already having three children.

"I will," the lady said. "Both of us have read your books and all your mother's as well and really enjoyed them."

"Thank you so much," Ursula said. "I love hearing that a reader likes my stories."

"Hope to see you around. I'll tell Cynthia that I got to see you," the lady said and hurried away when a bell rang to announce that another order was ready.

Remy picked up his spoon and dug deep into the parfait. "I feel pretty special."

"Why's that?" Ursula followed his lead and took a bite of her ice cream.

"I'm out with a celebrity," he answered. "Maybe that's

why Derrick hasn't taken his eyes off you since we walked past. He might be trying to wrangle a date so he can get at your bank account."

"Knowing that he's staring at the back of my head gives me the creeps, and he might get a surprise if he saw my bank account," she replied without even a hint of a smile. "What I have might last through this next year since I have free room and board at the Paradise."

"If it doesn't, you can always hop over the fence and help feed cattle and wash dishes. I'll pay you well," Remy teased.

"Then I could really walk around in Daisy's shoes," she joked right back at him.

"Maybe we could borrow two or three young'uns just so you could get the right feel." His dark eyes twinkled.

"Did Jack have children for Daisy to take care of?" Ursula asked.

"Mama said there were two, and rumor had it that they were hellions. Seems his wife had run away with another man and left them behind for him to raise. She divorced him too, which was uncommon in those days. I guess that's the main reason he needed to get married again," Remy answered.

"I'm pretty sure I can fake it," Ursula bantered.

"Oh, really?" He raised an eyebrow.

"I have managed to write a few works of *fiction*," Ursula said. "They are contemporaries and set in a large city and not a ghost town, but hey, love is love and happy-ever-after happens all the time. It'll be interesting to see if Daisy tamed those kids and if she fell in love with Jack for real."

"Do you really believe that?" Remy asked.

"Believe what?"

"That happy-ever-after happens all the time?" He looked straight at her without blinking.

"No, I don't," she answered honestly, "but when it does, it has to be wonderful."

"I can agree with that for sure," he said. "I'm really enjoying this evening, Ursula."

"Me too," she whispered.

Sometimes miracles happen in the real world, not just in romance novels, her inner voice said.

Chapter 3

URSULA COULD HEAR HER sisters gathered in the room next door to hers as she tiptoed up the stairs. Any other time, she would have been eager to join them, but that night she had Daisy's diary in her hands, and she couldn't wait to read a few pages. She eased her bedroom door shut and sat down in her rocking chair. For several minutes, she simply held the book in her hands. The edges of the spine were lighter than the front and back of the burgundy leather, but considering that it was well over a hundred years old, the book was in remarkable condition.

She held it to her chest, expecting to get a whiff of the leather scent, but that had long since faded. Ursula could feel Daisy's heart keeping time with hers for several seconds before she switched on the lamp and adjusted the shade. As she unwound the leather strap that held the book together, her pulse raced. She was holding a woman's deepest secrets, and that was not to be taken lightly.

She took a long breath, let it out slowly, and opened the cover to read.

I have led marches in New York for women's rights. I have

spent the night in a smelly jailhouse. I have had lovers, had my heart broken and broken hearts. I've buried my father and mother from the typhus. Soldiering has taken my two brothers. I've been alone through a long, dark year, but nothing has prepared me for what has happened today.

I didn't expect to fall in love at first sight, not when I could be classified as a mail-order bride, but from the half a dozen letters I received from Jack Dulaney, I thought I would get more than I did today when I married the man. He met me at the train station in Nocona, Texas, and we went straight to the justice of the peace and were married. Other than saying "I do" when the man prompted him, he didn't say another word to me and barely brushed a kiss across my cheek when we were pronounced man and wife.

He is quite handsome, and I was so looking forward to being a married woman, moving to Texas, and seeing my new home—until we got here. He had not told me that he had two children—a seven-year-old boy and a five-year-old girl—or that they were complete hellions. The house he dumped me out at would make the jail cell where I spent a night back in New York look like a fancy hotel. The moment he had unloaded my things, he left me with the children and the nasty house and left in his wagon pulled by a couple of mules. He didn't say where he was going or when he would be back. I could not live in such a filthy house, so I changed my dress and started cleaning. I tried to talk to the children, but they told me to get out of their house. I have made a terrible mistake.

Ursula moved from her rocking chair to her desk and began to take notes when she got to the part where Daisy had made it her mission to understand her new husband. Daisy had learned from past lovers that the way to get a man to open up about his feelings was to feed him well, so she started cooking three meals a day for Jack and his children.

"The first chapter I outlined is far too sappy," Ursula muttered.

Jack and Daisy had definitely not fallen in love at first sight, and the two kids sure didn't accept her as their new mother. Doors opened and shut in the Paradise sometime after midnight, but Ursula kept reading. Finally, her eyes ached so badly that she had to lay the book aside and rest them for a few minutes.

Sunrays streamed into her room and warmed her face when she awoke the next morning. Her face was glued to the last page in her notebook. She peeled the paper away gently and groaned when she straightened up. The aroma of fresh gingerbread wafted up from somewhere and filled her bedroom. She wasn't sure if it was from the kitchen or if it was just a figment of her imagination since she'd been reading about Daisy trying to please Jack with all kinds of baked goods. She groaned a second time and rubbed her aching neck.

She had barely gotten her bearings when Endora poked her head in the door and gave her a dirty look. What a way to start off Thanksgiving morning, she thought.

"Good morning, and Happy Thanksgiving, but what did I do to get such a stink eye?" Ursula asked.

Endora stopped at the top of the stairs and blocked the way down. "Did Remy kiss you good night? Was it a date?"

Ursula drew down her eyebrows and pointed a finger toward Endora. "I'm thirty-three years old, and that would be none of your business, little sister. I'm not sure if it was a date or not, but rest assured, I do not kiss and tell. It's time for you to pull on your big-girl underbritches and get over what happened to you. As long as you mope around and refuse to move on, you are giving Kevin power over you."

Endora's chin quivered. "I don't want you to get hurt like I did. I trusted Kevin, and I also trusted my so-called friend Krystal. You could suffer a heartbreak like I did if you don't be careful."

Ursula draped an arm around her sister's shoulders. "Honey, in one way or another, *all* your sisters have most likely had bad experiences with men, including me. We just decided to get past it and not let it define our future."

"How?" One pitiful tear ran down Endora's cheek.

"The first thing is to either shoot him or make peace with the fact that you really don't want to live in a small prison cell the rest of your life," Ursula answered. "You never did look good in orange. The second thing is to learn to see him as the jackass he really is, make yourself believe that you deserve a better friend than someone like Krystal and a better boyfriend than that sumbitch was, and put them both out of your mind. My advice is to make peace first and foremost. Want me to pray for him?"

"Hell, no!" Endora gasped.

"Well, I'm going to." Ursula bowed her head. "Dear Father in Heaven, I'm here to ask that You shoot down Your wrath on the man who hurt my baby sister. I know that You've said that vengeance belongs to You, so I'm trusting You to take care of this—and I would like for the punishment for Kevin to be at least equal to those boils that the Scripture talks about. But if boils is all You have to work with today, please give him a dose on the parts of the body that cheated on my little sister. If You're real busy and need some help, then just send me a sign, and I will be glad to step in and take care of things for You. Amen." She raised her head to see a hint of a sparkle in Endora's eyes. "Will that prayer work for you?"

Endora nodded. "Yep, it sure does, but why did you think about boils?"

Ursula stepped around her. "That's a story for another day. For now, let's get down to the kitchen before those other five eat all the gingerbread. If that happens, I'm blaming you."

"Then hurry up." Endora finally smiled. "After that prayer, I don't want you to be mad at me."

"You really don't." Ursula brushed past her and led the way to the kitchen.

When they arrived, Luna looked up. "So was it a date?"

"She isn't talking," Endora answered. "Evidently, she doesn't kiss and tell."

"Happy Thanksgiving, and it wasn't a date," Bernie declared. "If it was, she'd have a glow, and she just looks sleepy to me."

"Me too," Luna agreed.

Endora shook her finger at her twin. "You don't get to put a dog in this fight. You've been shamelessly flirting with Shane O'Toole for weeks now."

Ursula bit back laughter.

"What's so funny?" Luna asked.

"I believe that business of not having a dog in the fight is one of Aunt Bernie's sayings," Ursula said.

"Yep, it is." Bernie beamed.

"Well, it's a good saying," Endora declared, "and Luna *has* been flirting with Shane."

"Yep, I have," Luna agreed, "but I've gotten nowhere."

Ursula noticed that Luna had crossed her fingers, so *that* was a little white lie. She wondered just how far things had gone between her sister and Shane O'Toole.

"She"—Luna pointed at Ursula—"comes home one day and has a date the next night. Evidently, I need to take some dating lessons from her. How about you, Endora? You want to sit in on her class with me?"

"Hell, no!" Endora gasped. "I'm going to be the old maid aunt who spoils all y'all's kids."

"Oh no, you will not," Mary Jane disagreed as she set a second pan of gingerbread right from the oven in the middle of the table and then sat down beside Bernie. "That's my job, and I'm not giving it up. You can be the old-maid aunt, but the spoiling business belongs to me and your daddy."

"Ursula, darlin'," Bernie said in a sugary tone, "you are the oldest, so maybe you'd better get things rolling on those grandkids."

"Why shouldn't Luna take the first step?" Ursula shot back as she cut herself a huge square of gingerbread and covered it with warm lemon sauce. "First grandbaby always gets the most attention. Y'all should all be going full speed ahead for that honor."

"But you always told us that because you were the first-born, you got to do things before any of us other sisters," Luna protested. "You left the Paradise and went to college first. And now I understand your muse has been keeping you up, so you get to be famous with a breakout novel."

"I wouldn't want to take all the credit, so I'll leave the first grandbaby to you and Endora," Ursula teased.

"Listening to all y'all reminds me of when I came to visit when y'all were little girls," Bernie said. "Y'all were always competitive"—Bernie tossed in her two cents—"but I agree with Luna. Ursula should get married first and have the first grandbaby, then we need at least one a year for a long time. Two or even three would be nice some years."

"Holy smoke!" Endora gasped. "Other than Luna flirting with Shane, none of us even has a boyfriend."

"And you never will if you sit around bellyachin' about that rotten egg that did you dirty," Bernie told her and then glanced over at Mary Jane. "Feels wonderful to have them all home and arguing, doesn't it?"

"Yep, it sure does," she agreed.

Bernie cut herself a square of gingerbread and squirted whipped cream over the top. "I remember when y'all first moved here and Mary Jane hired Joe Clay to remodel this old place. I thought she was crazy for hiring a man who didn't even like kids."

"We had to work hard to change his mind," Luna replied. "But..." She glanced over at Ursula. "Ursula got another *first* thing when she got her bedroom done before any of us."

"Oldest to youngest," Mary Jane said with a nod.

Ursula glanced around the table at her mother, aunt, and two sisters. Was Endora ever going to rise above all her moodiness? Had Luna actually been flirting with Shane, or was Endora jealous and imagining things? Were all the rest of the sisters really waiting on her to settle down first and start a family, or were they just teasing her?

The questions didn't have to be answered that very moment. Being together again for another Thanksgiving was enough for now.

———

"Okay, fess up," Mary Jane said while she and Ursula made pumpkin and apple pies after breakfast. "How was the date last night?"

"Y'all said he had to kiss me good night for it to be a date. He didn't, so it wasn't," Ursula answered.

"You might fool your sisters but not your mother," Mary Jane told her.

"I like Remy," Ursula answered. "Always have. I'm surprised that we haven't run into each other throughout the years since his mother was our closest neighbor."

"Everything happens for a reason," Mary Jane told her. "Y'all must not have been ready to meet up again until now."

"You are probably right," Ursula agreed. "He's entrusted me with a diary that's been passed down through generations. I stayed up way too late last night reading the first few entries, and I got a very good personal insight into what this area was like during the time when Daisy lived here. It would have been back in the time when Madam Raven ran this place. I had the beginning chapter of my story all wrong. They didn't fall in love at first sight. Jack was somewhat of an old bastard who evidently just wanted a wife to cook and clean and take care of his kids. Right now, I don't like him too well. I only hope by the time I get to the end of the diary that there is a happy-ever-after."

"When Joe Clay found Miz Raven's old journals, I felt the same way as you do, but the more I read about the women who lived here, the more I learned that I had been wrong," Mary Jane said. "I was writing a Regency at the time, and when I talked to Norma, she said to put it aside and write the book that was taking over my heart. I'm hoping that your Daisy is just the beginning of a series that hits the market like mine did."

"What are y'all talking about?" Endora asked as she joined them.

"The new book I'm researching," Ursula answered. "Remy gave me a diary, and so far I'm getting a really good picture of what things were like here in Daisy's time and the difference in the way some men treated their women back then."

Pepper's growls announced Bernie's arrival before she made it into the house. When she breezed into the kitchen, Sassy scooted inside as if she was the queen of Paradise. Pepper realized the cat was there and tried to wiggle free of Bernie's arms.

"Why can't you and Sassy be friends?" Bernie snapped at him. "You liked the old stray cat that came up behind the bar."

Endora covered a yawn with the back of her hand as she headed for the coffeepot. "Pepper was king of the bar, and the alley cat was a peasant. Sassy is the queen here, and she's not going to give up her throne. It's a major conflict of interest, but give them time. They'll work it out."

Endora was supposed to be allergic to dogs, but Ursula always figured that what she was having as a child was just a panic attack. When Endora was just a little girl, a neighbor's dog got loose and chased her. Since then, every time she was around one, she had the symptoms of an asthma attack. According to Aunt Bernie, folks who were allergic to dogs could have a Chihuahua around them without any problems. Ursula had looked it up, and it was a myth, but she wasn't about to tell Endora or argue with Bernie about it.

"Endora, why don't you write a children's book about

a cat and a dog learning to get along," Ursula said. "You always were good at drawing so you could do your own illustrations."

"A whole series of books about Pepper the dog might be fun," Mary Jane suggested. "Pepper moving to the country. Pepper learning what a cow is. The possibilities are endless."

"That might be fun," Endora agreed.

"Do you hear that, Pepper?" Bernie beamed. "You are going to be a hero. They might even come after you to act in the movies they'll make from the books. Your name will be on posters, and you'll be the star of the show." She kissed the dog on the nose, and then she glanced over at Endora. "Don't you dare make Pepper a bulldog. He's a Chihuahua straight out of Mexico. One of your stories will be how he had to adapt from barking in Spanish to English."

Endora rolled her eyes as she carried her mug of coffee to the table. "I'll *think* about writing one book about Pepper, and I will draw him as a Chihuahua. But right now, I want to hear more about what Ursula is writing."

"Daisy comes to Texas from New York where she's gotten in trouble for marching for women's rights and decides to bring the fight to Texas," Ursula answered. "After paying fines and sitting in jail, her money is almost all gone, her family has all died, and she doesn't know what she's going to do until she sees an ad in a newspaper at the train station. She figures the Texas newspaper was left there by a traveler from that area and takes it as a sign when she sees an ad for a mail-order bride. She answers it and Jack Dulaney—that would be the man who lived next door to the Paradise—sends her a train ticket to come to Spanish Fort."

"That sounds like a match *not* made in heaven," Bernie laughed.

"Why's that?" Ursula asked.

"Daisy is a suffragette. Men back then were fighting as hard against women's rights as women were fighting for them," Bernie explained. "I'm going to tie Pepper to the porch post while we have breakfast, and then I'll take him for a walk."

"What does Daisy fighting for women's rights have to do with her falling in love?" Ursula asked, but she had been wondering the exact same thing.

"She's an independent woman. Like I said, men back then expected their women to stay home, cook, clean, and raise babies. Honey, Jack and Daisy are going to have to jump through hoops of fire if there's going to be a happy-ever-after in your book," Bernie answered as she left the room.

Mary Jane shook a little cinnamon on top of the pumpkin pies and then slid them into the oven. "She's right, Ursula. Your characters can't sit down on a blanket under a shade tree with a basket of fried chicken and fall in love. They have to face and overcome battles. Put them on a high limb of a tree and throw stones at them. That will keep your reader invested in the story until the very end."

"Are you starting to feel like you are Daisy?" Endora asked.

"Of course she is," Mary Jane answered. "She's got to feel

what Daisy does, cry when she does, get mad when she does, and even laugh when she does. If the character isn't real to Ursula, then she won't be to the reader."

"My characters are always in my mind, but I don't feel like I'm becoming the people I write about," Ursula admitted.

"How did Daisy feel when she first got to her new home?" Mary Jane asked.

"Utter bewilderment," Ursula answered. "I wept with her."

"You get that emotion into your first chapter, and you will do fine then," Mary Jane said with a smile.

"You have a case of transference," Endora said.

Ursula tilted her head to the side. "I have what?"

"You are transferring Daisy's life to yours. Is Jack a stand-in for Remy?" Endora asked.

"Hell, no!" Ursula declared loudly.

"Hell, no, what?" Bernie asked as she came back into the kitchen. "The rest of the family is watching the parade. I stopped for a minute to see what was going on. Looks like I missed something here. What are y'all arguing about?"

"Endora thinks I have a case of transference," Ursula answered. "That I have projected my character onto myself, and the hero of my new book is Remy."

"Want my opinion?" Mary Jane asked. "I think Endora is looking for a reason to make you doubt your own feelings. She can't bear the thought of you or Luna getting hurt like she did."

Endora crossed her arms over her chest. "I am not, and

even if I was, it's just because I love my sisters so much I don't want them to endure the pain I have."

Ursula stood up, bent down, and gave Endora a hug. "We love you too, darlin'. But we're grown women, and it's not your fault if we get our hearts broken along the paths that life leads us down. You don't have to protect us. All you have to do is get to feeling better and learn how to trust again."

"That might take a while," Endora whispered.

Ursula picked up her plate and headed for the kitchen sink. "Let yourself feel joy like we had when we were kids growing up in this house. You have to work on it yourself, Sister. Happy doesn't just fall out of the sky and sit on your shoulder."

"Don't I know it," Endora said with a long sigh. "Enough about me. This is Thanksgiving. What can I do to help, Mama?"

"You can make the cranberry salad. Recipe is in the notebook," Mary Jane told her and mouthed a thank-you to Ursula.

"The weatherman just gave us a news flash on the television. We've got good weather today and tomorrow, but Saturday it's going to turn off cold and Sunday we're supposed to get freezing rain and sleet," Joe Clay yelled from the foyer.

"We'll have to make hay—or in this case decorate for Christmas—while the sun shines." Remy's deep drawl floated to the kitchen.

Joe Clay mused, "Rae and Tertia should probably start home tomorrow before the bad weather starts."

Mary Jane wiped her hands on the tail of her apron and headed toward the living room. "Let's take a break and watch the parade for an hour and then come back to cook some more. Endora, the cranberry salad will wait that long. Come on, girls. Let's go claim a seat and spend some time with the family while we can."

Remy stuck his head around the doorjamb. "Hey, Ursula! Did you have time to read any on the journal?"

"Some of it." Ursula hung back with Remy while the rest of the family claimed seats in front of the television. "I'm fascinated by what Daisy has written and how much of her feelings she's put into words. But I will never take running water for granted again."

"Or indoor bathrooms," he said with a smile.

"Thanks again for letting me read it," Ursula said. She would rather stand in the foyer or maybe sit on the stairsteps and talk to Remy than go watch a parade on television, but her sisters would never stop teasing her if she did. And chances were that they would all leave tomorrow or Saturday at the latest.

"Ursula, come on!" Luna yelled. "You are missing the parade."

"Guess that's our cue," Remy said.

Before either of them could take a step in that direction, someone knocked on the door. Ursula took a couple of long strides and slung it open to see a tall man with thick blond hair that grazed his shirt collar and steely blue eyes.

"Hey, Shane!" Remy said so close behind her that the warmth of his breath on her bare neck sent delicious little shivers down her spine. "You are just in time."

"I'm Ursula, the oldest sister." She extended her hand.

"Pleased to meet you." Shane shook with her and then removed his coat and hung it on the hall tree beside Remy's. "As much as Luna talks about all her sisters, I feel like I already know you."

From the way his eyes went all dreamy when he looked at Luna, Ursula would be willing to bet that he and her sister were doing a whole lot more than just flirting. "Well, then it's time we all get to know you. Come on into the living room. The parade is on right now, and after that, there'll be ball games that we will all argue over and then Thanksgiving dinner."

"And I'm going to enjoy every single second of having folks around me to celebrate this day," Shane said and went ahead of them into the living room.

"What Shane said," Remy whispered. "Especially for the time I get to spend with you."

"Me too," Ursula said a bit breathlessly.

———

Mary Jane brought out trays of finger foods when the Thanksgiving Day parade ended—hot yeast rolls stuffed with pineapple cream cheese and ham, pumpkin bread, chips and several kinds of dip, and a fruit tray—and as luck would have it, the last play of the first football game of the day was done in time for them to set the table for Thanksgiving dinner.

With nine women and three men who were willing to pitch in, the turkey and all the trimmings were on the table at exactly four o'clock. When everyone was seated, Mary Jane asked Joe Clay to say grace, laid her hands on the table, and bowed her head.

Ursula took her mother's hand in her right hand and Remy's in her left one. She tried to listen to Joe Clay's short prayer, but the sparks dancing around the room made that virtually impossible.

When Joe Clay said, "Amen," Mary Jane raised her head and said, "Everyone keep holding hands. One of the traditions we started when we moved into the Paradise was to go around the table and have everyone tell one thing they are grateful for this year. I'll start. I'm thankful for my family and that we are all together today."

"That's two things, darlin'," Joe Clay said with a chuckle. "I'm thankful for the same things, but most of all for my beautiful wife."

"A new start," Ursula said.

"This family," Remy added and gave Ursula's hand a gentle squeeze.

She hoped that he couldn't hear the way her heart was thumping at no more than his fingers laced in hers or that he could feel her jacked-up pulse.

"This day," Luna said.

Ursula noticed that her sister stole a look at Shane who was sitting beside her.

"Good neighbors," Shane said.

Bo shrugged and then said, "Turkey and dressing."

"Ditto!" Rae added.

"Fun times," Ophelia said.

"Just the joy of life," Tertia said.

They all looked at Endora, who brought up the end of the line. "I'm grateful for the support of my family," she said.

"Amen to all of the above," Ursula said.

"Now, darlin'," Mary Jane said with her eyes on Joe Clay. "Would you please carve the turkey? I'm starving."

Mary Jane dropped Ursula's hand. Remy gave her left one a gentle squeeze before letting go. Did that mean something, or was he just being nice?

Chapter 4

"WHY ARE YOU WAKING us up at daylight? What day is it anyway?" Rae grumbled and gave Ursula dirty looks as she rubbed sleep out of her eyes. "I work the night shift at the police station, so my body is used to sleeping during the day."

"The day after Thanksgiving." Ursula handed her a cup of steaming hot coffee. "This should get you going this morning. And, Sister, there hasn't been a night shift at the Paradise since it was a brothel. If you ever move back home, you'll get along with Bernie really well."

"Why's that?" Rae sat up carefully and took a sip of her coffee.

"All those years of working in a bar at night has messed up her sleep pattern. But hey, y'all can stay up all night looking at brides' magazines and picking out wedding dresses."

"Are you asking me to be your maid of honor?" Rae asked.

Ursula sat down on the edge of the bed. "No, I'm telling you that Bernie wants one or all of us married. You and Luna can be next. Drink your coffee and wake up. Today is when we put up Christmas trees and decorations, and everyone gets up for breakfast, just like we all did when we were kids. Your personal Christmas tree is in the box right outside your door."

"I stumbled over the box last night when I came up to bed. We don't do our own trees until the rest of the decorations are up, right?" Rae covered a yawn with her hand and then took a sip of her coffee. "This is so much better than the thin stuff they have at the police station. Is Mama cooking?" She sniffed the air. "I don't smell bacon."

"Mama doesn't cook the day after Thanksgiving. Leftovers from dinner yesterday are everywhere," Ursula told her. "I had a slice of pumpkin pie with whipped cream on it this morning, and I can hear a turkey sandwich calling my name for lunch."

Rae set her coffee on the nightstand and got out of bed. "Am I the last one awake?"

"Yep," Ursula answered. "Daddy, Shane, and Remy are stringing lights in the pecan trees down the lane and on the sleigh out in the front yard. After that, they'll put up the lights around the edge of the roof and wrap them all up the porch posts. Mama is unpacking boxes in the living room with Endora and Bo. You better wake up and come on down or you'll miss all the fun."

Ursula stood up and started across the floor.

"Hey," Rae said.

Ursula turned around at the door. "What?"

"Thanks for waking me." Rae smiled. "I love all the fun of decorating, and I'm hoping that the holidays bring Endora up out of her sadness."

"Me too." Ursula waved. "See you down there in a few. There's still a slice of apple pie left if Tertia hasn't eaten it."

"I'll hurry," Rae said with a chuckle. "That's my favorite."

Ursula was making herself a glass of sweet tea when Luna toted a box into the house through the back door. BREAKABLE was written on the side. She took it straight to the living room and came right back.

"That was the last one in the barn," she said as she took the container of leftover turkey out of the refrigerator. "They're the ornaments that Mama kept from when we were all little kids. I'm having this and potato salad for breakfast. You want some, or should I put it back when I'm finished with it?"

"Nope, but I will pour each of us a glass of sweet tea," Ursula offered.

Luna brought her plate to the table and sat down across from Ursula. "I'm glad you're home and flirting with Remy. It takes some of the heat off me and Shane. Endora is determined that we all seven are going to be old maids like her and never even think of marriage."

"*I'm* not flirting, and you said you weren't—" Ursula stopped in the middle of the sentence when Endora breezed into the kitchen.

"Turkey for breakfast?" Endora frowned.

"You know I'd rather have leftovers as breakfast food," Luna answered.

"That's the one area where we are totally different," Endora declared. "I'm making hot chocolate for me and Bo. Anyone else want some?"

Ursula held up her glass of tea. "Not for me."

"Not me," Luna said, "but thanks for the offer."

"You seem to be in a good mood, Endora." Ursula hoped that her blunt speech the day before had helped.

Endora set about pouring milk and packages of hot chocolate mix in each of the mugs. "Yes, I am. Mama reminded me that this is the Jesus season and that love can't live in the same heart with hate. So I'm going to try to get rid of all the bad feelings I've been having—one day at a time."

"Good for you," Ursula said.

"But I'm not ready to trust men yet." Endora whipped around and pointed a long, slender forefinger at Luna and Ursula. "And I want you two to be careful and not make the same mistake I did." The microwave dinged, and she carefully took the steaming mugs out. "We just put up that old metal Christmas tree in the middle of the dining room table, but Mama says we all have to gather around and put the tiny little bulbs on it together."

"Just like we did the first Christmas we were here," Ursula said with a nod. "I love our traditions."

"Me too," Luna agreed.

Ursula had never made traditions of her own because she had always come home for the holidays. When she was in college, she spent the time between semesters at Spanish Fort. Then when she landed a job at the same college, her schedule hadn't varied very much from when she was a student. Since the family had moved into the Paradise all those years ago, she had put up her own small tree in her bedroom, but she never even thought about decorating one in her dorm room or her apartment.

"What were we talking about before Endora arrived?" she finally asked.

"I was saying that…" Luna scanned the doorway and lowered her voice. "Shane and I are doing more than just flirting. We'd like to date openly, but…"

"But Endora is your twin, and y'all have been together since before birth," Tertia finished the sentence for her.

"And you don't want her to feel like you are leaving her out," Ursula said. "Even though she was engaged."

Luna shrugged. "I know, I know."

"Are we talking about Endora?" Rae asked as she came into the room.

"Yep," Luna answered.

Rae grabbed the last piece of apple pie, added whipped cream, and took her first bite on her way to the table. "Has she decided to move on and forget that sorry sucker?"

"I think she's making progress," Luna said.

"It's going to take a while for her to feel good about *you* dating. You need to just rip off the Band-Aid, girl, and tell her how you feel." Rae covered a yawn with her hand. "Maybe if she sees you happy, she'll realize that all men aren't like the one who did her dirty, and you deserve to be happy."

"I agree," Ursula said. "We all love Endora, but we can't stop living our lives for her. If you and Shane have a connection, then go for it. I can see the chemistry between y'all, and what if he's really the one, and you regret not doing anything about it? We're getting too old to have to look back at decisions we made with regrets." She wasn't sure if she was thinking about Daisy's words or if she was preaching to herself.

"Part of that chemistry we saw belonged to you and Remy," Rae declared. "I'm more than a little jealous of the both of you and Luna. If you don't stake a claim on Remy, I may rush in ahead of you and take him for myself."

"Not possible," Luna disagreed. "He had a crush on her in high school, and I don't think he's ever gotten over it."

"Okay, enough!" Ursula scolded as she pushed back her chair and started out of the room. "This is our Christmas tradition day to make the Paradise look better than it ever has before. It's not one of those talk shows on television."

She found Endora in the living room working on decorations with Mary Jane. Her youngest sister was setting up the nativity scene on the fireplace mantel. Mary Jane was busy taking the old Christmas tree out of the box and laying the limbs out in piles.

"Mama, you should buy one of those prelit trees that are already put together," Endora said. "All you have to do is take them out of the box and pull them up from the bottom."

"Where's the fun in that?" Mary Jane asked. "This tree has been with us since our first Christmas at the Paradise. I remember you girls sorting the limbs according to color and our first kittens breaking a few ornaments when they batted at the ones on the low branches. It was Joe Clay's and my first tree together, and I'll use it forever or until the limbs get too worn out to stay on the base."

Ursula opened one of the boxes marked Ornaments, removed the tissue paper from each one, and then laid them out on the coffee table. The first one—baby's first Christmas—was engraved with her name. There were six more just like it hiding in the box somewhere, each with one of her sisters' names on it.

Ursula thought about the ornament she was holding. Her mother had been younger than Endora and Luna when she hung it on her tree the year that her baby daughter Ursula was six months old. By the time Mary Jane was Ursula's age now, she had seven daughters.

And you sit there with that ornament in your hand, a sexy cowboy across the fence from you, and dragging your feet. By this time next year, you should be ordering something pretty for your baby's first Christmas, Bernie's voice scolded in Ursula's imagination.

"Where is Aunt Bernie?" Ursula asked.

"She's hasn't gotten here yet. The rest of the bunch is outside helping your daddy and Shane and Remy," Mary Jane answered.

Ursula laid the ornament aside, but the thoughts in her head went round and round like they were on a fast-turning merry-go-round. She wondered if she would ever buy one for her baby's first Christmas and have it engraved. What name would go on it? Maybe something like Abby or maybe Will? Or would she name her baby after a grandmother or grandfather?

The name Mary popped into her head. Mary Jane had been named after Bernie—Mary Bernadette. As much as Ursula would love to name her daughter Mary, she figured she should leave that one for Ophelia to use since her full name was Mary Ophelia Simmons.

"We're coming in for a cup of coffee to warm us up." Joe Clay's big, booming voice filled the room when he, Shane, and Remy entered the house. "The girls are still working on putting up the red bows around the porch." Joe Clay met Mary Jane in the middle and wrapped her up in his arms, then tipped up her chin with his fist and brushed a kiss across her lips. "This is my favorite time of the year, darlin'."

"Mine too," she said.

Ursula could see that for just a brief magical moment, they were in a world of their own. *That's what I want,* she thought. *I want to feel like they do even after twenty years of marriage. I want something as simple as seeing each other again to be new and fresh and for my husband to look at me like Daddy looks at Mama.*

As if on cue, Remy walked up beside her.

"Good mornin'," she whispered.

"Right back at you." He flashed a brilliant smile. "Being a part of today is awesome."

"And to think I've taken it for granted," she said and suddenly felt as if she and Remy were the only ones in the living room. Was that an omen?

Luna came into the room, nudged Ursula on the shoulder,

and whispered, "You think Remy and Shane would help us do our little personal trees? In our bedrooms?"

"I would love that, but you know the rules," Ursula answered out of the corner of her mouth.

Boys had never been allowed to put a single foot on the second step of the staircase—not even after the sisters were all grown and away from home. If they brought home a boyfriend to stay for a couple of days over a holiday, Mary Jane rented a motel room for them in Nocona.

=====

"Do you think you might come over to my house after church on Sunday and help me put up my tree?" Remy asked Ursula as they made their way to the kitchen.

"I'd love to," Ursula answered. "I could bring Daisy's diary back then too."

"I told you to keep it as long as you want," Remy said. "You might need to backtrack and reference something while you're building your outline."

"Thank you," she told him with a smile. "Now, who wants coffee and who wants hot chocolate?"

"Chocolate for me," Joe Clay answered, "and if there's any apple pie left, I'll have some of that rather than cookies."

"You're out of luck on that apple pie," Ursula told him. "Rae got to it first."

"Pumpkin or pecan?" Joe Clay asked.

"Either or both?" Ursula asked.

"Both, since there's no apple pie," Joe Clay said.

"Coffee is fine for me, and can I take it with me? Luna and I still have to put lights around the cutouts of Santa and Mrs. Claus down at the end of the lane," Shane said.

"I'll take my coffee to go too," Luna said.

"I've invited Shane and Remy to go with us to cut down a cedar tree for the porch tomorrow," Joe Clay said and slid a sly wink toward Ursula. "I might need some help with that cranky old handsaw."

She had no doubt that Joe Clay could bench-press a Brahma bull, so he didn't need help cutting down a Christmas tree.

"Oh, and I put a big ball of mistletoe in one of the rocking chairs out on the porch. Remy found it on a limb in one of the pecan trees. I thought your mama could use part of it to decorate with," Joe Clay said.

Ursula's thoughts quickly jumped from finding the right tree for the porch to standing under the mistletoe and gazing into Remy's eyes just before a long kiss. Warmth filled her whole body, and she felt heat crawling up—again—from her neck to her face.

"I'm sure we can find a place for it," she said and then whipped around and headed out into the foyer.

All of us girls feel like we are teenagers again when we come home, she fussed at herself, but I'm acting like I'm sixteen and mooning over Remy again.

Mary Jane peeked around the doorjamb into the living room and held up a big ball of mistletoe. "I'm so glad y'all found this. It's beautiful. What I had packed away is so dried up that it's falling apart. Ursula, you are in charge of breaking off small pieces to hang in every doorway. We'll need red ribbons at the top of each stem, and maybe a jingle bell or two."

"Think either one of us will be able to take advantage of this?" Luna asked.

Ursula led the way into the living room. "Depends on whether we want lectures from our baby sister. Would it be your first kiss from Shane?"

"That's 'need to know,' and no one does, not even my big sister," Luna answered as she picked up two disposable cups of coffee and headed toward the foyer with Shane right behind her.

Ursula sat down on the floor next to a box with RIBBONS printed in bold letters on the outside and patted the space next to her. "It's beginning to look a lot like Christmas," she singsonged.

"Ohhh, mistletoe," Ophelia squealed. "I'll help put ribbons on it. Maybe I'll get a kiss or two at our big community party this year."

"What if Old Man Versey takes up residence under it?" Ursula teased. "Mama says we're putting them in every doorway. He could stand under one or another of them all evening with that big toothless grin and a little dried snuff in his gray beard."

"I'm not kissing anyone if that's the best I can get." Ophelia shivered.

Endora snarled her nose. "Me neither. Like I've said

before, I'm going to be the old-maid aunt in this family, and the rest of you would do well to follow my example."

"There's got to be babies before you can be an aunt," Mary Jane said and opened a box with lights inside. "Endora, help me stretch these out and make sure they're all in working order."

"Mama, why do you use these big old lights that have to be tested every year?" Ophelia asked. "You could trash them and buy some of the twinkling lights that you just put on the tree and plug in."

"These were the lights my grandmother put on her tree when I was growing up. Her mother had used them when my grandmother was a little girl. I inherited them when she passed away, and I've used them every year since then," Mary Jane answered. "Your father hated them."

"That's enough reasons for me to love them," Ursula declared. "I'll help check every bulb if you need me to help. Have you got extras if one is out?"

"I bought dozens of them years ago," Mary Jane answered. "And you and Ophelia have a job to do with the mistletoe. Endora can help me with this."

Ursula picked up a spool of red-and-green-plaid ribbon and cut off a long length to make a bow. "Hey, is this the same stuff you used to tie in all the twins' hair the first Christmas we were here?"

"Yep." Mary Jane nodded and smiled. "Good memories."

"Not for me," Endora declared. "Luna acted up at the church Christmas program, and since we were identical, I got blamed."

Ursula made a bow for a sprig of mistletoe, but her mind was on the possibility of having twins. She'd never thought of the fact that she could have multiple births, but it didn't scare her. Her mother had raised two sets, born only a little more than a year apart, at the same time she had three other daughters and very little help from her husband. Ursula was following in Mary Jane's path when it came to writing, so she had no doubt that if she did the same thing with children, she would manage—especially if she had support from her future children's father.

Chapter 5

A FEW DARK CLOUDS shifted over the sun periodically on Saturday when everyone at the Paradise loaded up in vehicles and headed to Saint Jo for the annual Christmas Festival on the square. "Okay, girls, now you know the rules," Joe Clay teased as he glanced up in the rearview mirror at Ursula and Ophelia. "Don't talk to strangers. If anyone offers you candy…"

"We know, Daddy," Ursula said with a nod. "Don't take anything from strangers, but we've gone past the candy stage."

"Then don't take a drink from anyone," Joe Clay said, "and that means that you open your own beer."

"Yes, sir." Ophelia saluted and then shook her finger at her parents. "And the rules go for you and Mama too. Y'all don't get to stay in a hotel room for a little time alone while we run wild all over the square."

"Well, crap!" Mary Jane said with a fake smile. "That's exactly what we planned to do."

"What happens at the festival stays at the festival, darlin', and as far as you two go"—Joe Clay turned around slightly in his seat—"we'll meet you in the parking lot at three thirty so we can get back home and finish up the final decorations. And remember, if we can't get a room, then neither of you can."

"On a serious side," Ophelia said, "I asked to ride with y'all because I wanted you to know that I had a long talk last night with Endora. I told her that we can't undo the past, but we don't have to let it define the future like she is doing."

"And?" Mary Jane turned in her seat enough to see her daughter.

"She said she would work on it," Ophelia answered.

Joe Clay drove down the lane and made a right-hand turn. "I hate seeing her so miserable. She's always been so feisty. I should've gone down to south Texas and confronted Kevin myself."

"What good would that have done?" Ursula asked.

"It would have shown my baby girl that her daddy didn't put up with a guy treating her like that," Joe Clay answered.

"I wouldn't let him," Mary Jane said in the serious tone that she usually reserved for correcting the girls. "Endora found out about it over spring break. We knew about the two vacancies at the Prairie Valley school, so we told her and Luna about them and suggested that they move back home so Endora wouldn't have to work with Kevin and Krystal."

"Working in the same school system with both of them would be rough," Ursula said. "I can't imagine having to do that for another two months."

"Me either," Ophelia said. "It's a good thing I was

deployed at the time, or Daddy and I would have gone down there together."

Ophelia had never been one to throw around threats. She had served two enlistments and was trying to decide whether to stay in for the full twenty years to retirement or get out the next year. She didn't take crap from anyone, and even when they were kids, if someone was hateful or ugly to any of her sisters, she was there to take care of it.

"That's done and over with," Ursula said. "In the past, like you told Endora. Now, let's talk about you and whether you're going to come on back to Spanish Fort when this enlistment is up."

"Don't know yet," Ophelia answered. "I'm tired of the job I do. I sit in a small room and manage drones all day or all night, depending on what shift I'm on. I'd like a different environment, but not many people need someone with my skills in this area."

"Forget the skills," Ursula told her. "Do something different."

"I'll come home for a couple of months when my enlistment is up and see what shakes out," Ophelia agreed. "I've got enough leave time to do that, and then I'll make a decision."

"So you'll be home for the whole summer?" Mary Jane asked with excitement in her tone.

"Yep. My enlistment is up the first of May, and I'll be home for Mother's Day. Think y'all can stand five of us for the whole summer?" Ophelia answered.

"I don't know," Joe Clay said with a fake sigh. "What do you think, Mary Jane?"

"It'll be tough, but we'll give it our best shot." She pointed at the swarm of people milling about in the town square. "Looks like everyone in the county has turned out for the festival."

Joe Clay snagged a parking spot only half a block away from the square. "You would hear whining all over this part of Texas if folks didn't bring their kids here today."

Ursula unfastened her seat belt and opened the truck's back door. "Why's that?"

"The Saturday after Thanksgiving is the first day that Santa Claus comes to town," Mary Jane answered.

"See y'all right back here at three thirty, and don't eat—"

"Too much cotton candy." Ophelia finished the sentence for her. "See y'all later. I'm going to see who I might recognize from the old days."

Both sisters got out of the truck at the same time. Ursula waved at her folks and disappeared into the crowd. People were everywhere, some going from one vendor to another, others just stopping to hug or visit neighbors or friends. Little girls gathered in groups, looking like pictures from magazines in their Christmas finery as they waited to have their pictures taken with Santa, who was supposed to appear sometime between one and two o'clock.

Ursula remembered those years when she had to help corral both sets of twins until after their photograph was taken with Santa. Hair bows had to be straightened and sashes retied before their turn to sit on Santa's lap.

"Hey!" Luna touched her on the shoulder. "What are you doing first?"

"Where did you come from?" Ursula asked.

"I saw you and Ophelia coming this way," Luna answered. "What are you going to do first?"

"I'm going to stake a claim on a park bench and watch the people," Ursula answered. "Are you going to sneak off with Shane?"

"Not with Endora glued to my side," Luna said with a sigh and nodded toward the funnel cake wagon where her sister was making a purchase.

Ursula patted her on the shoulder. "Get on out of here. I'll distract Endora long enough for you and Shane to disappear."

Luna gave her sister a brief hug. "I owe you."

"And I will collect"—Ursula nodded—"but please don't let Endora be right about Shane or we'll never hear the end of it."

"Never happen," Luna declared and disappeared toward the hotel.

Ursula was more than a little jealous of her sister and wished that she and Remy were that far in their relationship.

She found a place on an empty bench, sat down, and took a notebook out of her oversized purse to take a few notes. She had learned long ago to ignore the crowds when she needed to grade papers on the university lawn. From what she'd read in the old journal, back in Daisy's day, folks had often come to town on Saturday to buy supplies, and pretty often there was a cattle drive through town. But after Daisy arrived in Spanish Fort, she had quickly found out that Jack expected her to stay home while he hitched up the mules to the wagon and went to town. After she had marched for women's rights to vote and even spent time in jail, submission to what he wanted seemed like she was taking more than one step back. She voiced her opinions, and even though he didn't agree with them, he was warming up to Daisy just a little. Maybe having a clean house, good food, and better-behaved kids was working the charm.

"Penny for your thoughts." Remy sat down close enough to her that their shoulders touched.

"Just imagining this as how Spanish Fort might have looked when everyone came to town to buy or trade things back in Daisy's day," she answered. "I try to imagine thousands of heads of cattle coming through town and the men stopping to buy supplies and even visit the brothels."

"You really *are* deep into this book, aren't you?" Remy asked. "But finish what you are writing before you forget something important."

"Thank you. Give me just a minute, and I will close the cover to the past and writing a novel during that era and enjoy this day in the here and now," she replied.

"No rush, but when you finish, would you like to walk around the square with me and maybe get a snack?" he asked.

"Yes," she answered, closed the book, and slipped it into her purse.

He extended his hand. She put hers in it and allowed

him to pull her up. She told herself that the electricity that sizzled between them was because she hadn't had time for a relationship of any kind in the past couple of years.

He kept her hand in his. "So which way first?"

"How about a stroll around the vendors, and then maybe we could find a seat in the hotel lobby and have a cup of something to warm us up. I really like their salted-caramel hot chocolate," Ursula answered.

"With me, it's a toss-up between the caramel and the double-Dutch chocolate," Remy said.

They had only made it a few yards when she heard someone yell Remy's name in a high, squeaky voice that sounded vaguely familiar. She turned her head to see Vivian Samples jogging from the cotton candy vendor toward them.

"Dammit!" Remy said under his breath.

"Remy, darlin'," Vivian hollered when she was still at least ten feet away and making her way through the crowd like she was a policewoman in hot pursuit of a bank robber. "I hoped you would be here."

Ursula thought the woman was going to run right into them, knock both her and Remy on the ground, and then attack him like a hungry hound pup. If she landed on top of him, cell phones would whip out faster than lightning. Everyone would take so many pictures of the spectacle that the towers around Saint Jo would probably explode, and Instagram would blow up within hours. She tried to untangle her hand from Remy's and take a few steps back, but he held on tightly.

Vivian came to a halt so close to Remy that they were

practically nose to nose, cupped his face in hers, and kissed him on the lips. Moving her hands from his face to his chest, she said, "I've been waiting for your call for two weeks, darlin'. We had such a lovely time on our date, and you said you'd call. I know you've been busy with finals at your job, but now you've got a whole month off, and my calendar is free. I'm going to a little dinner party tomorrow night. Just a few friends and then we'll play charades. You can be my plus-one."

Remy took a step backward and held up his and Ursula's clasped hands. "I should have called and told you that although we had a good time at the potluck, I..." he stammered.

"I see." Vivian's expression turned from pure joy to red-hot anger in an instant. "The queen of Spanish Fort comes back, and you kick me to the curb."

Remy lowered his and Ursula's hands. "I bought your basket at the church fundraiser, so we sat together and enjoyed your fried chicken dinner. I never intended that it would go any further than that."

Vivian popped her hands on her hips. "You said you would call me, and you didn't."

"I'm sorry," Remy apologized. "You were the one who told me to call you, and we would set up another more private date."

"But you didn't say no," Vivian growled. "So I took it that you agreed you would call."

The cold wind was carrying Vivian's voice across the square, and people were beginning to stare. Any minute now, Ursula expected the phones to come out for a few videos of the argument. Her thoughts shifted from her own uncomfortable dilemma to Daisy. Did she ever get to go to town or make friends? She must have stayed on the farm because she eventually had children—or else Remy wouldn't be beside her in this awkward situation right now.

"I bet you would have called me if Ursula hadn't come back to Spanish Fort," Vivian hissed and stormed away into the crowd.

Remy turned to face Ursula. "I'm sorry about that. I'm no saint. I've had girlfriends, and even a couple of serious relationships, but Vivian was not one of them. She's been chasing me for a couple of years, and apparently thought she'd caught me when I bid on her basket at the church fundraiser. I guess I raised some expectations there…"

Ursula laid a hand on his arm. "You don't owe me an explanation, but I feel like maybe we both need to go right to the hotel lobby and get you a double-Dutch chocolate with maybe a splash of Jameson in it to get the taste of that kiss off your lips."

Remy wiped his mouth with his free hand. "I could go for that."

They had made it across the courtyard and were headed for the hotel when Endora caught up to them. "Well, hello!" she said and grimaced when she noticed that Ursula and Remy were holding hands. "I've lost Luna, and I'm tired of the crowd. I was about to see if there's a table in the hotel so we can sit out of the cold wind for a spell. Want to join me?"

"Love to," Remy said. "I'll buy the first round of what-ever you ladies want to drink."

"Thank you," Endora said. "A cup of hot chocolate sounds good. I can't believe it's turning so cold."

Ursula pulled her denim jacket together and fastened the snaps. "I can. The weatherman said we're in for a winter storm tomorrow. I just hope that all the ice and sleet doesn't ground the planes and cancel Bo and Ophelia's flights. Bo said that she's got a couple of gigs in Nashville next week."

"She's been out there five years now," Endora said. "Think she will ever get a contract?"

Remy opened the door to the hotel and stood to the side to let the ladies enter first, but he kept Ursula's hand in his. Endora headed for an empty table for four in the back corner of the lobby, but Remy stopped right inside the room.

Ursula scanned the place but didn't see Vivian or anyone else she recognized. "Something wrong?" she asked.

"No, just grabbing one more minute of just us," he answered. "There are too many people here today for us to spend alone time together."

"Remy Baxter, are you asking me for a date?" Ursula teased.

"We've been on a date," he reminded her.

"According to my sisters, you have to kiss me good night for it to be a real date," she flirted.

"We'll have to remedy that real soon, then." He took

a step toward the table where Endora was already seated. "How about a walk tonight if the weather holds until then?"

"I might have to help with the last of the decorations when we get home, but I could be ready at six thirty," she replied.

"Pick you up then," he said, let go of her hand, and pulled out a chair for her.

"I'll be ready," she agreed with a nod.

"Ready for what?" Endora asked.

"If it's not sleeting or freezing rain, we're going to take a walk this evening," Ursula answered.

"And if it is?" Endora asked.

"Then we're going to take a ride in my truck down to the river and watch the trees ice over," Remy answered.

A vision of a make-out session so hot that it fogged the windows of his truck put a blush on Ursula's face. She shook the picture from her mind and glanced over at her sister.

Endora would make a terrible poker player because whatever she was thinking was written as plain as a bright, sunny day on her face. And right then, she was not happy, even though she had evidently tried to be nice earlier.

"So, Ursula," Remy asked. "Would you be interested in a part-time job? My supervisor at the university put out a memo that they are looking for an English comp teacher for next semester."

"Not right now, but thanks for thinking of me," Ursula answered. "I'm hoping that this book does well and that I can write a series of books set right around here during that time and maybe even make this story the first of a long-running series."

"Me too," Remy said. "But I didn't want you to be mad at me for not telling you about the opportunity."

A waitress made her way over to the table. "What can I get you folks, other than a place to get warm?"

Ursula had to work hard to shake the idea of spending the afternoon in a hotel room with Remy. She forced herself to think of something else—birds chirping, a stack of papers to grade, decorating her own personal tree—to get her mind off what she and Remy would do in that room.

"Hot chocolate," Endora said.

"Salted-caramel hot chocolate with extra marshmallows and a cup of black coffee on the side," Ursula added.

"Make mine a hot chocolate with a splash of Jameson," Remy said.

"Have your orders right out," the waitress said. "All on one ticket or individual?"

"I'm treating today," Remy answered.

The waitress hurried off to wait on another table.

"Look!" Endora pointed out the window. "The fire truck is bringing Santa to the festival."

Ursula was glad to see Endora get excited about *something* and stop shooting dirty looks across the table at her. "I thought he wasn't supposed to arrive for another hour."

"I heard that they were bringing him early just in case everything goes south with the weather," Remy said. "He does all the picture business outside. That might be tough if it's sleeting."

"It sure felt like it could start spitting something frozen any minute out there," Ursula said. "We don't usually get the snow and ice before New Year's."

"But a white Christmas would be nice," Endora said with a long sigh.

"Yep, it would," Remy agreed. "It's been years since we've had snow on Christmas. I'm hosting a snowman-building party at my house for all of us if it sends down enough to even make a snowman."

It was way too soon to think about cuddling up with Remy in front of a blazing fireplace while it snowed outside—they hadn't even had a real first date or a first kiss yet—but Ursula couldn't shake from her mind the image of the two of them sitting in front of a roaring fire or get rid of the warmth flooding her body at the idea.

———

"Ursula's got a date…" Luna singsonged that afternoon when they all got back to the Paradise. "And I'm glad it's her and not me. I wouldn't take a walk in that cold wind out there with Drake Milligan."

"Who's that?" Ursula asked.

"Just one of the hottest new country stars," Luna answered.

"I'll have to look him up," Ursula said and then started upstairs. "I'm going to finish decorating my tree and change my clothes, and then I'll come down and help with supper.

I hate that the weather got so bad that Ophelia, Bo, Rae, and Tertia had to leave so early. Now they'll have to decorate their trees when they come home for Christmas."

"I'm making Mexican turkey casserole to go with a pot of pinto beans and cilantro rice for supper tonight. It's pretty much already done," Mary Jane said. "But whoever wants to can come help set the table."

"I'll be right back down." Ursula gave her mother a hug and then went on up to her room. She removed her jacket, slipped off her boots, and threw herself on the bed. Her thoughts had shifted all day from being with Remy to comparing the crowd and all the hustle to the way Spanish Fort must have felt right after Texas became a state. Could Endora be right about transference? Was she slipping into Daisy's character—like actors did when they made a movie about a celebrity—and casting Remy in the role of Jack?

She slammed her right fist into her left palm and growled. *No! Remy would never treat me or any other woman like Jack did Daisy at the first. Even if times were different back then, all men surely didn't treat their women like that. He must have been either shy or not over the embarrassment of his first wife leaving him like she did. Times have changed and women have rights now, and… I feel like Ursula, not Daisy, when I'm with him. That's when my heart beats double time, and it's my back that gets those delicious little chills chasing up and down it when he holds my hand. I'm not her when that happens, and from what I've read so far, she didn't get those kinds of feels with Jack—at least not where I am in reading the diary at this point.*

She picked up the diary and read:

Jack told me today that my fried chicken was the best he had ever eaten. The children sat up to the table and had a semblance of manners. I was just glad neither of them got into an argument and threw their mashed potatoes at each other like they did the first night I was here. He still hasn't come to bed with me to consummate the marriage. I wonder if his wife left him because he has problems in that area. Or maybe he really loved her—after all, they had two children—and he would feel like he's cheating.

Ursula didn't mean to fall asleep, but she did. She awoke with a start when she felt the bed move. She cut her gaze over to the other side to see Luna stretched out beside her.

"Wake up," Luna said. "Mama has called us all down to supper. I'm bullfrog green with jealousy right now."

"Because Mama made my favorite casserole?" Ursula sat up, rubbed her eyes, and moved the diary from the edge of the bed to her nightstand.

"No, because *you* have a real date with Remy, and that means you'll get out of cleaning up after supper." Luna turned to look at her sister. "But mostly it's the date. Shane and I were able to sneak a few minutes in his truck while you and Remy kept Endora busy. And by the way, thank you so much for keeping her in the hotel lobby for a while. I keep telling Shane that after Christmas Day, we can go public with our relationship, and I'm hoping all y'all being home for the holidays will help Endora come out of her funk even more than she has up until now."

Endora knocked on the open door and sat down on the end of the bed. "What's this about Vivian embarrassing herself? I just heard about the whole fiasco. Did she actually kiss Remy right in front of you? How did that make you feel?"

"I wanted to slap her, but Remy was holding my hand," Ursula said. "That girl was clingy in high school and evidently hasn't grown out of it. Remy said they had a fundraiser at the church. The men bid on picnic baskets with supper in them without knowing who brought what. He bid on one, and it turned out to be Vivian's. She considered that a date."

"I bet she went home and made an appointment with a bridal shop to try on dresses," Luna said. "You aren't doing that, are you?"

"Hell no!" Ursula snapped. "Remember what Mama told us about opportunities?"

"'When opportunity knocks, invite it in,'" Endora answered and headed out of the room. "Mama sent me to get y'all. She's disappointed that the rest of us aren't here, so let's not disappoint her."

"'It's easier to see if you like what opportunity offers when it's right outside the door rather than having to chase it down the road for a mile after it's gone,'" Luna finished the saying when Endora was gone.

"I'm inviting it in, but that doesn't mean I'll let it stick around if I don't like it," Ursula said as she slid off the bed and started for the door. "Endora can lecture me if she sees me looking at white dresses and wedding cakes, but until then, she's going to have to live with the fact that I'm going on a date with Remy tonight."

Luna followed her. "I want to be like you."

"You want to be living back at home at thirty-three, taking a chance on a dream that might never happen?" Ursula asked.

"Yep, and being brave enough to go on a date with someone without thinking about the flack you'll get for it and for following a dream without looking back," Luna answered.

"Well, thank you, but it's just a date, not a lifetime commitment," Ursula declared. "And FYI, we should all do the exact same thing. Speaking of following dreams, what would you do if you didn't teach?"

"I only went into that field because Endora wanted me to," Luna declared as they made their way down the stairs. "I'd rather be a clerk in a store than deal with kids every day. In this day and time, a teacher doesn't just deal with kids. They have multiple sets of parents and even grandparents to have to work with, lots of times on a daily basis."

"Do I hear plans already being made?" Ursula asked, glad to have the attention moved away from her.

"Maybe I do," Luna said with a grin. "If you can survive living here at the Paradise as an adult, and if your book looks like it's going to be big hit, and if you and Remy do more than date…"

Ursula held up a palm. "That's a lot of *ifs*."

"You've got a lot to prove," Luna said. "After all, you are the oldest, and you are setting the example for the rest of us."

"Some days, I wish Ophelia had been born before me," Ursula said with a long sigh.

Chapter 6

URSULA GRABBED THE DIARY, like she did when she had a moment, and read a few paragraphs that evening while she waited for Remy to arrive. Like always, she took notes as she went through a passage that mentioned Daisy talking to Madam Raven over the fence.

I met the neighbor lady today while the kids and I were out for an afternoon walk. We talked about women's rights and how we both hoped that we would see women vote in our day. When I got back home, Jack told me that I was never to speak to those women again.

That's when I had had enough of the whole arrangement. I told him that I would talk to whomever I pleased. He was sullen all evening and left the house right after supper.

Luna knocked on her door and then peeked inside. "Remy is downstairs."

Ursula laid the book aside, even though she wanted to know what happened next. "I'll be right down." She took time to run a brush through her dark hair before she crammed a stocking hat down on her head and picked up her heavier coat and put it on.

Remy stood at the bottom of the stairs in his jeans and fleece-lined denim coat with a plaid shirt showing underneath it. He locked eyes with her, and she felt like one of the princesses in the books she had read as a child.

"You might need gloves," he suggested when she reached the last step.

She pulled them out of her coat pocket and shoved her hands down into them. "I'm ready if you are."

"Yes, ma'am," he said.

"You kids don't stay out too late," Luna teased on her way from the living room to the kitchen.

"What's my curfew?" Ursula shot back.

"Midnight will do fine since you are over sixteen," Luna answered.

"I've been wondering," Ursula said when they were outside, "why you never came to our big Christmas parties here at the Paradise. The whole town was invited."

"I didn't want to see you with another guy," Remy answered. "And after we were grown, when I was in a serious relationship, I didn't want my date to see the way I would have looked at you."

Mary Jane always quoted the old adage about truth being a virtue, but Ursula wasn't quite sure how to handle so much honesty in the first five minutes of her date. She had expected mild flirting, maybe a kiss or two, and perhaps more conversation about Daisy.

"I'm not the same girl I was in high school," she finally managed to say.

He gently squeezed her hand. "I'm not the same guy either. That boy wouldn't have had the nerve to even ask you to go for a walk with him."

"I'm not a perfect person," she said. "I make mistakes, and I have a little bit of a temper, and it's very hard for me to give second chances."

"I don't have a halo either." He chuckled. "Mama says I'm mild tempered, but I'm a brooder, and I hate injustice to anyone."

"I don't keep things inside," Ursula said. "I just blurt them out and deal with the fallout afterward."

"I've heard that opposites attract." Remy chuckled again as they reached the end of the lane. "Turn around and look at the Paradise all lit up and shiny. What memories does it bring back?"

"The first one is when we were little girls," she told him as they reached the end of the lane and turned left. "That was the first Christmas after we moved here, and our father, Martin, came to take us with him for a couple of days. None of us wanted to go, but Endora and Luna had just turned seven years old, so leaving Mama was toughest on them. Endora already had Joe Clay wrapped around her little finger, as they say, and he promised her that when we got back, we'd have the prettiest house in the whole area. He kept his promise, and when our father brought us home, everything was lit up and beautiful."

"And other times? Other memories?" he asked.

"Until I left for college, I loved going somewhere in the evenings and coming home to see it all fancy," she replied. "The past few years, Daddy would be sure all the lights were on when I left to go back to Tyler, and it made me sad to know that I wouldn't get to see it again for another year. What about you?" she asked. "What's your first memory of all those lights you saw next door to your house?"

"We were in junior high school that year when y'all moved into the house," Remy answered without a moment's hesitation. "I would lean on the fence or sit on the top rail and tell myself stories about the dark-haired, green-eyed princess who lived in that castle."

"Were you the prince who was going to rescue her someday?" Ursula teased.

"Nope, I was the stable boy who loved her from afar," he answered.

"That's not right." Ursula stopped and argued with him. "I'm not a princess. Never have been. And you've never been the stable boy. I had a big crush on you too, and I'm glad you didn't come to the parties."

"Why?" Remy asked.

"Because I'm a poor poker player. Whatever I feel or think is written on my face, and if you'd brought a date, well…" She left the sentence hanging.

"That makes me feel good," he said as he stopped in front of the old redbrick store building. "Shall we sit down and rest a spell before we start back?"

A rusty, corrugated metal roof covered the porch that had three steps leading up to it at the front. The lettering on the sign above the porch had long since faded until it was barely legible, but all the windows were still intact. The building hadn't been there in Daisy's day—but what had been on that spot? Ursula would have to do more research… She pulled out her notebook and made a quick note while Remy patiently waited.

Ursula shook thoughts of writing from her head with an effort. "That wasn't very nice of me," she whispered. "Sometimes I disappear into my imaginary world, and without even thinking, I write a quick note so I won't forget something. Forgive me?"

"Nothing to forgive." Remy chuckled. "As long as you come back to me when you are done, it's all right if you need a moment."

"Thank you," she muttered. "It takes a special person to understand a writer who seems to always have characters in their head."

"I like that you think I'm special," he said with a grin. "I'm just glad there's a full moon to give you a little light, so you can see to write down those important thoughts."

She stretched her long legs out and rested her feet on the bottom step. "I wonder where we might have been if we'd been brave enough to act on our feelings back then."

He eased down beside her and rested their hands on his knee. "That wasn't our time. We were too young for a lasting relationship."

"Is *now* our time?" she asked.

"Could be, but we'll never know if we don't take a chance and see. I'm glad we have some time alone, Ursula." He dropped her hand and draped an arm around her shoulders, pulling her so close to him that she could feel his warmth even through their coats.

Dark clouds shifted away from the full moon, giving her enough light to see his dark eyes boring right into hers when she looked up at him. "I'm willing to take that chance if you are."

"I am." He used his free hand to tip up her chin and stare deeply into her eyes.

She barely had time to moisten her lips when his closed over hers. The moon and the stars disappeared behind the clouds again, giving them almost total privacy in the shadows of the old country store. The electricity between them lit up the area just for them without needing help from the universe.

Ursula tried to think of something to say when the kiss ended, but she couldn't find the words, so she just laid her head on his shoulder. She just wanted to stay right there on the cold concrete porch, wrapped in a warm private bubble.

Finally, Remy broke the silence. "I don't want this moment to end. It's everything I imagined back when we were just kids."

"I know," she whispered. "Talking to you is so easy, and thanks again for understanding about my note-taking."

They sat in silence for several minutes before Ursula

finally straightened up. The beautiful, romantic moment was over, but she didn't mind as long as she and Remy could spend more time together.

"This may seem anticlimactic after that mind-blowing kiss, but I was wondering... What happened to *your* father?" she asked.

"My father's name was Jerome Terrance Baxter," Remy answered, "and he went by his initials, J. T. He worked for an oil company, and Mama says that she fell in love with him and got pregnant with me before she knew that he already had a family up in Oklahoma. By the time I was born, he was dead—an oil rig accident. Mama gave up her job in Nocona where she met J. T. and moved back up here to Spanish Fort so my father's folks could help her raise me. She went to work at the school in the cafeteria, and my grandparents helped take care of me when I was born. When I was in kindergarten, they moved to California to live with my uncle who had never married or had kids. He got cancer and needed some help. He died a couple of years later, but they stayed, and then they died out there a few years ago."

Ursula couldn't imagine raising a child as a single mother or the heartache that Remy's mama must have felt when she figured out that she had fallen for a married man. That would be even worse than what had happened to Endora.

"Now your turn? Tell me more about Martin," Remy said.

Ursula smiled at the memory of the morning when all seven sisters had come downstairs to find Joe Clay at the breakfast table. "The first question Daddy asked when he saw the seven of us gathering around the breakfast table was if we all had the same father. Other than Luna and Endora, none of us look alike. Not even Rae and Bo, and they're twins—just not identical."

She started to lay her head back on his shoulder but changed her mind. She wanted to see his reaction when she told him how they'd answered Joe Clay that morning. "So being the oldest, I went first. I told him that my father was a fun-loving student who read me books and took me to the park while Mama worked."

"If that's true, then why did you say that Joe Clay did all the things that daddies do with their kids?" Remy asked.

"My relationship with Martin only lasted while Mama worked and put him through medical school," she explained. "By the time Ophelia was born, he was an intern and working long hours. He tried to be there for us when he was home, which wasn't often. Then Tertia came along. We were all named after heroines in whatever book Mama was writing at the time, but Tertia does mean third, and it seemed fitting since she was the third child."

"I'm beginning to get the picture. With each child, he got busier and busier, right?" Remy asked.

"Yep, but he did tell Tertia that she was supposed to be a boy, so she would have to be his son. He took her fishing once or twice, and she learned to play softball and basketball, but he seldom made it to one of her games," Ursula said.

"And the twins?"

Ursula just shook her head. "He wanted a son but didn't get one when he and Mama got a third daughter. He said he was giving up, and there would be no more kids. But Mama says the birth control pills failed, and Rae and Bo were born a year later. His story then was that he had to work long hours to support five daughters, and he had a vasectomy right after they were born."

"But…"

Ursula held up a hand. "He didn't go back and get tested to see if everything worked with the surgery. One year later, Mama had Luna and Endora, and our father did a DNA test to be sure they belonged to him and had another surgery to be sure there would be no more kids. He filed for divorce not long after that, leaving Mama with seven little girls. It took a while for Mama's lawyer to get everything straightened out, but as soon as the papers were all signed, she sold the house we were living in and bought the Paradise. The rest is history. We all had the same biological father, but he was never much of a daddy. Now we all have a real daddy in Joe Clay."

"That's a story for a book for sure," Remy said.

"No one would believe it if I wrote it. Sometimes, the truth is stranger than fiction." She shivered.

"It's starting to sleet, and you are cold. We should start back," Remy said as he stood up and pulled her up beside him.

"I know, but I don't want this night to end," she admitted.

He took the first step, and a bit of sleet stung when it hit her face. "I wish we didn't have to wear these gloves. I'd rather feel your hand in mine, but I don't want either of us to get frostbit fingers."

"We probably wouldn't need them on the short walk back to the house, but it's a good idea for us to protect our hands. Especially you, since you've got a book to write," he said.

"Daisy's really getting into my head more and more, just the way a heroine of a romance novel should. I can't stop wondering about her life and looking for signs of her history all around us. But I haven't given her a thought for the past few minutes now." Ursula finished putting on her gloves and tucked her arm into his.

Remy laid one of his hands on hers and said, "Darlin', the fact that you haven't thought about anything but us is the icing on the cake for this date."

She'd thought the icing would be the kiss that had rocked her soul and came close to knocking her socks off.

"For you to shoo your characters away for *me*, that means that we really do have a chance," he finished.

"I kind of hope so," she said and wondered if she was diving into this way too quickly. The year that she brought a boyfriend home from college for the Christmas party, her mother had advised her not to think that long-term relationships were built from a flash in the pan, and she sincerely hoped that this was more than just a hot beginning that would turn into a cold ending.

"Looks like the weatherman might be right," Luna said from the corner of the porch when Ursula and Remy arrived.

"Looks like it," Remy said. "I had a wonderful evening, Ursula." He brought her hand to his lips and kissed the knuckles. "I'll see you tomorrow after church."

"Why don't you plan on having dinner with us?" Luna asked. "You and Shane would be more than welcome. Mama is making fried chicken. The Thanksgiving leftovers are all gone, thank goodness. I love them the first day and even the second, but by the third, I'm ready for something different."

"I'd love to. Fried chicken is my all-time favorite food. Can I pick you up in the morning for church, Ursula?" Remy asked.

"I'd like that," she said. "I'll be ready by a quarter 'til eleven."

"I'll be here." He dropped her hand and disappeared around the corner of the house. Ursula sat down in the rocking chair next to her sister and listened to him whistling a Christmas carol all the way to the fence separating their property.

"That was so romantic." Luna sighed.

"A kiss would have been more romantic," Ursula grumbled. "What are you doing out here in the cold anyway?"

"I needed a little bit of privacy to talk to Shane. We'd just ended our call when you and Remy arrived," Luna answered. "We're going public with our relationship at our Christmas party, and I'm *not* going to teach school next year."

"I thought you were standing back and waiting to see how I cope with the change," Ursula said.

"I don't want to wait a whole year." Luna shoved her

phone in her pocket and stood up. "By the end of May, Shane will have a small combination convenience store, gas station, and place to buy fishing and hunting licenses built down on the river next to his house. I'm going to run the store for him while he guides fishing tours."

"That sounds awesome. The folks here in town will be able to get a loaf of bread or milk without having to drive all the way into Nocona," Ursula said.

"And beer and wine," Luna added.

Ursula pushed up out of the chair and headed across the porch behind her sister. "I thought this county was dry."

"Beer and wine can be sold in a convenience store, but not liquor," Luna said. "And please, keep the news of me handing in my resignation quiet for a little while. I love Endora. She's my other half, and I want her to be better before I make this change."

"Be sure this is what you want before you jump into it," Ursula urged.

Luna held the door open. "You too. Age before beauty."

"Wisdom before impulse," Ursula shot back as she marched into the house.

———————

On Sunday morning, church services seemed to last longer than the spring semester at college. There was no way Ursula could keep her mind on the hymns with Remy's shoulder pressed against hers. When the preacher started talking about Jesus's Sermon on the Mount, her mind drifted back to the night before. While the preacher talked about being poor in spirit and the meek inheriting the earth, Ursula replayed every single moment—from what was said to the sizzling-hot kiss that heated up all of Montague County, Texas.

After the final amen was said, Remy stood up and extended a hand to Ursula. She tucked her hand inside his and he gently pulled her to her feet. "If you were given a test on the sermon today, would you pass it?" he whispered.

She shook her head. "I'd fail miserably. He said something about a sermon on the mount, but that's all I can remember. How about you?"

"You'd make a better grade than I would," he said with a smile. "I couldn't concentrate on anything but you."

"Me too." Ursula got out just before Luna touched her on the shoulder.

Bernie eased in between Luna and Ursula. "I'm riding home with you and Remy," she announced, "and we're going out the side door. Pepper probably needs to get outside and water down a bush so bad that he's holding his little hind legs together. I'll never understand why churches won't let folks bring their dogs to the services with them. When our beloved animals die, we say they cross over that rainbow bridge, which is doggy or kitten heaven, so why wouldn't they be welcome in church?" She tugged Ursula's arm. "Come on. I'll show the way out of here without having to stand in line and shake the preacher's hand. Lord only knows how many germs are spread that way, anyhow."

Remy chuckled and followed along with the two ladies.

"Besides," Bernie said. "I'm hungry, and while I let Pepper out to do his business, you and Remy can set the table for dinner."

"Yes, ma'am," Remy said.

Since they didn't have to wait for folks to stop and visit in the parking lot, they were on their way fairly quickly and were the first ones back to the Paradise. Remy parked, then got out of the truck and hurried around the back side.

"I've done my part to give y'all some time alone," Bernie said. "You are welcome!"

Remy slung the door open and helped Bernie get out. "There you go, Miz Bernie."

"That's Aunt Bernie to you," she scolded and headed back to her trailer. "And thank you for the ride."

"You are so welcome," he said as he closed the door and then opened the one for Ursula. "She's a hoot. My grand-mother was nothing like her."

Ursula slid out of the seat. "That's because she's an aunt, not a granny. And she's run a bar for more than fifty years. She kept a sawed-off shotgun under the bar, and nobody messed with her."

Remy kept her hand in his. "Did she ever use the gun?"

"A couple of holes in the ceiling proved that she did," Ursula answered. "Everyone was more than a little afraid of her—at least that's what my grandma said. She reminds me a whole lot of what I'm reading about Daisy."

They entered the house and stopped to remove their jackets. "What makes you say that?" Remy asked.

"Determined, bullheaded, and bossy. I'm to the part in the journal now where Daisy has met the madam who worked at the Paradise," Ursula answered and cocked her head to one side. "I guess some other family members followed us out the side door."

"How's that?" Remy asked.

"I hear a vehicle coming down the lane," she answered.

So much for having a few alone minutes with Remy. Before Ursula could say another word, Luna and Shane burst through the door.

"We snuck out like y'all did," Luna said.

"I told her that Santa would put her on the naughty list, but she wouldn't listen," Shane teased.

"She never was too good at the listening thing, even as a child," Ursula said.

Neither of the couples had more than a moment alone because the rest of the family rushed through the back door before they even made it to the kitchen. The next half hour went by like time had wings, and soon they were sitting around the table passing platters and bowls of food.

"I'm glad to see that there's a little community church in town now," Shane said. "When I came to visit my grandparents, we drove all the way into Nocona for services."

"I know," Mary Jane agreed with a nod. "When the girls were little, we did the same thing."

"Who knows? We might even get back on the map if we could get some businesses in here other than oil pumpers and cattle ranching," Joe Clay said.

"I'm doing my part," Shane said. "Come spring, I will be working as a fishing guide. Grandpa ran the business out of the house and Granny took care of the books. I'm going to do things differently. I'm going to build a small convenience store right beside my house. It will also have a couple of gas pumps and folks will be able to buy fishing and hunting licenses right here in town. If the weather permits, my contractor says it will be done by the end of May."

"That's awesome," Luna said.

Ursula was proud of her sister for acting surprised.

"I don't fish or hunt," Bernie said, "but, honey, it'll be real nice not to have to drive all the way to Nocona for a bottle of wine."

"Congratulations," Remy told him. "We should have a grand opening on your first day."

"And advertise in the newspapers all over the county." Joe Clay grinned. "It'll sure be great to fill up a gas tank right here in town. We might not have a big population, but I bet everyone around here will give you some business."

Endora picked up the platter of fried chicken and started it around the table again. "I heard that there's a winery going in between here and Nocona. You have to turn off the road for a mile or so to see the grape arbors. They'll be ready to bottle their first crop this next summer. They make different kinds of wine, including strawberry and watermelon, from fruits from down in the Rio Grande Valley, and they grow their own grapes for their special brand."

"I checked them out a few weeks ago. The watermelon

wine was a little too sweet for my taste," Remy said, "but the green apple and the elderberry were just right."

"I should buy a case or two for our Christmas party," Mary Jane said.

"That would be great," Endora said.

Ursula wondered if getting a little tipsy on wine just might help Endora. "What kind do you think you'd like?"

"The watermelon to start with," Endora answered.

"Then I'll bring a couple of bottles to the Christmas party," Shane said.

"Thank you." Endora said the words, but her tone didn't agree with them.

"Endora, you and Ursula can help me bring in the coconut cake and coffee for dessert," Mary Jane said.

Ursula pushed back her chair at the same time Bernie did.

"You sit still, Mary Jane," Bernie said. "I'll help Endora and Ursula."

As soon as they were all three in the kitchen, Endora whipped around with an angry expression and shook her finger at both of them. "I know you are in here to fuss at me, and I don't want to hear it."

Ursula slapped her sister's finger away. "You are a twin, so you know that Luna is falling in love with Shane. She has to feel like she's walking a tightrope with no safety net. She doesn't want to hurt you, and yet she wants to listen to her heart. What if Shane is the one, and you're keeping her from fifty years or more of happiness?"

"I don't need or want your advice." Endora glared at Ursula.

"Well, well, well." Bernie did a head wiggle. "There's the spitfire I know as Endora Simmons. But darlin' girl, you might not need advice, but you do need to adjust your attitude. Shane and Remy both are good men, and trust me, after sixty years of working behind a bar, I can spot a bad one the minute they walk in the door."

"How?" Endora shifted her gaze over to Bernie.

"By their eyes," Bernie answered without hesitation. "Now let's get this dessert to the dining room. I'll take the cake. Ursula, you bring the dessert plates and clean forks. Endora, your job is the coffee, and if you spill a drop on Remy or Shane, I intend to move into your bedroom with you for two weeks."

Bernie led the way back into the dining room with the three-tiered cake in her hands. "Thanksgiving is over, and this cake is a lovely way to kick off the Christmas season. It's made from my mama's recipe that's been passed down through the years, and we only get it at this time of year. Too bad we don't have a bottle of that elderberry wine to go with it."

Ursula passed the dessert dishes around the table, then took her chair and said to Remy, "You mentioned trying the wine from the new place. What's your favorite? Wine? Beer? Soda?"

"Sweet tea with meals. A cold beer in the evenings," he answered.

"Or coffee with cake like this?" Shane said from across the table.

The conversation started with favorite wines, sweet or unsweet tea, and then circled around to favorite desserts. The words all blended together into nothing but noise as Ursula let her mind go back to what Bernie had threatened Endora with—moving right into her bedroom. That would take away the devil's tail and put a halo above his head, for sure.

"Mama, we hate to eat and run, but I promised Remy that I would help him decorate his tree," Ursula said when she finished the last of her cake and coffee.

Mary Jane waved her away with a flick of her wrist. "I've got plenty of help for cleanup. Go on and have a good time."

Remy pushed back his chair and stood up. "Dinner was wonderful. If you'll teach Ursula how to fry a chicken like that, I'll propose to her tomorrow."

"Better start practicing getting down on one knee," Joe Clay teased. "Every one of these girls can cook just as good as their mama. She made them learn to cook, and I made them learn how to change the oil in their cars and a flat tire."

"Who taught them how to fight?" Shane asked.

"With seven of them, they didn't need any extra help in that area," Mary Jane answered.

"We could tell stories about those times all night long," Joe Clay said, "but we'll save that for another time."

Ursula stood up and kissed her mother on the forehead. "Thanks, Mama."

"Anytime, but remember," she whispered, "if you aren't home by midnight, send me a text so I won't worry."

"I'll be home long before that," Ursula promised.

They left by the back door and walked around the house to Remy's truck, where he opened the door for her like a southern gentleman. To have been in such a hurry to get out of the house, she suddenly didn't know what to say to Remy.

"I know I've said it before, but I really do enjoy being around a big family." He started the engine and drove down the lane. "That said, I love being alone with you even more."

"To have been so shy in high school, you sure are a romantic now," she told him.

"Not really." He grinned and made a right-hand turn toward the south. "I just don't want you to ever feel like I'm taking one single moment with you for granted."

"What about when we have our first fight?" she asked.

"I hear make-up sex is wonderful." His grin got even bigger.

"I wouldn't know," Ursula said. "When I break up with a guy, I'm done. It's over and there's never been any make-up sex involved."

"That's been my experience too," Remy said. "I guess if and when we have our first fight, we'll have to see how it works. But tonight, let's decorate a tree and the rest of the living room and then have a glass of elderberry wine. It's chilling in the fridge right now."

"From the new winery?" she asked.

He nodded as he parked, got out, and rushed around to open the door for her. Oh, yes, sir! He was a romantic, and she loved every minute of it.

Remy's white, ranch-style house had a couple of bright-red metal lawn chairs on the front porch. Both the chairs and the roof had real icicles hanging from them. When Ursula stepped out of the truck, a cold north wind whipped up under her denim skirt. Her slick-soled boots slipped on the icy grass, and she started to fall. One second, she was reaching for anything to slow her way to an embarrassing tumble. The next, Remy's strong arms had caught her and pulled her to his chest. Adrenaline rushed through her body, and her heart pounded.

"Whoa, darlin'," he said. "If you get hurt, Miz Mary Jane might not let you come back over here to play." He scooped her up in his arms like a bride and carried her to the porch. "I hate to set you down, but I've got to open the door."

"I'm good now," she said, "but your back is going to hurt tomorrow for sure."

"If it does, I'll just remember how I got the pain and figure it was well worth it." He flashed one of his brilliant smiles.

Remy threw the door open and stood to the side. Ursula walked in to find glowing embers in the stone fireplace. A sofa faced the fireplace, and beyond that were the small dining area and galley kitchen. A short hallway leading to an open door into a bathroom at the end was to her left.

"It's not fancy, but it's all mine now," he said.

"I love it," she told him. "It's so cozy and peaceful."

He closed the door behind him, helped her remove her coat and hung it on a rack at the end of the sofa, and then took her in his arms. "That's exactly the way I feel, especially after I get back when I've been gone all day." He brushed a soft kiss across her lips and then took a step back. "I'd like to cuddle on the sofa all afternoon, but we told your mama that we were decorating a tree. I wouldn't ever want to lie to her—or you."

"Tree first. Cuddle later," Ursula said. "We've got until the clock strikes midnight."

"Deal!" He pointed to a box with a faded picture of a Christmas tree on the side. "It's Mom's old one like your folks have. We'll have to put it together before we start decorating."

She sat down on the floor, opened the box, and pulled out all the limbs. "First we separate them by color on the tips, then we assemble it"—she talked as she worked—"and the lights go on first."

"Wine while we work?" he asked.

"I'd rather have a beer," she answered without even looking up. Getting the tree all done had to be first, but what she really wanted to do was get into that cuddling stage with lots and lots of those passionate kisses.

He went to the kitchen and brought back two longneck bottles of beer. "You are definitely a woman after my own heart."

She took a bottle from him when he offered it, twisted the top off, and took a long drink before setting it on the coffee table. "Why's that? Because I know how to put a tree together?"

"No, because you like beer better than wine," he answered

and plopped down beside her. "Mama never waited for me to get home from college to put up the tree, so all I did was help with the lights and decorations."

"It'll be a sweet tribute to them. I'll show you how," she argued.

"I'm teachable." He slid a sly wink toward her.

Chapter 7

REMY PUT THE BASE of the tree together and set it in front of the double windows that looked out onto the porch. When it was finally fluffed out, it took up a good part of the small living room with just enough room at the top for the star. Then he went back to the kitchen and brought out a box with LIGHTS written on the side.

Ursula opened it up to find twinkly lights that were neatly wrapped around cardboard, but her mind wasn't on the business at hand. Earlier in the day, she had read the part of Daisy's diary where Christmas was right around the corner, and Jack had brought in a tree for her and the kids to decorate with homemade ornaments. She felt as if this might be the turning point in their pseudo marriage and hoped it was because she had started to love the children, Bessie and Clark.

"You don't have to test the lights," Remy said. "We made sure they were all in working order before…"

Ursula heard the buzz of his voice, but in her mind, the tree in front of her was the small cedar that Jack had cut down out in the field behind the barn. She could visualize a paper chain that Daisy and the children made with old newspapers and some popcorn garland.

"Ursula, are you hearing me?" Remy asked.

"I'm sorry. I was woolgathering again," she answered. "What did I miss?"

"I was saying that Mama always made me put away the tree before I went back to school every year, and the lights had to be checked," he answered. "I'm a neat freak. My grandparents drilled 'Everything has a place, and everything in its place' into me as a child. I guess it stuck."

"I'm glad that opposites attract," she said with a shrug. "I'm not a messy person, but the dinner dishes can wait until morning. Is that going to scare you away?" She mentally closed the diary and put it away.

"No, ma'am. It will take more than a few dishes in the sink to do that," he answered. "Let's work like Mary Jane and Joe Clay did over at the Paradise. I'll hold the lights and follow you as you unwind them and put them on the tree."

She rolled up on her knees and then stood up. "We'll start at the top and work our way down to the bottom so that the plug end will be near the outlet. I've been meaning to ask you something," she said as she tiptoed and wrapped the end of the green strand around the very top of the tree.

"I'm an open book," he said.

"It took a while for us to fit in here in Spanish Fort," Ursula said. "I always figured it was because Mama was kind of famous, and folks thought we would be uppity. But your mother was our closest neighbor, and to my knowledge, she and my mother never…"

"Remember how shy and backward I was in high school?" he asked.

Ursula nodded. "What has that got to do with being neighbors?"

"Nothing, but my mother was an even worse introvert than I was. My stepdad brought her out of it somewhat, but if she hadn't had to work to support me, she would have been a true hermit. She loved to read, to take long walks alone, and to do all kinds of handiwork like knitting and sewing. She didn't visit with anyone except for the cooks in the school cafeteria," he explained.

Ursula made a mental note to ask her mother why she didn't try to get to know basically the only neighbor they had. "I see, but you're not an introvert anymore."

"Going to college changed that," he said.

His arm brushed against hers, and a wave of heat that had nothing to do with the blazing logs in the fireplace chased through her body. To keep her mind off the diary, Ursula thought of the old song that she and her sisters sang about going round and round the mulberry bush, the monkey chasing the weasel. Endora had called it the *mulmerry* bush.

"I wasn't an introvert by any means, but going to college changed me too." Ursula pushed a mental delete button on all her wandering thoughts and turned them toward Remy. "When we were bused down to Nocona to go to high school, the place intimidated me, but I bluffed my way through the experience until I was comfortable. Then I went to Tyler and…" She finished up the last length of lights and took a step back.

"And the place intimidated you even more, right?" he asked. "I'm saying that because going to college, even as far as Gainesville, was the hardest thing I'd ever done. Mama made me stay in the dorms, and I could only come home on weekends. I had to endure a roommate and eat in the cafeteria with other people. I practically lived in the library the first few weeks because my roommate was a partyer. The whole dorm didn't really need air-conditioning. The way his door fanned open and shut with different women coming and going could have cooled the whole place."

Ursula remembered the same kind of situation with girls in her college dorm and the guys who were constantly in and out of their rooms. "I couldn't even come home every weekend, but I was fortunate. My roommate dropped out after the first two weeks, and I had the place to myself."

"Same thing with me," Remy said. "My roommate finally moved into a house with a bunch of other guys, so I was alone after the first semester, but the dorm was so noisy that I still spent most of my waking hours in the library," he said as he headed toward the kitchen again and returned with two boxes. One was marked #3 ORNAMENTS, and the other #2 GARLAND.

"We are opposites and yet quite a bit alike," she said as she corralled her thoughts away from Daisy and how she must have felt so alone at times with just the children and a husband who she had trouble getting to know.

"Looks like it," Remy agreed. "I'll hold this garland like knitting yarn, and we can play ring around the rosy again while you drape it on the tree."

"Why are these two boxes marked with numbers?" she asked.

"Mama knew last year that she and Alan would be leaving when the school year was finished, so she tried to make it easy for me," he replied.

"Why didn't she take all this with her?" Ursula's hand brushed his, and suddenly the heat in the room seemed to jack up several degrees. Her pulse kicked up like she'd been running the last mile of a marathon, and sweat beads popped up on her forehead. She had never thought that decorating a Christmas tree would be like foreplay and found it frustrating because she had never been a bed-hopping bunny.

"She didn't take all this stuff with her because the place Alan inherited was fully furnished, and she wanted me to have…" He paused. "Are you off in la-la land again?"

"Nope, I was thinking about you," she answered, "and wishing that we'd gotten to know each other when we were younger."

"Me too. Seems like years have been wasted, but then maybe it's like that old Rascal Flatts song that talks about the broken roads that led us back together," he said.

"Yep, and here we are." She smiled. "I bet Miz Vera wanted you to have familiar things that would make you comfortable through the holidays since she wouldn't be here." Ursula remembered what her mother had said about the old lights that had been passed down from her family.

"Yes," he said. "I've never talked to anyone as much as I have you, Ursula. Not even my mother, and we shared everything."

"Everything?" She wiggled her dark brows.

"Well, not absolutely everything," he admitted with a chuckle. "She and Alan wanted to go to Wyoming, but I wouldn't be surprised if they didn't think it would be a good thing to leave me and his daughter who lives in Bowie to teach us to survive without them being so close."

"Raising kids has to be a tough job, but someday, I want to have them anyway," Ursula agreed and finished draping the last of the gold garland on the tree.

"Me too," he said. "And now for the ornaments and the little things that we put on the mantel. Then we'll plug in the lights and see how it all looks." He slipped an arm around her shoulders and gave her a quick hug. "Thank you so much your help. I was dreading having to do this alone."

At the mention of the word *alone*, her mind started to drift over to Daisy. She reeled it back in and mentally put her writing in a box and closed the lid.

"You are so welcome, Remy." She removed the first of the ornaments from the box and hung it on the tree. "You can enjoy the noisy family next door and then come home to peace and quiet. I don't have the latter option. Don't get me wrong. I love every one of them, but I miss alone time."

"I'm here anytime you want to get away," he told her.

"And if I'm not and you just want to admire our tree, the spare key is under the mat on the back porch."

Our tree? A shiver scooted down her spine. She had a book, maybe a series, to write. She couldn't rush into a relationship right then, no matter how much she was attracted to Remy.

"Are we going too fast?" Ursula blurted out.

"Nope," Remy answered. "I'd say we've taken this decorating job pretty slow and got it just right. I'm going to send a picture of our tree to Mama and Alan. She was afraid, since I'm alone this year, that I wouldn't put up a tree or even celebrate the holiday."

Daisy popped up out of the box Ursula thought she had put her in and seemed to have sad eyes. In Ursula's imagination, they were dark like Remy's. She made a mental note to make sure of that and then shoved Daisy into the back of her mind—again.

"I'm not talking about the tree," she said, but she hadn't missed the fact that he'd said *our* tree again, and not *my* tree. "I'm asking if this thing that is between us is going too fast. Is it a flash in the pan that will fade after this holiday magic, or is it lasting? I wouldn't want to start something, have it fizzle out, and then have everything be awkward between us as neighbors or friends."

Remy took her by the hand and led her over to the sofa. He pulled her down to sit beside him and turned to look right at her. "I've liked you—a lot—for twenty years. I want to see where this goes, but I'm not rushing you or what this is between us. It can travel at whatever speed you want it to, and I'll be happy with whatever you decide. I won't even mind a speed bump every now and then, as long as we continue to travel together. Does that come close to answering your questions?"

She laid her free hand on his cheek and leaned forward to brush a soft kiss across his lips. "It does and thank you. Now we had better get the rest of the ornaments on the tree or else…"

"Right after this." He pulled her so close that she could hear his heart pounding in unison with hers. He freed his hand from hers and ran his palm ever so gently down her cheek and kissed her. The first one was soft and tender, but then it deepened into something that sent desire shooting through her whole body. She felt totally limp and on fire at the same time.

That first steamy kiss in front of the old store had just been the opening act to the one that they shared at that moment. She'd been kissed many times before, but this was different. It reached down into her soul, and she wanted more and more of the amazing sensation that had never happened in the past.

"And now…" He panted just as hard as she did when the make-out ended. "Lady, you have left me breathless, but we'd better finish our job. I want a selfie of the two of us to send to my mother and Alan."

"Did your mother know…" Ursula had to catch her breath before she could finish the sentence. "That you had a crush on me?"

"She did, and she told me not to wish for the impossible," he said with a grin. "Did your mother know about me?"

"No, but she would have told me the same thing," Ursula said. "You were the smartest kid to ever come out of Prairie Valley school. Our principal at the time said so at our graduation."

"We were quite the pair." He chuckled. "You thought I was too smart. I thought you were too rich and famous."

"Surprising what twenty years can do, isn't it?" Her heartbeat had slowed down slightly, and her legs didn't feel so wobbly when she stood up.

"Makes me wonder what the next twenty will do," he answered and untucked his shirt and eased up off the sofa.

"We never know, but the prospects are good right now," Ursula replied.

When they had finished with the tree, Remy brought out the last box. "This is going to seem egotistical, but it is part of the tradition in this house."

"I've never thought of you as having a big ego," Ursula smiled. "What are you talking about?"

"You'll see," he said as he began setting small, framed pictures on the mantel. "Mama had my picture made on Santa's knee every year until I refused to do it anymore. As you can see, the only way they could get me to be still in the first ones was to let me wear Grandpa's cowboy hat, so that became the tradition," he explained as he continued to set up the photos.

Ursula watched him grow from a tiny baby to a grown man right before her eyes. The old cowboy hat aged right along with Remy. "This is awesome. I want to do this when I have kids."

Remy took a step back to stand beside Ursula. "I was afraid you'd think it was silly, but Mama loved it."

She nudged him with her shoulder. "I passed the first test, then. Where's that old hat now?"

He pointed to the hat rack behind the door. "Right there."

She crossed the room, picked the hat off the rack, and set it on top of the tree. "What do you think?"

"I love it. This can be our first tradition." Remy's grin said as much or more than his words. He pulled his phone from his hip pocket and held it up. "Stand closer to me for a picture to send to Mama."

"I should brush my hair before we take a picture."

"You are beautiful just like you are." He drew her close to him and snapped several photos.

"Can I see them before you send them?" she asked. "Did you get the cowboy hat on top of the tree in the picture?"

"Sorry, darlin', they're already in Mama's hands, and yes, I got the hat in the photo. Mama is going to love that. You want me to forward them over to Miz Mary Jane and Joe Clay?" he asked.

"Yes, please," she answered.

Endora would see them, but at least everyone would know that she was truly helping with a Christmas tree and not dragging Remy back to the bedroom. But then again, Luna would be disappointed that she didn't take advantage of the evening for more than a few scorching-hot kisses.

She wandered over to the mantel and studied the pictures to get her mind off the vision of Remy with only a sheet pulled up over his muscular body that popped into her head.

She got a fresh blast of heat from his body pressed against her back when he walked up behind her and slipped his hands around her waist.

"Neither Granny nor Mama liked being in big crowds. Most likely that's where Mama got her introverted personality, but once a year, she and Granny would bite the bullet and take me over to Wichita Falls to the mall to have my picture taken with Santa. Mama framed them and they always went on the mantel during December. When I was about ten, I didn't want to sit on his knee anymore, so you'll see that she took my picture in front of the Christmas tree"—he pointed to the tenth photograph—"and put it up there with the rest of them. I insisted that the tradition stop when I went to college, but she wasn't having any of that idea."

"I love every one of them. You were such a pretty baby," Ursula whispered, turned around, and wrapped her arms around his neck.

"Boys aren't pretty." He chuckled.

"Boy babies are, and some sure grow up to be sexy men," she whispered as her eyes fluttered shut and she tiptoed to kiss him again.

———

The clock in the foyer struck ten times when Ursula walked into the house. As the old Christmas story went, not a critter was stirring. She tiptoed back to the kitchen for a snack before heading up to bed and was surprised to find her mother sitting at the table with notebooks spread out before her.

"Where is everyone? Isn't it a little early for it to be this quiet?" she asked.

"Luna and Endora had to get ready for classes tomorrow. I heard from Rae and Tertia earlier. They were whining about not getting to be here for all the decorating fun. From your glow, I'd say your date went very well."

Ursula nodded and opened the freezer, took out a container of butter pecan ice cream, and got two spoons from a drawer.

"Huh-oh!" Mary Jane whispered. "Did you and Remy already have an argument?"

"No, we didn't, but I want to talk to you, and I'm hungry, so we can share ice cream while we visit," Ursula said. "Do you realize that I only had you all to myself for the first two years of my life, and then Ophelia came along, and I had to share? We haven't had many moments like this since then." She sat down beside her mother and opened the container. She stuck two spoons in it and set it between them. "I need some advice."

Mary Jane organized her papers and shoved them to the side, then dug deep into the ice cream. "I'm listening."

"When we were young, did you know that Remy and I had a crush on each other? You never asked me about it." Ursula asked.

"That's a question, not advice," Mary Jane answered. "But the truth is, I was so busy with you girls and the remodeling and writing that first book about the women who lived here when this was a brothel that I didn't always talk about every single thing back then, but after that first year, I knew that Remy used to sit on the fence and look over this way. I figured he had a crush on you, but you never mentioned him and none of your sisters ever teased you about him, so I figured it was best to let it be. Why are you asking me this?"

Ursula finished the ice cream that was in her mouth before she spoke. "I had a big crush on him, but he was so smart that I never thought he'd be interested in me. And he said that he had a crush on me, but I was too rich and famous for him to believe I'd go out with him. I hate that anyone would ever feel like that about us, Mama. We might live in the biggest house in Spanish Fort, but this place would be nothing in Dallas or Houston or New York City. You would never have let us act like we were entitled or too important for other people to even talk to us."

"No, I wouldn't," Mary Jane said. "But remember that you were both very young back then. He intimidated you with his intelligence and aloofness. You did the same to him because of where we live and what I did for a living. Folks don't realize that writing is a job—a hard one most of the time. I read a little quote from someone once that said writing was ten percent inspiration and ninety percent perspiration."

"Amen," Ursula agreed.

"But now you and Remy are adults," Mary Jane went on, "and how you feel about each other in this day and age is what is important. I've written this story many times."

"It always turns out well in books," Ursula said. "I've been home less than a week, and I feel like I'm falling in love. But that can't be possible, can it? What if this is just what you used to warn me about—the heat going cold after a while?"

"Sometimes, characters get a happy-ever-after with an old love," Mary Jane answered. "Sometimes they find a new relationship that gives them their happy-ever-after. In my stories and your stories, the two main characters always find happiness."

"Am I falling too fast and trying to build a foundation on nothing more than an old crush?" Ursula asked. "When did you know that you were in love with Joe Clay?"

"Looking back, probably after a couple of weeks of watching him work and seeing his kindness toward you girls," Mary Jane answered. "I knew for sure by Christmas, and I've never regretted telling him how I felt."

"What do I do, Mama?" Ursula asked. "I'm trying to break into a brand-new writing genre and fall in love at the same time. And I'm not being nice to Remy by thinking about Daisy and her diary when I'm with him. How do I manage two things at once? Or maybe the question is, can I manage both at once?"

"You compartmentalize like I told you before," Mary Jane advised.

Ursula remembered the words that she had heard in her head. "How do I do that?"

"When you are with Remy, you leave your work behind. When you are working, you focus on that. Honey, I did the same thing basically twenty years ago during the Christmas season. It's possible and doable."

"How is it possible?"

"It doesn't come natural. You have to work at it," Mary Jane answered.

"But…" Ursula started.

Mary Jane laid a hand on her arm. "There are no buts in love, darlin', or in meeting deadlines either. My advice is simple—follow your heart."

Chapter 8

URSULA STARED AT THE computer screen for a full five minutes. How could it only be the first day of December? Since she had come home less than two weeks ago, her life had done a complete turnaround.

She blinked a few times and then went back over every single thing she had written in the proposal and the first chapter of her story about Daisy. Commas were all in the right places. The synopsis was laid out in a good arc from beginning to end. Enough emotion was included in the first few lines to draw a reader into the story—hopefully, even with a few tears.

She had taken her mother's advice and focused on the job at hand for the past two days, but Remy had kept peeking out of the box where she had put him to distract her, much like Daisy did when she was with him.

"What if..." She began to doubt herself on both issues. What if Remy got tired of her staring off into space and thinking about whatever story she was writing? What if her muse grew bored with her not giving all her attention to her career? Lord have mercy! How on earth did a person manage two lives at once?

She took a deep breath, attached the documents to her letter to Norma, and hit Send before she could change her mind. Now, it was out of her hands, and her agent could hopefully sell it to a publisher somewhere. She took a long shower, washed her hair, got dressed for the first time in two days, and went downstairs.

"It's alive!" Joe Clay teased when she reached the kitchen.

She gave him a quick hug and then went over to give her mother a longer one. "Thank you both for everything these past couple of days. For bringing me sandwiches and sweet tea and letting me work without interruptions. Y'all are the best." She stepped back, got a chunk of lasagna out of the fridge, and heated it in the microwave.

"Honey, I'm used to living with an author," Joe Clay said. "When your mother is focused on a deadline, I know to leave her alone until it's done, because when she's done, I will get all her attention for a while. And that's worth waiting on."

"Thank you, darlin'." Mary Jane beamed. "It takes a special person to live with an author." Then she frowned at her daughter. "Lasagna for breakfast?"

"Best time of day for it, especially after the days I just spent getting my proposal ready," Ursula said. "After I eat, I'm going over to Remy's. I may cook dinner for him today."

"He's a good man," Joe Clay said as he put on his work coat and headed out the back door. "Just between me and you, kiddo, I think he likes you."

"Think so?" Ursula blew her daddy a kiss just as the microwave dinged telling her that her breakfast was ready.

He caught the imaginary kiss midair and shoved it into his coat pocket.

"Mama, were you worried or antsy when you sent in that first book about Lili?" she asked.

Mary Jane poured herself a cup of coffee and sat down at the table. "Of course. Daisy is your Lili, and she is guiding you into brand-new territory, just like Lili did for me. I can't explain it, but I understand, and I never thought I would be having this conversation with you twenty years later."

"Thanks," Ursula said.

"There's the remnants of a hummingbird cake on the counter if you want some dessert," Mary Jane said, "but right now, I'm going to my office where I will be working on my own project while your younger sisters are at school and Bernie is sleeping. She's a good bit like having a baby in the house. When she's awake, there will be noise." She started that way and turned back at the doorway. "Has Luna confided in you about Shane?"

"Just that she likes him and plans to let the cat out of the bag pretty soon about their dating. She's trying very hard to be a good sister to Endora," Ursula answered. The part about her sister not teaching next year was Luna's story to tell when she was ready.

"That man is good for her. I hope something comes of their dating when it's out in the open, and I really hope that it's not just excitement because of the secrecy," Mary Jane said, and with a wave of her hand, she left the room.

Ursula blew on the next bite of lasagna before she put it in her mouth and stared out the kitchen window at the naked trees. The ice had melted off the roads while she was holed up in her room, but the tree branches on the shady side of the house still sparkled in the sunlight.

"It's colder than a mother-in-law's kiss out there," Bernie shivered as she came in the back door and removed her hat and gloves. Static caused her red hair to stand up like she'd grabbed a bare wire. She headed straight for the coffeepot and poured a mug full. "I swear, the wind down here is as bad as in Oklahoma. It blows constantly from Halloween to July Fourth, but don't ever try to beg, borrow, or steal a breeze from July until the end of September."

"Why do you figure that is?" Ursula asked.

"Because it gets so damn—I mean, danged—hot durin' that time that the wind would cook the skin right off a person's bones," Bernie answered as she carried her mug to the table and sat down. "Learnin' not to cuss has not been easy, and not havin' a drink first thing in the morning is tough." She blew on her coffee and took a sip. "But, darlin', it's worth it to have all y'all around me. How's the writing going?"

"I sent in the first chapter and the outline," Ursula answered.

"How's the romance going?" Bernie's eyes twinkled.

"I don't kiss and tell," Ursula answered.

"An old friend of mine told me that you can't ride two horses with one ass. I expect that it's tough trying to have both worlds, isn't it?" Bernie asked.

"Yes, it is, but I don't want to give up either one," Ursula replied.

"You are strong. You are smart. You are gorgeous. You can figure it all out if anyone can," Bernie told her.

"I hope so," Ursula muttered.

―――――

"This is a fantastic surprise," Remy said as he came through the kitchen door into the house that day at noon. He crossed the room and wrapped Ursula up in his arms before he even took off his coat.

Her arms snaked up around his neck, and she tangled her fingers in his hair and rolled up on her tiptoes to meet his lips halfway. She wasn't even surprised when she went weak in the knees and had to lean in close to him for support. Would this always be the way things were between them if they got really serious? When the kiss ended, he buried his face in her hair but kept her in a tight embrace, and his cold face and warm breath, like fire and ice combined, sent desire dancing through her body.

"I've missed you so much," he said.

She leaned back and smiled up at him. "You kept sneaking out of the box."

"What?" Remy asked.

Ursula told him about her mother's advice to compartmentalize. "I was working hard, and I sent the proposal and first chapter in this morning, but during that time, you kept peeking out of the box I had put you in. Seems that I'm not very good at tunnel vision."

"Part of me is sorry that I interrupted your work, but

the other part is glad that you didn't forget me," he said as he sniffed the air. "I see a pot on the stove, but I smell something cinnamon and maybe bread cooking?"

"I made a fast trip to Nocona and bought everything for a pot of chili. Corn bread is in the oven, and a cinnamon Bundt cake for dessert is cooling."

"I think I might have died and gone to heaven. Having dinner ready to eat is a big treat for me, and from the size of that pot you've made, there'll be enough for supper too." He took a step back and headed down the hallway toward the bathroom. "I'll get washed up and set the table for us."

A man who was willing to help in the kitchen was one in a million, Ursula thought. The guys she had dated in the past had been more than glad for her to cook, but not one of them had ever offered to help out—or to wash dishes afterward either.

"What have you been doing all morning?" she called out.

"Working on the tractor," he answered when he returned to the kitchen. "It's old and hasn't been used in years, but with a little TLC, it will still get me through a couple more years. Grandpa sold all the cattle when he and Grandma left, but I bought a few head when I moved back at the end of last summer. I've been talking to Jake, the guy who owns the winery south of town, about leasing the acreage next to me so I can grow my own hay next year."

She took the cast-iron skillet of perfectly browned corn bread from the oven and set it on a hot pad in the middle of the table. "That's a big undertaking."

"Yes, it is, but I've got spring break and all summer when I don't teach, so I think I can manage it. If the tractor holds up, I won't have to buy equipment for a while." He got bowls and two glasses from the cabinet. When the table was readied, he put ice in the glasses and filled them with sweet tea from a gallon jug he had gotten out of the refrigerator.

Ursula carried the pot full of chili to the table and set it beside the corn bread. "When we just serve dinner out of the pots that we cooked it in, Joe Clay says we're eating country style."

Remy pulled out a chair for her and then sat down beside her at the small round table for four. "My grandma said the same thing, and Grandpa loved pot meals."

The front of his chambray shirt had oil stains on it, and the creases of his jeans were white with wear. His work boots were scuffed and showed signs of wear at the heels, but to Ursula, he was just as sexy as he had been in the starched and creased jeans, plaid shirt, and shined boots he had worn to church on Sunday.

"You cooked, so I'll say grace," he said as he took her hand in his and bowed his head. After a short prayer, he said, "Thank you for cooking and just for being here when I came in from working. I could get used to this kind of living in a hurry." He picked up her bowl and filled it with chili before he did the same thing for himself.

His helping her before himself was another first in Ursula's experience. The men she had previously dated were more like Jack—demanding and selfish. But she shouldn't compare the past with the present, or as Bernie said, "Don't measure one person by another's half bushel."

Remy took the first bite and rolled his eyes toward the ceiling. "This is the best chili I've ever put in my mouth, and I'm not just saying that. What's your secret?"

"Chocolate and beer," she answered. "Cajun seasoning and a few jalapeños to give it some fire. It's my grandmother Marsh's recipe. When she went to the nursing home, she passed her cookbook with her handwritten recipes down to Mama."

"Chocolate?" he frowned.

Ursula cut wedges of corn bread and put one in each of their bowls, then added a chunk of cheese to the side of hers and passed the relish tray over to Remy. "Just half a bar of milk chocolate for a pot this size. I've never learned how to make it in smaller batches, but it does freeze well."

"Well, darlin', I don't expect this to last long enough for any of it to make it to the freezer," Remy told her. "Now, tell me all about Daisy in the first chapter of your book."

Compartmentalization went right out the window.

He didn't just ask about her work but paid attention when she talked about Daisy's emotions when she realized she had married a man who was in serious need of some schooling.

"Your however-many-times-great-grandmother was a spitfire. After that first Saturday when he went into Spanish Fort to the store and the bar without her, she laid down the law. I can't believe that anyone who had her genes was ever introverted," Ursula told him.

"Can I read the first chapter?" he asked.

"For real?" she gasped. "Do you read historical romance?"

"What you told me are just the bare bones." He took a long drink of his tea. "I want to read the words, if that's okay, or is that against the rules?"

Chalk up one more check mark on the plus side for Remy for being interested in what she did.

"I will email it over to you this evening, on one condition," she told him.

"And that is?" he asked.

"If I can go out to the barn with you and help with whatever you're doing this afternoon. If you're interested in what I do, then I want to be a part of what you do," she answered.

"Deal!" he agreed with a smile.

―――――

Ursula was glad she'd worn jeans and a plaid flannel shirt over a T-shirt that day and that Remy insisted she leave her "good" coat in the house and wear an old mustard-colored work jacket out to the barn. After an hour of working on the old green tractor, she had grease smudges on her cheeks, and if it hadn't been for gloves, she would have had broken fingernails.

"This is right the opposite of sitting in front of a computer all day," she said.

"Grading papers, writing, teaching classes day after day is mental work," Remy said. "This is physical, and it works the kinks out of our bodies that come from all the stress that we have in our other jobs." He stopped on his way over to get another tool from the workbench in the corner and kissed her on the forehead. "You are still beautiful with tractor grease on your cheeks."

Ursula rubbed a knuckle across her cheek and then looked at the results. "You must have grease in *your* eyes, but thank you for the compliment."

"You are very welcome, but it's the truth, not just a compliment," he said as he finished up what he was doing and opened the barn doors. Cold wind, with the promise of rain or maybe even more sleet, rushed into the barn.

She wondered how many times, if any, Daisy went out to the barn to help Jack and then forced herself not to go there.

"We should take her for a spin around the property and see if I can remember everything Grandpa taught me about shifting gears," Remy suggested.

Ursula buttoned up her coat, jammed her stocking hat down over her dark hair, and climbed up into the seat. "Is this like a horse-drawn carriage?"

Remy nodded and settled in behind the wheel. "It will kind of feel like that, only we're sitting up a little higher." He took a deep breath and started the engine.

"You look relieved," Ursula said. "You didn't think it would work?"

"I haven't done anything with this old thing in years, and I am really glad that it's purring for us." He shifted the transmission into gear and drove it out of the barn.

"Grandpa used to tell me that Mabelle"—Remy patted the dashboard—"had a temper that would rival Grandma's.

Some days, she required a little extra patience, and some days, she just didn't want to work at all, no matter how much he babied her. I think she likes you and didn't want to make me look bad in front of you."

"You will never look bad in my eyes." Ursula slid across the bench seat covered with an old blanket and snuggled up against Remy.

Remy patted the steering wheel. "Did you hear that, Mabelle? I think the lady likes me."

"I only make chili for guys who I really like and those who tell me where to find the key to the back door," she teased. "But I will confess that you're the only one who has told me the secret of the extra key."

"Then there are a lot of stupid men out there around Tyler, Texas," Remy said. "And, honey, I will have a key made just for you anytime you want it, and one more thing, you don't have to go to the store for food. I keep a well-stocked pantry and freezer. Anytime you get a notion to cook, I'll be grateful for both the food and the company."

She laid a hand on his knee. "Is that an offer for me to move in with you?"

"Any time," he nodded. "But timing is totally up to you. There are three bedrooms in the house. You can have one and use the spare one for an office if you aren't comfortable with actually living with me."

"Don't you use one of those rooms for an office?" she asked.

He shook his head. "My grandparents, my mama, and I each had a room. When my grands left, Mama turned their room into her sewing and craft room. Now she and Alan have moved north, and that room is totally empty as well as their bedroom. I use the kitchen table when I need to work on lesson plans, which is seldom now that I've taught the same classes for years. Everything is computerized these days, so all I need is my laptop."

"Thank you for the offer," she said.

She wondered what he would do or say if she said she would rather sleep in his room and reminded herself that their relationship was way too new to even think about that.

"Like I said, anytime." He slid a long, sexy wink her way.

Endora had been wrong about her getting so involved with Daisy that she was becoming the character. Yes, she loved all the characters in the story she was writing and enjoyed all the emotions that they stirred up when she wrote about them. But she was Ursula when she was with Remy. Even with grease stains on her face and wearing a stained, old work coat, she was free to be herself.

If this relationship went up in smoke, she vowed to never, ever let herself get entangled with someone else who made her feel any less than what Remy Baxter did.

"Penny for your thoughts," Remy said.

"Do you want the truth?" she asked.

"Always," he answered.

"I like who I am with you," she told him. "You take me as I am, and so far, you haven't wanted me to change."

"Never." He laid a hand on hers. "I like you just the way you are, darlin'."

"And that's exactly what makes this between us so special." She rested her head on his shoulder.

"Yes, ma'am, it surely is," Remy said and draped an arm around her shoulders.

Chapter 9

"THIS WAS SURE SHORT notice," Endora complained as Ursula got dressed for her date with Remy. "He had plenty of time to ask you before the last minute. It's just not right to only give you one day to get ready for a big party."

"He hadn't planned to go until yesterday," Ursula snapped right back at her, "and I'm always ready for a party. Besides, he said he would come to the Paradise for our Christmas celebration with me, and it seems only fair that I go with him."

"And besides all that, she wants to get all gussied up and go out," Luna said from the office chair in front of her sister's desk. "I'm jealous, and deep down, you are too, Endora. We both like to socialize."

Endora sucked in a lungful of air and let it out in a loud whoosh. "I don't want a brother-in-law or"—she shifted her gaze over to Luna—"two of them. This has always been a girls' house. Boys don't belong here."

Ursula whipped around to face her baby sister. "You're acting like a fifth grader. You are a grown woman, and to expect all six of your sisters to never have a relationship is downright selfish. And besides, we aren't going to move boys into the Paradise, Sister. We plan to fall in love and move in with them."

Endora gave Ursula a dirty look and stormed out into the hallway. In a few seconds, she slammed her bedroom door with enough force to rattle the pictures on the walls.

"Looks like you made her mad," Luna said.

"She's had her fifteen minutes of whining," Ursula declared. "I love her, but none of us are doing her a bit of good by mollycoddling her."

Luna nodded in agreement. "I've decided the same thing, so you are preaching to the choir, Sister. Shane and I will announce that we are dating at our Christmas party here at the Paradise. She's probably never going to speak to me again."

"Yes, she will. You are twins, and she can't bear to not have you in her life. I can see that she's in the anger stage of grief, and that's fine, but—"

Luna butted in, "But, Lord, please let the last stage of acceptance arrive soon."

"Amen!" Ursula slipped a pair of ruby studs into her ear-lobes and handed Luna a matching necklace. "Would you help me with this?"

Luna stood up and fastened it around Ursula's neck. "You look stunning. That dark-green dress matches your eyes, and the touch of red really gives it a Christmas feel."

"Thank you." Ursula smiled and brought out a green velvet cape that matched her dress. "This is last year's dress for the party we had here, but I didn't get to wear the cape because I didn't go outside at all. No one at the college where Remy teaches has seen it, so I figured I'd get double duty out of it."

"Can I borrow the whole affair for the party this year?" Luna asked. "I'll make an excuse to go outside, just so I can wear the cape for a little while."

"Sure," Ursula answered. "With your blond hair, this will look so good on you that Shane's eyes will pop right out of his head."

"Don't know about that, but I hear Remy's truck outside, so you better throw that cape around your shoulders and put your shoes on," Luna told her. "Give me time to get downstairs. I want to see his face when you start down the steps, and Mama will want to take pictures."

"Good Lord!" Ursula fussed. "I'm just going to a faculty party. It's not a big deal."

"Yes, it is," Luna said as she headed out the door. "This is your first really big date with Remy, so it's a *huge* deal. I can't wait until I can have a real, honest-to-God date with Shane."

"I've had dates with Remy." Ursula remembered the walk to the old store, decorating the tree, and even just two days ago, making dinner for him, and then the tractor ride—and all the making out before they heated up the chili for supper.

"Not like this," Luna threw over her shoulder as she disappeared down the stairs.

"You sure cleaned up good, Remy." Bernie's voice floated up the stairs. "If Ursula falls down the stairs and sprains her ankle, I'll be glad to go with you tonight."

"Well, thank you, Miz Bernie." His deep Texas drawl followed right behind Bernie's comment.

"None of that Miz Bernie sh...crap." Bernie's tone changed. "I told you to call me Aunt Bernie."

Bernie's tone told Ursula that the old gal was in her element and that she would say that the universe heard her pleas and granted her wishes. That way, she could take full credit for the date.

Ursula had never been known for gracefulness, so she picked up her shoes and carried them down the stairs. Remy stood at the bottom of the stairs with his eyes glued on her, and she suddenly felt that maybe she was overdressed. Everything went so quiet that the only thing she could hear was her own heart beating.

He held out his hand when she reached the bottom step. "You are breathtaking. Would you know if Joe Clay has a ball bat or a tire thumper I could borrow just for tonight?"

Ursula put her hand in his. He brought it to his lips and kissed her knuckles.

"Why?" Luna asked.

"So that I can beat the other professors away from your sister," he teased.

"That won't be necessary," Ursula said. "Not for me, but maybe I should load my purse with rocks so I will have a weapon for all the women who'll be trying to steal *you* away from *me*." She let go of his hand and sat down in the ladder-back chair beside the hall tree.

Remy dropped down on one knee and put her shoes on for her.

Bernie laid a hand over her heart and sighed. "Now that

there is a real prince, and, Ursula, you are even prettier than Cinderella."

"Thank you, Aunt Bernie," Ursula answered.

The kind of romantic soul that Remy was couldn't often be found in today's fast-paced world, and she wondered if women of royalty ever felt a spike in their pulse when a man touched their bare skin.

"Wait for it. Wait for it," Luna whispered.

"What?" Ursula asked.

"Y'all come on in here and stand in front of the Christmas tree," Mary Jane said. "I want a picture of you before you go."

"And there it is," Luna whispered again. "I told you there would be pictures."

Remy gently pulled Ursula up and ushered her into the living room with a hand on her lower back. "Would you forward a copy of the pictures to me? I'd like to frame one for the mantel. Mama displayed all the photos of me on Santa's lap during the holidays, and then one of me in front of the tree when I got too old for that. This will be this year's addition."

"I sure will," Mary Jane agreed.

Remy pulled a rocking chair over by the tree, sat down in it, and patted his knee. Endora made it into the room just in time to see Ursula sit down on his lap and smile for the camera.

"I can't believe you're having a faculty party this early in December," Luna said. "At the elementary school, we have our party on staff development day the day before we are out for the holidays. This year, that is December twentieth."

"We'll all split seven ways to Sunday after the finals next week," Remy said. "Last tests are given on Friday, and semester break begins on the eleventh. Second semester begins January third."

"For a break that long, I might consider teaching college classes." Endora hugged Ursula and whispered, "You look so happy. I hope it works out for you, but in case it doesn't, I'll be here ready to listen, and I won't even say 'I told you so.'"

"Thank you," Ursula said.

"I feel like a kid going to the prom," Remy said as he ushered her outside with his hand on the small of her back. "I should have brought you flowers or, at the very least, a corsage."

"You put my shoes on for me. You kissed my hand," she whispered as he helped her into his truck. "That's better than all the flowers you could have brought."

"Honey, you have not been treated right in the past if that was a big thing," he said. "I've missed you the past couple of days, but I had to be at the college both days, lecturing for finals. I have to admit that you did more than just peek out of the box several times a day. You crawled right out and sat on my shoulder. But after next week, I'll be home for almost a month, and I won't have to compartmentalize at all."

She wished that the pickup had a bench seat like the old tractor so that she could slide over next to him and feel his body next to hers. Damned old consoles made it hard to flirt. She thought of Bernie trying so desperately not to swear but then wondered if that coffee cup she carried around most of the time was really filled with just coffee.

"I'm glad that I got out of the box," she said. "That's payback for all the times when you did the same thing when I was writing. But today I finished the second chapter and sent it in. Norma—that's mine and Mama's agent—says she loves the first chapter and the proposal, and she can't wait to read the rest of the book. She's already submitted it to five different publishing houses. I'm not holding my breath, but I did cross my fingers. To have her submit this soon is a good sign."

"Why would you hold your breath? I told you two days ago when I read the first chapter that this was going to be a bestseller right out of the chute," Remy said as he drove south toward Nocona.

"Because it is a historical, and that's brand-new territory for me. I'm new in that field and have no track record, and it's tough to break into something different from what readers are already used to seeing from a writer. Maybe I should set them up in my next reader newsletter. I might be able to get some of them talking about their own family tree," she explained.

It's just like breaking into new relationship territory with you, she thought. Having someone pay so much attention to her, tell her that she was beautiful even with grease on her face, and look at her like Joe Clay looked at her mother— that was almost scary. What if she messed it up and had to live with the regrets the rest of her life?

Be yourself and listen to your heart. Her mother's advice came back to her again.

"If all your readers are as struck by the first chapter as I was, they won't be able to put the book down," Remy said.

"And that's with no prejudice, and I would be totally honest with you if I thought it was garbage."

"I believe you would," she told him.

"It's the only way to be," he said and connected his phone to the Bluetooth in his truck. "I made us a special playlist for the drive tonight."

Could he get any more romantic? she asked herself and wished again that she could rip out the console and throw it out the window.

Blake Shelton sang the first song on the list, "God Gave Me You." The lyrics talked about God giving him the lady to help him with the ups and downs.

"But we've only had ups and no downs," Ursula said when the song ended.

"When that changes, we'll remember the ups and get over the downs," Remy told her as he made a turn onto Highway 82 and drove toward Gainesville. "To expect that everything between us will always be perfect would be crazy. We'll eventually have an argument, but when we do, I'm going to think about tonight and the day that you were willing to crawl up on an ancient old tractor with me and ride around the fence line."

"I'm going to think about how much you enjoyed that chili and how you made me feel when you looked up the stairs at me," she told him.

The next song was "H.O.L.Y." by Florida Georgia Line. The letters stood for "high on loving you," and Ursula almost shed tears when she thought about Remy picking a beautiful love song from a man to a woman.

Remy smiled across the seat at her. "I might not be too good at expressing the way I feel sometimes, but songs can do it for me."

"You come across really well to me," Ursula whispered. "No complaints here."

"That's great," he said and leaned over to give her a quick kiss on the cheek. "I never want you to doubt how I feel about you. I always wondered if you ever came back to Spanish Fort and weren't married or in a relationship if I would be brave enough to ask you out."

"Now you know," she told him. "And I'm so glad you did. Now, tell me a little about these people I'm about to meet. Are they all old professors who squatted in Gainesville and they built the college around them?"

"Some are," he said, chuckling. "Some are about my age. Some are in between the older ones and me. All ages. All types, and every one of them is going to be jealous of me tonight," he answered. "Probably a lot like the ones you taught with out in Tyler."

"Any of them ever try to fix you up with a date?" she asked.

"Some of the guys that I play a pickup game of basketball with on the first Sunday afternoon of each month *have* tried to fix me up, but I keep saying over and over again that I am waiting for the right woman to step into my world. That happened the day before Thanksgiving when I saw you get out of your car. Joe Clay told me you were moving back for at least a year, but I wasn't expecting to be there when you arrived."

"Well, darlin'," she said, "I wasn't expecting to find you unmarried and standing right in front of me either. Are all the women in this part of the state stupid?"

"I wouldn't know about that," he told her as he turned into the Gainesville County Club parking lot and snagged a parking place not far from the front door. He helped her out of his truck and then took her hand in his, brought it to his lips, and kissed the knuckles—one by one. "I'm the luckiest man in the state tonight, Ursula, and having you join me is a dream come true. Don't let anyone talk you into leaving me."

"Not a chance," she told him. "I don't trade sirloin steak in for bologna…darlin'."

When they were inside, a young guy handed Remy an envelope. "You'll find your name tags inside, Mr. Baxter. Y'all enjoy the evening. If you haven't been here before, just follow the signs to the banquet room. Almost everyone"—he pointed to only a few envelopes left on the table—"is already there."

"Thank you, Liam," Remy said. "How are you?"

"A bit stressed over finals," Liam answered.

"You'll do just fine," Remy assured him.

"So we're going to make an entrance?" Ursula asked.

"Oh yeah, we are." Remy grinned.

When they'd gone past the first sign and made a turn down a hallway, Ursula asked, "Was that one of your students?"

"Yes, it was," Remy answered. "Liam was a dropout and is now retaking the course because it's a requirement for his major. He was the pretty boy on campus that all the girls swarmed around like bees to honey. That first semester, he came close to flunking out, and he's had to really work hard to bring his grades up."

"If you hadn't been so shy, you could have been like him during *your* first semester," Ursula said.

"Well, thank you." Remy's smile got bigger.

"Mr. Baxter!" A young girl at the table in front of the banquet hall squealed and looked up at him with adoring eyes. "I'm so glad to see you here."

"Glad to be here, Kasey," he said. "Ursula, this is Kasey Andrews. She served as my student aide last year, and she graduates in May. Kasey, this is my date, Ursula Simmons."

"Pleased to meet you, Miz Simmons. Mr. Baxter was my favorite teacher," Kasey said. "Y'all have a good time."

"Nice to meet you too, Kasey," Ursula said.

"Could I take your cape and hang it up for you?" Kasey asked.

"Not right now," Ursula answered with a smile. "I can always drape it over the back of my chair if it gets too warm."

"Yes, ma'am," Kasey said, but her eyes were still on Remy.

"Methinks that the girl has a crush on you," Ursula whispered as they made their way through the double doors into the banquet hall.

"How did you handle that kind of thing?" Remy asked.

"With kid gloves," she answered, "but I've got to admit, I can't blame Kasey for flirting with you. You are mighty handsome all fancied up this evening, but I thought you were just as sexy in your stained and faded jeans when we worked on the tractor."

Remy leaned over and kissed her on the cheek. "Same to you, darlin'."

He opened the envelope and handed Ursula the tag with her name in the middle and decorated around the edges with images of Christmas tree lights. She peeled the back off and slapped it on the left side of her dress just above her heart. Remy was doing the same thing with his when a tall, lanky guy with gray in the temples of his red hair and a long, thin face tapped Ursula on the shoulder. She read Lester Bailey on his name tag.

"What is a gorgeous creature like you doing with Remy?" he teased.

"He asked me, and you didn't," Ursula shot back.

Lester chuckled. "You've met your match, Baxter."

"Yes, I have." Remy shook hands with Lester. "Darlin', this is one of my colleagues. He teaches biology, and if you will look at that gold band on his left hand, you'll see that he's married. Where is your wife, Lester?"

"Getting her second margarita," Lester answered. "There's a free bar, and she's taking advantage of it and the fact that her mother is watching our five kids tonight. It's not often that we get an evening away from them. I'm headed over to the bar for a beer. Can I get you anything?"

"No, thank you. We're going to find our table first," Remy answered.

"See you around, then," Lester said and walked away from them.

Remy weaved his way through the people, stopping to introduce Ursula to several of his colleagues. She wouldn't remember all their names the next morning, but she would never forget the way the women all looked at Remy—like they could have him for breakfast, dinner, and supper.

All the tables were decked out with bright red table-cloths. Twinkling lights and tiny ornaments decorated the small Christmas trees in the middle of each round table, all of which had eight place settings. Remy groaned when he saw the cards of the other people who would be joining them.

"What's the problem?" Ursula asked.

"That guy"—he pointed to the name card beside Ursula's—"is a player. The person beside him will be one of his many date-for-the-night women. This couple"—he swung his finger around to the next couple—"is on the verge of a divorce, and they'll either be snippy or icy to each other all evening. The last couple can't stand the others who are seated with us." He pointed to the first cards. "The player and the wife of that one had an affair, and everyone on campus knows about it. This is why I hate these things. The students, like Liam and Kasey, help with this kind of thing, and they have no idea what their professors' private lives are like."

"Well, darlin', this is easy enough to fix." Ursula snatched their name cards off the table and stepped over to a table beside the wall. "Is this one better?"

"Much, and you are a genius as well as gorgeous," he

answered with a smile as he picked up Lester and his wife's cards and took them to the other table.

He stopped and talked to people on his way back to her, and from the way folks treated him, he seemed to be well liked. But Ursula would far rather have been curled up in his arms watching a Christmas movie on television that evening than being there having dinner with all his colleagues. Remy finally made it back to her side, pulled out a chair for her, and then sat down beside her. "We don't have to stay until the party is over at eleven o'clock, unless you want to."

"Will there be dancing?" Ursula asked.

"There hasn't been in the past," he answered. "But I see a DJ setting up on the stage so there could be tonight."

Ursula was wondering if Daisy and Jack ever got to the place in their relationship where they danced together, but then she caught a flash of red out of the corner of her eye. When she shoved her writing out of her mind and turned, she saw Vivian bent down and whispering in Remy's ear. Her skintight satin dress showed enough cleavage to bury Santa and two of his elves inside and hugged her body so snugly that the zipper up the back had to be groaning in pain.

Remy shook his head—twice—but Vivian just smiled and kissed him on the cheek. When she stood up, she winked at Ursula and then disappeared into the crowd.

"So sorry about that," Remy said. "She came as her brother's plus-one tonight. He works in the admin office."

"No problem." Ursula forced a smile. "What did she want?"

"To dance the last dance with me," Remy answered.

"When I told her no, she asked for the first dance, and I told her that all my dances belonged to you."

At first Ursula wasn't sure if the next flash of red came from Vivian's dress or her own jealous anger, but when she focused, she could see the woman leaving the room. "Thank you for that," Ursula said. "Excuse me for just a minute. I need to find the ladies' room before this party gets into full swing." She pushed back her chair and stood up, then bent down and kissed Remy on the forehead. "Don't start without me."

"Wouldn't dream of it," he said. "The ladies' room is right out the doors we came in and down the hall a short distance."

"Be right back," Ursula whispered in his ear and hoped all the women who were blatantly staring at him realized that he was taken.

Is he? Aunt Bernie was in her head—again.

"Damn it, Aunt Bernie, get out of my head," she muttered as she made her way down the hall to the ladies' room. Ursula took a few long breaths and then opened the restroom door to find Vivian leaning into the mirror and applying a fresh coat of lipstick. When she finished, she turned around slowly and gave Ursula a smug smile.

"Are you stalking me?" Vivian asked.

"Are you stalking Remy?" Ursula fired back.

"Yes, I am, and I'm willing to fight for what I want," Vivian answered. "You're not his type, and you will never make a decent ranch wife. When the dust all settles, it will be me who is living in his house and sleeping in his bed. I'll be the one who has his children. Have your fun and then break his heart. I will be waiting in the wings to put all the pieces back together for him while you go off and be famous."

Ursula opened her mouth to say something, but before she could utter a single word, Vivian blew her a kiss and hurried out of the room.

Ursula stepped into a stall, put the lid down on the toilet, and sat down. Doubt crawled into her chest and lay there like a ton of concrete. Maybe Aunt Bernie and Vivian were both right. Ursula's career as an author would always come first and keep her from being a good ranch wife. Jealousy the color of her dress covered the doubts like a layer of pure ice.

She doubled up her fist and shook it at the stall door. "No! If Vivian wants a fight, I'll give it to her," she whispered.

"Did you see that fancy woman Remington brought to the party?" a feminine voice asked.

"Oh yeah, but Vivian has already made it well known that she's going to marry Remington, so that woman, whoever she is, doesn't have a snowball's chance in hell. Vivian has no morals or inhibitions when it comes to going after what she wants," the other one said.

Ursula held her breath and leaned forward to look through the slim crack between the door hinges and the edge of the stall. Both of the women had gray hair and were dressed in black.

"I'm sure she's out there now, flirting with him," the first woman said.

"Then let's get through with what we came in here for and go watch the fireworks," the second one said in a scolding tone. "We didn't come to a party to gossip in the bathroom."

Ursula heard two stall doors close and then she quietly slipped out, washed her hands, and tiptoed out of the restroom. If Vivian wanted a fight, then she had better pack a lunch, because Ursula would give her one, and it would take all day and part of the night.

Chapter 10

"You've seemed a little distracted all evening," Remy said as he walked Ursula from the truck to the door. "Were you thinking about Daisy's story?"

"I'm sorry," she apologized. "I had a lovely time tonight, Remy. The food was good, and the dancing was wonderful. And yes, I did think about Daisy a few times. I try to compartmentalize, but sometimes I fail." No way would she ever admit that the ordeal with Vivian had given her doubts.

He drew her close to him when they reached the door. "Will it always be this way?"

"Mama says it takes practice to completely put something away and not think about it. I know I just need to work at it harder," she answered.

"Just keep practicing," he said as he leaned in to kiss her good night. "See you tomorrow?"

She opened her mouth to say that she would be working all day but then snapped it shut and just nodded. "Call me?"

"I will," he said and gave her another long, passionate kiss.

She stood on the porch and waved at him while he drove away, but in her mind, she was already opening up the diary to read the next passage that Daisy had written.

She could almost hear Aunt Bernie's scolding voice fussing at her, but she ignored it as she took off her shoes and tiptoed up the stairs. She changed into a pair of pajama pants and a T-shirt and opened the diary.

Jack came home so drunk that he didn't know what he was saying. At least I hope he didn't know, but now that I look back on it, I wonder if he was in full control and wanted to make me mad enough to leave. If so, he succeeded when he told me he'd been to one of the cheap brothels in town and that there would be no grocery money that week. My temper got the best of me as jealousy filled my breast. I thought we were making progress and that someday we would have a proper marriage. I called him names that would make the devil blush, and he declared that no woman would talk to him like that.

He drew back a fist to hit me, so I picked up a cast-iron skillet and used it on his hard head. He was lying on the floor when I left by the back door and went straight to the Paradise. If he wanted to act that way, then he could damn sure go to hell. When I knocked on the door, Madam Raven invited me right in and made me a cup of tea. She assured me that she could use help with cooking and cleaning, and I could live in the small place above the carriage house where the butler used to stay.

Ursula laid the book aside, opened her computer, and began to write the next chapter. After the night she'd just had, she could sympathize with Daisy. Evidently, the woman had fallen in love with Jack, and he had broken her heart. After an hour, she stopped abruptly. Daisy tried to be a ranch wife and mother to those children and had failed. If she tried to do the same thing, would she fail?

She closed the computer and went to bed, but nightmares plagued her all night and she awoke with a demon of a headache. She took a couple of pain pills and started downstairs, but the place was so eerily quiet that she wondered if she was still dreaming. Aunt Bernie proved that Ursula was wide awake when she reached the kitchen and found the old gal sitting at the kitchen table playing solitaire.

"The princess awakes," Aunt Bernie said as she placed a nine card on a ten. "I thought maybe you might have spent the night over at Remy's and would be coming in the back door this morning."

"Nope," Ursula answered and headed for the coffeepot. "Where is everyone?"

"Here and there," Bernie said. "It's just me and you for now. You look like warmed-over sin on Sunday morning, girl. Did you and Remy have a fight?"

"No, but I had one helluva argument with myself, you, and Vivian," she answered and then went on to tell Bernie about her fears, doubts, and jealousy and ended with, "What if he doesn't call today? What if I just lost the best chance at happiness I will ever have?"

"Go upstairs, put on your big girl panties, and go talk

to Remy. Don't spend the day worrying about it. Quit your stewin' about it in that slow cooker of doubt and figure out what y'all mean to each other," Bernie said. "Go on. Get. I'm about to beat Sol, and then I have to go walk Pepper. His little bladder is probably about to explode."

―――――

"We need to get one of those stiles to make crossing this fence easier," Ursula said to herself as she climbed over the fence and headed across the pasture. Dark clouds waltzed across the sun, threatening rain—or the way the temperature was falling, perhaps even ice or sleet.

The brown, frozen grass crunched under her feet as she crossed the pasture. Cows were huddled together, trying to keep warm. Just looking at them made Ursula shiver and look forward to cuddling in front of the open fire with Remy after they had had a long come-to-Jesus—or maybe she should call it a come-to-Bernie—visit.

She checked under that mat on the back porch for a key, but apparently both she and Remy had forgotten to put it back. Was that an omen that this wasn't going to work between them after all? He needed a ranch wife, and she needed to be an author? Could the two ever meet in the middle?

She heard voices before she reached the end of the house, and then she saw a bright-blue pickup sitting in the driveway. She wanted time alone with Remy, so she peeked around the corner to see Vivian blowing Remy a kiss as she left the porch. Remy waved and then hurried back into the house.

He was wearing only pajama pants and a smile. His hair left no doubt that he had just crawled out of bed.

Scalding-hot tears welled up behind Ursula's thick lashes and flowed down her cheeks. She whipped around and jogged all the way back to the fence. She sobbed so hard that a couple of cows started her way, but she just ran faster. She could hardly see when she put her foot on the bottom rail. The damned thing had a sheet of ice on it, so she slipped and fell flat onto her back.

She lay on the cold ground, gasping for breath and still crying when her phone rang. She fished it out of her hip pocket, saw that Endora was calling, and answered it on the fifth ring. "What are you doing home before noon on a school day?" she asked.

"We had a water leak at the school. No bathrooms. No school. Where are you?" Endora asked. "Did you spend the night at Remy's?"

"No, but I wish I did." Ursula's voice caught in her throat. "I'm at the fence between his place and the Paradise."

"Are you crying?" Endora asked.

Ursula didn't figure there was any reason to lie so she answered honestly. "Yes, I am."

"I'll meet you in the barn tack room," Endora said. "That's closer than coming all the way to the house."

"Thank you," Ursula agreed and wept all the way from the fence to the barn.

She was just entering the side door into the tack room when a flash of lightning zigzagged through the sky, and her phone rang. She dragged it out of her hip pocket and found a text from Remy: I miss you. Call me when you are awake.

She shoved the phone back into her pocket. Her mind was running in circles. Her face was wet with a fresh bunch of tears. Her heart hurt more than it ever had before.

Endora raced across the small room, hugged her sister, and then took her hand and led her to the old sofa against the far wall. "Did Remy die?"

"No, he's alive and well, and please don't say 'I told you so,'" Ursula said.

Endora grabbed a roll of paper towels from the end table, peeled off a fistful, and handed them to Ursula. "I promise I won't. What did he do?"

Between hiccups, more tears, and sobs, Ursula told her all about the night before and what she had witnessed on his front porch that morning. "It's not all his fault, Sister. I've been so engrossed in my writing that I'm distant and..."

"Whoa!" Endora held up both palms. "Did it ever occur to you that you might have jumped to conclusions about what happened this morning?"

"How can you say that?" Ursula snapped.

"I'd love to say, 'I told you so,' but in all honesty, I can't," Endora answered, "and I can't believe that you didn't plow right into Vivian and give her the fight she's been looking for. What's the matter with you anyway? You've always been the strong sister, not the weakling sitting here with me. Stop your bawling, put on your fightin' gloves, and march right back over there, but don't go in with a chip on your shoulder, or"—she stopped for a breath—"or saying that this is all your fault either one."

"When did you get so smart?" Ursula dried her eyes.

"I think Aunt Bernie is rubbing off on me," Endora said. "I'm still in the anger stage of this grief process. I don't know how long it will take for me to make it to the end and just accept that Kevin was worse than a toad frog, but I'm workin' on it."

"It's raining," Ursula said, but she remembered that she'd vowed to herself at the faculty party that she wasn't going to let Vivian win over Remy without a fight. It was time to put up or shut up.

"So what?" Endora told her. "That should cool you down before you get there. Go on, get! You don't know how hard it is for me to be honest about this. If you don't go soon, I'm going to call Aunt Bernie to come out here and talk sense to you, or maybe Mama *and* Aunt Bernie."

———————

Not even the cows made a sound in the pasture as Ursula made her way to the back of Remy's house and knocked on the door. When he didn't answer after the third knock, she tried the knob. It turned so she went inside, dripping cold water on the throw rug inside the door. She could hear water running in the shower and Remy was singing "In Case You Didn't Know" at the top of his lungs. The lyrics talked about her having his heart a long, long time ago. Was he thinking about Ursula or about Vivian, though? Was he washing the smell of Vivian from his body before he came to see Ursula?

"No! I won't go there," she whispered.

"Ursula?" Remy's voice jerked her back into reality. "What are you doing here? Good Lord! You are wet and shivering. Here, come closer to the fire, and"—he jerked a blanket from the back of the sofa and wrapped it around her shoulders—"I'll get a towel from the bathroom for your hair. Did you walk over here in this freezing rain?" he asked as he hurried down the hall without waiting for an answer.

He wore a T-shirt and a different pair of pajama pants than he had had on earlier that morning. His dark hair was still wet, and he hadn't shaved. His eyes were worried, but then they should be if he'd spent the night with Vivian.

"I did." She raised her voice above the lump still in her throat.

He returned with a towel and wrapped it around her hair, then led her over to the fireplace. "Sit on the floor, and I'll work on your hair until it's dry. What's this all about? Are you breaking up with me?" Remy asked.

"I don't know," she answered. "Maybe you should be breaking up with me."

"Why would I do that?" he asked.

"I was here, Remy," she said. "I saw Vivian leave."

Remy reached across the sofa and took her hand in his. "Why didn't you just come on into the house and talk to me? Don't you know that you can trust me? Trust is the foundation for a relationship."

"You were half-naked, and she…" Ursula's voice caught in her throat.

"And she had nothing but a skimpy, sexy thing under her coat," he said, "but I didn't even let her in the door. I told her that I was dating you and had probably been in love with you for twenty years. Then I told her to leave." He tossed the towel on the floor and gathered her into his arms. "Give me your trust, and I will never betray you, and that's a promise that could be written in stone."

"Is that a proposal?" she asked.

"No, darlin', it's a vow," he answered. "When I propose, you won't have to wonder about it. You will know it's real."

She buried her face in his shoulder. "But she really would make a better ranch wife than I would. I'm preoccupied with…"

He laid a finger on her lips, then tipped her chin up for a kiss. "I'm not looking for a ranch wife. I can kick any bush between here and Houston and find a woman willing to do that. I want you."

"Is this our first fight?" She was breathless when the kiss ended—just like always.

"I was kind of hoping it was," he said, "but I guess it's just one of those speed bumps that we talked about, isn't it?"

She leaned back enough to look up at his face. "Why would you want us to have a fight?"

"Like I told you before, make-up sex is supposed to be amazing." His teasing lightened the heavy mood in the house.

"You don't hate me for being distracted with this story?" she asked.

"Darlin', I could never hate you, and if you are passionate about your career, then you'll be passionate about falling in love with me," he whispered as he tightened his grip on her.

"We decided to go slow and be sure about this relationship, remember?" she asked.

"Slow is in the heart of the beholder." His eyes glittered, and then his heavy lashes came to rest on his cheek as he moved in for another kiss.

She felt as if a bucket of rocks had been lifted from her chest. She pushed away from him, stood up, and took his hand in hers. "How many dates have we been on?"

"Real dates or supper dates?" he asked.

"All of them combined," she answered, amazed that she could even speak the way her heart was pounding. "I figure it's got to be at least ten or fifteen, maybe even up around twenty. If we had been going out once a week, that would be about six months' worth, right?"

"Yes," he nodded.

"And this is our first speed bump? That's pretty good." She stood up and reached for his hand.

"I agree, but where are we going?" he asked.

"To your bedroom to see if speed-bump sex is good," she answered.

Remy hurriedly got to his feet, scooped her up in his arms, and carried her the rest of the way down the hallway. He closed the bedroom door with his bare foot and laid her on the bed. "Something tells me that this is going to be a day to remember."

"A precious memory for the ages," she agreed.

Chapter 11

LUNA TIPTOED UP THE stairs just before midnight. December second would forever be branded in her mind as the day she and Shane broke up. She could hardly see through the tears of both sadness and anger streaming down her face. How dare he imply—no, demand was a better word—that she had to choose between him and her twin sister. She stomped her foot on the third step so hard that she got off-balance and had to grab on to the banister to keep from tumbling backward down the stairs. Endora had been right about all men being jackasses, but she wasn't ready to hear *I told you so*. She thought of the lyrics of a Kelsea Ballerini song, "Miss Me More," but even that didn't bring her any closure or comfort.

"What in the hell are you stomping around about?" Bernie asked from the top step where she was propped up against the banister with a bottle of Jameson in one hand and a glass in the other.

"I just had a fight, our first, with Shane, and we might have just broke up," Luna answered.

"Well, darlin', let's go downstairs and get you a glass. I don't mind sharing my whiskey, and it sounds like you need a good stiff drink," Bernie said.

"I agree!" Luna whipped around and started back down the stairs.

Bernie followed her and set the bottle on the table, but Luna didn't wait for her aunt to get a glass down from the cabinet. She turned up the bottle and took a couple of long gulps.

"Well, that should take a little anger out of you," Bernie said and then set the glass in front of her. "If it helps to drink it right from the bottle, that's fine with me."

"Why did we have to argue tonight?" Luna moaned.

"Before or after sex?" Bernie asked.

"Before." Luna turned up the bottle again.

"No wonder you are angry." Bernie leaned in closer. "I'd be mad too. What was the fight over anyway?"

"Endora," Luna groaned. "What else?" She went on to explain that Shane had said she wasn't her sister's keeper and if she loved him, she would put him first.

"Then I'm on Shane's side." Bernie poured herself another shot and handed the bottle back to Luna. "You should have come clean about Shane with Endora from the first time you were attracted to him, girl. You might have just lost the best relationship you will ever have."

"Don't I know it," Luna whined. "What am I going to do?"

"Well, the first thing you should do is have another drink and then go to bed before you are so drunk you can't get up the stairs to your room. When you wake up with a hangover in the morning, I'll bring you the cure that I've used for years. You will take a shower, put on some perfume, and fix your blond hair all pretty. Then you will go knock on Shane's door and talk to him."

"Why don't I go right now?" Luna asked.

"Because I won't let you drive when you've had that much whiskey, and you and Shane both need a little bit of cooling-down time," Bernie answered. "So pull your bikini underbritches out of your crack, and…"

"They're not in…" Luna started and then stopped. "Oh, you're talking about getting over being mad before I go to bed. I love Shane, Aunt Bernie." She swiped a tear away from her eyes.

"Yes, I am, and I'm learning that you are not a happy drunk," Bernie said. "Have one more for the stairs, and then we're both going to call it a night, or morning, or whatever to hell time it is."

"You aren't supposed to drink whiskey before breakfast or cuss," Luna scolded and then turned up the bottle again.

"'Hell' is not cussing. It's a destination, and this Jameson is after supper, not before breakfast." Bernie picked up the half-empty bottle and headed for the back door. "Good night, Luna. Do I need to stick around and make sure you get to bed?"

"I'm not drunk," Luna protested. "See!" She tried to touch her nose with her forefinger, and it landed on her left cheek.

"Come on, baby girl," Bernie said with a laugh. "I'll get you up to your bedroom and be there in the mornin' to wake you up. Good thing tomorrow is Saturday. You'd be an old bear in the classroom if it was a school day."

———

Luna heard her sisters' voices as they passed by her door on the way down to the kitchen for breakfast. The aroma of bacon and coffee wafting up the stairs made her stomach turn over. Just the mere thought of putting food in her mouth brought on a gag reflex. Had she really drunk all that whiskey the night before? She remembered falling into bed and Bernie taking off her shoes. The heated argument with Shane played in her head like a Technicolor movie. "What have I done?" she groaned.

"Good mornin', Sunshine," Aunt Bernie singsonged as she pushed the door open into Luna's bedroom. She set a tray on the table and then opened all the curtains so the bright sun could flow into the room. Luna grabbed a pillow and covered her eyes, but Bernie pulled it away. "Sit up and eat this banana."

"I can't," Luna moaned, and then she reluctantly sat up before Bernie could force her to. She grabbed her aching head with both hands.

Bernie sat down on the edge of the bed, peeled the banana, and handed it to her. "Yes, you can."

Luna pushed Bernie's hand away. "I need aspirin and caffeine."

Bernie shoved the banana so close to her mouth that she had to take a bite. "That comes later. First the banana, then what you said, and then some of the scrambled eggs and dry toast."

"I don't even like bananas," Luna moaned, but she took it from Bernie's hand.

"Neither do I, but when I've done something stupid like we did last night, I use the cure," Bernie told her.

Luna took a second bite. "It's punishment, isn't it?"

"Maybe, but you'll feel better soon. You can't go talk to Shane with a pounding headache, and by damn...dang...I don't intend to lose my prophecy that I'll have you and Ursula married by summer," Bernie declared. "Do you want me to have to start all over and pick out another boyfriend for you?"

"I can't let Shane see me like this," Luna muttered.

"Hence the cure," Bernie snapped at her.

"Don't yell!" Luna put her hands over her ears.

"Then do what I say," Bernie growled. "I've got places to be, and it's almost time for Pepper's midmorning snack."

"Good God!" Luna exclaimed. "What time is it?"

"Ten o'clock," Bernie answered. "Neither of us are going to make it to church, but Jesus knows we still love him. So follow my orders, and go take a shower. You smell awful and your hair is a fright. You're so right about Shane not needing to see you like this."

"You are mean," Luna said.

"But I'm right," Bernie fired back. "Coffee and aspirin now and then the eggs and toast."

"Okay, okay!" Luna fumed.

"I'm leaving. Pepper needs me," Bernie said and headed for the door. She turned around just before she reached it and smiled. "Thanks for last night and for confiding in me."

Luna nodded and followed the orders. Her headache was nearly gone by the time she finished her shower and got dressed in clean jeans and a sweatshirt. She used a curling iron on her hair and even put on some makeup.

"Good morning," Ursula greeted everyone as she came through the back door.

Luna glanced up at the ceiling. She sent up a prayer of gratitude and thankfulness to God or Fate or the Universe for sending Ursula to save her from a million questions.

"Did you go out early to help Remy with chores?" Mary Jane asked.

"Yes, I *did* help with chores this morning," Ursula answered, "but I spent the night with him also."

Everything went silent for a full minute, and then Endora said, "Did you have to kick Vivian out of his bed?"

For a moment, Luna forgot about her own issue and wanted to know why Endora asked that question about Vivian.

"Not really, but she did her best to get there. Remy and I had an argument, but we worked through the issue," Ursula said. "And I may spend more nights over there, since boys aren't allowed upstairs." She shifted her gaze to Endora. "I didn't have a knock-down, drag-out with Vivian, but I would have." She went on to tell a short version of what had happened and ended with, "And my baby sister helped me have the courage to march right back over there in the freezing rain. I don't intend to let the past define the present and ruin whatever future I might have."

Luna did a fist pump. "Preach on, Sister."

"I want to get to where you are," Endora admitted and then sighed. "I'm not there yet, but I'm working on it."

"Endora, do you remember what I told all of you when you were little girls?" Mary Jane stood up and brought a full pot of coffee to the table. "Back when you got your feelings hurt or when someone made you angry?" After she had refilled everyone's cups, she sat back down.

"You told us to go up to our rooms and pray for the person who upset us," Ursula answered for her sister.

"I will not pray for Kevin and Krystal. I can't forgive them—not yet," Endora said through clenched teeth.

"Until you can, they will have power over you. You have to forgive them to take the hardness, anger, and hurt from *your* heart. I'm speaking from experience," Mary Jane said.

"Amen," Bernie said as she picked Sassy up off the floor and hugged her. "Forgiveness is heapin' coals of fire upon the person's head that did you dirty. And it heals your heart at the same time so that you can get past what happened. Y'all don't tell Pepper that I loved on this cat, though. He's not the forgiving kind."

"I like Remy a lot and have no problem with Ursula taking the next step in a relationship with him," Mary Jane said. "My advice to all of you as grown women would be to be sure about your own feelings and to be careful about the man you choose to spend your nights with. You would never want him to think that you are not worthy of respect."

"Yes, ma'am," Ursula said. "Thank you, Mama, and I've

never been surer about anything. That means"—she waved her hand to take in her sisters—"y'all better get on the ball. I'm going to marry Remy Baxter, probably not soon, but that's how sure I am about this relationship. You do know what that means, don't you?"

"That you'll get to be first again," Endora groaned. "You'll wind up with the first grandbaby, and the child will be just across the pasture fence from Mama and Daddy. But hey, if I tell this story to Bo, she might figure out a way to turn your story into a song and finally get a foot in the door in a recording studio."

"You are welcome," Ursula said with a smile. "Now, I'm going to go up to my room and get busy on another chapter." She pushed back her chair and stood up.

Bernie whistled shrilly through her teeth and then started clapping. "I believe Ursula deserves a standing ovation, and this just might be the best Christmas present any of us will get this year. Now, let's start looking for a good man, like Remy or Shane, for you, Endora."

"Oh, no!" Endora gasped. "I'm making progress, but I'm still way too angry to even think about another relationship."

"So you're going to let Luna beat you to the altar?" Bernie raised her eyebrows. "You've always done everything together. I always figured y'all would have a double wedding."

Endora threw up her palms defensively. "She's on her own this time."

Ursula laid a hand on Endora's shoulder and gave it a squeeze. "I really think Remy and I have a chance at something real and lasting, and I appreciate the support from all y'all, but especially from you."

"You are welcome, but if you are wrong, I will say, 'I told you so,'" Endora said.

"And I won't say a word when you do," Ursula said.

"Neither will I," Luna said.

"Moving on is not easy," Mary Jane said with a sigh.

"Are you speaking from experience?" Ursula asked and thought of Daisy, who was now living in the butler's old apartment. Was moving on difficult for her?

"Yes, I am," Mary Jane said with a long sigh. "When your father left us, I had trust issues until Joe Clay came along. I'm just glad that you found out what kind of man Kevin was *before* you married him, Endora. And, Ursula, I'm glad that you were brave and went back to confront Remy. Rumors are worse than reality sometimes."

"You're preaching to me as well as Ursula, Mama, only I haven't talked to Shane yet. Evidently, last night was the night for arguments. But I've always thought Father was mad at you for having too many daughters," Luna said. "Did he cheat on you too?"

Ursula leaned against the doorjamb where marks had been made to show each of the sisters' growth from the time they moved into the house until they left home for college. "Of course he did," she answered for her mother. "Y'all were just little kids, but I remember the night that our father came home and told Mama he was in love with another woman and wanted a divorce."

"I didn't tell you that," Mary Jane whispered. "Did your Aunt Bernie…"

"Hey, I might let Luna get drunk and help her get to bed, but I didn't tell that story, Mary Jane," Bernie protested. "I wouldn't betray your trust for anything."

"Bernie didn't tell me anything," Ursula said quickly. "I was just a kid, and I had come out of the room that I shared with Ophelia and Tertia to sneak a cookie. Our father came home and told Mama that they needed to talk. It wasn't long until Christmas, and I thought maybe he was going to tell you that we could have a kitten, so I hid behind the recliner and eavesdropped."

"How did you survive emotionally, Mama?" Endora asked. "And why didn't you tell us?"

Mary Jane reached over and patted Endora on the shoulder. "Like Ursula said, you were all just little kids, and you didn't need to know that about your father. The news didn't come as a surprise to me. Those last two years, your father had spent less and less time at home, and after you and Luna were born, he rarely spent a night in bed with me. I suspected that he was having an affair, but I kept hoping the whole time that I was dead wrong."

Luna glared at her older sister. "I understand that Mama didn't want us to think less of our father, but why didn't you tell the rest of us, Ursula?"

"I was just a little girl, and y'all were too young…" Ursula said.

"But you could have told us when we were all older,"

Luna argued. "Mama, do you think we could have gotten a cheating gene mixed in with whatever tendencies we inherited from him, and we'll wind up being unfaithful to our spouses when we are older?"

Mary Jane shook her head. "Lord, no! That's not an inherited thing."

Endora threw a hand over her forehead in a dramatic gesture. "Thank God! I would never want to cause anyone's heart to break the way mine has."

"The cat is out of the bag about me and Ursula," Luna told her sister, "but now you can see from Mama's experience that you *can* live through what Kevin did to you—that there are good men out there like our daddy."

"Amen," Mary Jane agreed with a smile. "Let's talk about something other than the past now. Ursula needs to get busy on her writing, and, Luna, you need a nap."

"Not before I try to make things right with Shane."

"Oh, no!" Endora crossed her hands over her chest. "Before you do that, you've got to tell us about getting drunk and why Aunt Bernie—"

"Shane and I had a big fight last night, and I threw my key to his house at him. Then I came home and got drunk with Aunt Bernie. End of story," Luna told them.

"She never could hold her liquor," Ursula declared.

"Yes, I can," Luna argued. "But I'm not arguing with you today, Sister Famous Author."

"What was the argument with Shane all about?" Ursula asked.

"I'll tell you the whole story after she's gone," Bernie said. "She needs to get on out of here and go make nice with her boyfriend."

"I'll see y'all all later." Luna followed Ursula up the stairs and got her purse from her room. When she turned around to leave, Ursula was standing in the doorway.

"I guess last night started out crappy for both of us," Ursula said.

"Yep, it did," Luna agreed. "Shane said that he was tired of being all secretive about us and basically said that I had to choose between being with him and telling Endora. Not in that exact way, but the meaning was clear. He told me that if we were going to have a permanent relationship, he had to come first."

"He's right," Ursula said. "Remember that part of the Bible that says something about forsaking all others and clinging to your mate."

"I'm not a clingy type," Luna argued.

"None of us are," Ursula told her. "Mama raised every one of us to be independent. We've all proven we can stand on our own two feet and face off with anyone or anything. We don't *need* a man to complete us, but we would like to have someone in our lives to love and support us unconditionally."

"Like Joe Clay does Mama? Do you think they ever had an argument?" Luna asked.

"I'm sure they've had plenty of arguments. I'm learning that it takes a special person to live with an author, and that's without seven little girls thrown into the mix. Go on and fix things with Shane, Sister, but be sure to take a box of matches with you."

"Why?" Luna asked.

"If there's no chance for y'all to make up, then burn the imaginary bridge from the Paradise to his place. If you don't need the virtual matches, toss them in the river. But you'll have them on hand if it is time to end the relationship and move on."

"I'm terrified," Luna said. "We both said some really mean things."

"If it's real love, it will withstand more than one argument."

"How did you get so smart?" Luna took a step toward the hallway.

"I'm not smart," Ursula said, laughing. "I heard all that in a song. I guess this means that you aren't going to church this morning?"

"Nope, I'm going to try to salvage a relationship."

"You'll sure feel better when you do." Ursula patted Luna on the back as she left the room.

Luna braced herself for the cold wind, but only a chilly breeze greeted her when she walked outside. The storm that had raged all night had passed now, and only a few wispy clouds cluttered the sky. She got into her car and sat there for several minutes, playing one scenario after another over in her mind. How would Shane react to her showing up on his porch? Would he slam the door in her face? Could they recover the passion they had had before the argument?

Joe Clay startled her when he opened the door and slid into the passenger seat. "Is your car being cantankerous about starting in this cold weather? Want me to pop the hood and take a look?"

"No, it's not that," Luna said. "I messed up, Daddy."

"With Shane?" Joe Clay asked. "Is it about Endora?"

"Yes to both," Luna admitted. "I'm on my way to straighten things out with him—if I can."

"He called me this morning," Joe Clay admitted. "I listened to his side of the disagreement, and, honey, he has a point. He's dating you, not you *and y*our twin sister. Think about Kevin. When Endora was in love with him, you didn't expect her to put you first and foremost. I've been putting off having a come-to-Jesus talk with Endora, but I think the time has come."

"She's trying, Daddy, and most of this is my fault for letting her come first," Luna said. "But, Daddy, why does falling in love have to be so tough?"

"It has to be tough so you can see if it's really love or if it's just lust," Joe Clay told her. "Want to tell me your side?"

"No, I trust Shane to have been truthful," she answered. "This is as much my fault as it is his. My temper got the best of me too."

Joe Clay leaned across the console and kissed her on the cheek. "He wanted to come up here to the Paradise and talk to you. I told him to stay put and give you some breathing room."

"I can't breathe until I get this settled," she said.

"You got to have air to survive, darlin'," he said with a grin as he opened the car door and stepped out, "so I guess you better get on down toward the river."

Luna started the engine, rolled down the window, and yelled, "Thank you, Daddy!"

She was about to put the car in gear when Bernie opened the passenger door and got inside. "I can see by the way you've been just sitting here that you are having doubts. So, darlin', I'm your wingman if you've changed your mind. We can go to the nearest bar, get drunk again, dance on the tabletops, and have a hangover so bad tomorrow that even bananas look good. I'll treat us to however many drinks it takes to drink that man out of your mind. I want my favorite niece to feel better."

"I thought Ursula was your favorite," Luna said.

"She was, but you need me, and that makes you my favorite right now," Bernie told her. "Now get this buggy moving. Having fun and drinking away your sadness is just down the road."

"And I also thought you were worried about your prophecy not being right," Luna argued.

"I am, but I'd rather be wrong than—"

Luna didn't let her finish what she was saying. "Aunt Bernie, I'm going to Shane's right now to try to work things out. I was just trying to figure out what to say to him."

"Well, praise the Lord and pass the whiskey," Bernie said. "I thought for sure you would call it quits once you got in the car. If things don't work out, just give me a call, and I'll meet you at the end of the lane, or come to my trailer. What happens out there stays out there, and I've got enough liquor in my cabinet to fill a bathtub, but…" She put her finger to her lips. "Don't tattle on me to Mary Jane. Drinkin' buddies stick by each other."

"It can be our little secret since I'm your favorite," Luna promised.

She had barely reached the end of the lane when Ursula called. "Just checkin' on you."

Luna braked and shifted gears into park. "If you've got any connections with heaven or the universe, you could put in a word for me. I'm terrified that even if we do work things out, everything will be awkward between us."

"You can work through that better than a broken heart," Ursula told her. "I'm here if you need to talk. If you don't call, I'll figure that everything is good."

"Thanks, Sister. I love you," Luna said and ended the call.

Five minutes later, she was parked in front of Shane's house and felt as if she was frozen in place. She couldn't force herself to get out, and she couldn't go home until she did. Finally, after several long breaths, she managed to open the car door. It took another full minute before she took the first step, but even then, she felt as if her boots were filled with concrete. Her pulse raced like she had run a mile in under three minutes by the time she made it to the front porch.

She stared at the fish-shaped, brass door knocker for a

while before she took the cold thing in her hand. Was that an omen that the red-hot fire between her and Shane had grown cold?

"Mississippi one. Mississippi two," she counted as she waited. One scenario after another played through her mind, none of which had one of those happy-ever-after endings.

At the end of Mississippi twenty-five, Shane still had not come to the door. She had to face the fact that if he was in there, he didn't want to talk to her. She couldn't go back to the Paradise without closure, so she headed down the path behind the house toward the river.

She and Shane had gone there sometimes to sit under a gigantic weeping willow tree and talk about the new store and their future. At the very least, she could draw back the leafless limbs, sit in the same spot where the two of them had spent time, and accept the fact that it was over since he wouldn't even open the door and invite her inside.

The wind coming off the cold river water chilled her to the bone even more than the cold fish. She pulled her coat tighter around her chest and turned the collar up. A bunny startled her when it darted across the path in front of her. Before the adrenaline rush could die down, she stepped on a stick and thought it was a snake.

"What's the matter with me? I know that snakes hibernate in the winter," she muttered as she drew back the curtain of drooping bare limbs.

"Yes, they do." Shane looked up from the very spot where they always sat.

Speechless, Luna couldn't remember a single scenario that had played through her mind. She was afraid to blink for fear that he was nothing but a figment of her imagination.

"Did you come to get the things you've left behind?" he asked.

"Do you want me to take them?" Her voice sounded hollow in her own ears.

"No, but I won't keep you from taking them if that's what you want," he answered.

"Can I sit down?" she asked.

He looked out through the weeping limbs toward the rusty-colored water. "I don't own this land or this tree."

She eased down onto the cold earth. "It's not easy for me to admit that I'm wrong," she whispered, "but I was, and I might be just as stubborn and wrong again in the future. If I am, I'll own up to it, but there could be times when I want to be mad for a few hours before I do." She took a deep breath before she blurted out, "I don't want this to be the end for us."

"Me neither, Luna," he said with a long sigh and turned to look deeply into her eyes.

Of all the scenarios that had played through her mind, this was the one she had hoped for—no, prayed for—and even ate a banana for that morning.

"I'm an only child," Shane said, "so I don't know anything about sibling love, much less about the bond between twins. My grandparents were both only children, and so were both of my parents. I don't even have close cousins. I like spending time with your family and being on the fringes of that close bond, but…" He paused.

The pregnant moment hung above them so heavy that it seemed to press down on her chest so hard that every breath became more painful.

"But?" she finally asked. Had she heard hope in his voice? Did that tiny little three-letter word have some meaning?

"But I'm still in the same frame of mind I was last night," Shane said. "I want us to be a couple right out there in public."

"I can do that. I also have a *but*." She almost smiled. "That didn't come out right."

A grin tickled the corners of his mouth. "And that is…?"

"You can come first, but please don't ever try to draw me away from my family," she answered.

Shane reached across the distance and took her hand in his. "I don't want you to give up your family. Someday, if we work out, I want to be a part of it, and, darlin', I was miserable without you."

"I don't want any ifs in our relationship," she told him as she scooted over closer to him. "I just want whens. I can't promise that we won't disagree at times, but I do promise that I'll stay until we settle our argument."

He draped an arm around her shoulders. "And I promise to do the same." He reached into his pocket and pulled out the house key that she had thrown at him the night before. "If we have a disagreement, go toe-to-toe with me, but don't leave me again. I love you, Luna."

"I love you, Shane." She took the key and shoved it into her pocket. "Can we go home now? I'm freezing."

"Yes, darlin', we can go home." Shane stood up and extended a hand to help her.

She put her hand in his and hoped that Bernie's prophecy really would come true.

Chapter 12

"WAKE UP, SLEEPYHEAD," SHANE whispered in Luna's ear.

Without opening her eyes, she rolled over and laid her head on his chest. All was good with the universe—until she glanced over at the old-fashioned analog clock on his bedside table.

"Good grief!" she gasped and sat straight up in bed. "Is it really the middle of the afternoon?"

Shane gently ran his hand down her bare arm. "We were exhausted, so we took a long nap. Are you hungry? I'm not much of a cook, but I can make a mean peanut butter and jelly or bologna sandwich."

She cuddled up next to him and used her fingertips to comb the soft brown hair on his chest. Hot desire started at her fingers and shot through her body.

"I'm starving, but not for food just yet," she whispered.

"Well, darlin', nothing says that we can't have dessert before our sandwiches." He flipped her over on her back, gently brushed her hair out of her face, and covered her mouth with his in a long, lingering kiss.

When his phone rang, he slapped it off the nightstand in a single motion and deepened the kiss even more. Then

Luna's rang. Without opening her eyes, she attempted to turn the phone off but sent it flying across the room from the bedside table.

A noise from the porch completely broke the mood. Luna rolled away from Shane, slung her legs off the edge of the bed, and cocked her head to one side. "That sounds like someone is trying to pick the lock on the front door, Shane."

"Probably just a possum or a raccoon scratching on the screen," Shane grumbled.

Luna jerked on her underpants and grabbed the T-shirt that Shane had taken off earlier. She pulled it on over her head as she started out of the bedroom. "The third is the charm."

Shane slipped on his jeans and zipped them as he followed behind her. "I'll take care of this. Third what?"

Luna headed down the short hallway toward the kitchen. "Phone call to you, one to me, and now we have a burglar. That's three, so it must be a sign that we need to be up and getting busy, not making wild, passionate love."

"But the sun isn't shining so we can't make hay?" he teased. "And I'll bet you that our burglar has a fluffy tail and two black eyes. I've seen a raccoon around the house a few times lately."

"Shh…" Luna put a finger to her lips. "If it's a bunch of kids playing tricks, I want to catch them and give them a piece of my mind for interrupting us."

Shane barely beat her to the front door, but she was right behind him when he slung it wide open. "It's not a raccoon, but it's not a burglar either." He chuckled.

Luna tugged at the tail of his T-shirt and sent up a silent prayer that Endora wasn't the one standing on the other side of the old wooden screen door.

Luna held her breath as she peeked around Shane's shoulder and looked down at a black-and-white puppy staring up at her with its mismatched eyes—one blue and the other brown.

"I didn't ask for a puppy for Christmas. Did you?" Shane asked.

"I haven't asked for one recently, but I wished for one every year when I was a little girl." Luna couldn't take her eyes off the puppy. Its little tail thumped against the wooden porch, and it seemed to be begging for her to bring it in out of the cold.

"And you didn't get one?" Shane teased as he opened the door. "I thought you were a princess who got everything she wanted, especially at Christmas."

"Endora thinks she is allergic to dogs, so every time someone dumped puppies at the Paradise, we had to take them to the shelter. Mama figures that it's just panic attacks since a big dog chased her when she was little more than a toddler. She associates dogs with that fear, and she can't breathe. Aunt Bernie has her convinced that the old myth about Chihuahuas curing asthma is true," she explained as she gathered up the pup into her arms and giggled when it licked her on the face.

"That's too bad. That kind of fear can be horrible. It's a lot like PTSD," Shane said. "But it looks like since Santa

Claus didn't get the memo that you wanted a puppy, he decided to come early this year."

"Can we keep it, please? It'll have to stay here, but I'm already in love with the little critter," Luna begged.

"We've got a fenced backyard, so I don't see any reason why we can't adopt him," Shane answered.

When his phone rang, he jogged back to the bedroom and returned in a couple of minutes. "Looks like it's raining puppies today here in Spanish Fort. That was Remy on the phone. He said that someone had dropped a puppy off at his house, and whoever is dumping dogs today was headed this way with what looked like more in the back of a blue pickup. He was worried they were taking them to the river."

"No!" Luna gasped. "You don't think that…"

"We would have heard a vehicle passing the house," he said before she could finish. "There's only one way down to the river and one way out," he told her, "and that's the gravel path between this house and where we'll build our store. If they turned puppies loose down there, they would have had to drive back this way. I figure they're just driving around this area and dropping them off at houses one at a time."

"That's so cruel," Luna said. "They could be hit on the road. If people don't want puppies, they should take their mama dog to the vet or, at the very least, take the babies to the shelter."

"Hey, you are preaching to the choir," Shane said. "I agree with you, and I'm glad that Granny and Grandpa fenced in the backyard when I was a little kid. We can put the little guy back there until…"

"It's not a little guy. It's a little girl," she told him. "It's cold outside, so we'll have to get her a doghouse and we'll have to come up with a name for her."

Shane followed her back to the bedroom. "Then I guess we're going into Nocona this afternoon to buy one of those igloo doghouses. Since you are starving, we could have a burger at the Dairy Queen. We can figure out a name for this precious little girl on the way. I can be dressed in five minutes. I'm thinking that Holly would be a good name since that's the name I had picked out if Santa brought me a dog on Christmas."

Luna set the puppy on the floor while she got dressed. "Like Blake Shelton says in his song, you can name the dogs, I'll name the kids."

"Hey, now!" Shane grabbed a flannel shirt from the back of a rocking chair and put it on. "Why don't we call it a joint effort on both dogs and kids."

"I can live with that," Luna agreed.

"But she really does looks like a Holly to me," Shane agreed. "We should get on the road if we're going to make it to the store in Nocona before it closes."

Luna picked up the pup and carried her through the house. "You'll only have to stay out in the yard a little while, Holly darlin', and we'll bring you a toy to sleep with so you don't miss your siblings."

She took the puppy all the way into the middle of the

yard and sat her down. Holly immediately began snooping around, found a small stick, and started playing with it.

"You don't think she'll be too lonely out here all by herself, do you, Shane?" Luna asked.

Shane didn't answer but pointed and then opened the gate to let another pup into the yard. "Looks like we've got twins, only they're not identical. Looks like their mama might be a Catahoula, but their poppa is a mutt from what this critter looks like. That's probably the reason they're out delivering Christmas puppies today."

"Why would anyone just throw away sweet little things like these?" Luna asked with a sigh. The second puppy ran over to bump noses with Holly.

"I wonder if Remy and Ursula got one or two?" she asked.

"If they're lucky, they got two dumped on them. One will whine and bark all night without a friend," Shane told her.

"What are we going to name Holly's twin?" she asked.

"Probably something to do with Christmas," Shane said as he followed her inside. "Or maybe just Mutt, since he's so ugly he would make a freight train take a dirt road."

She whipped around and shook her finger at him. "Don't say that about our new baby. He might be just like the ugly duckling that grew up to be a beautiful swan," Luna said, "but I kind of like Mutt. So we have Holly and Mutt."

"Or maybe we could name him something like Comet or Blitzen for Santa's reindeer?" Shane asked.

Luna shook her head. "Mutt fits him better. I should tell

Ursula to put a dog in the story she's working on right now. It could be a puppy like Mutt or maybe an old redboned hound that stayed behind when his master got killed in a gunfight."

"Why not a Catahoula or a mixed breed like Mutt?" Shane asked.

"Because both of them are too pretty," she answered as she picked up her phone from the floor and scanned through the text messages.

One was from Endora asking her if she was going to help decorate cookies. Another was from Ursula telling her that a puppy had wandered up in Remy's yard, and one had showed up over at the Paradise. Since Endora had the pseudo allergy, Remy had said they could bring that one over to his place, so they now had two dogs and Remy intended to train them to watch the cattle.

She looked at the pictures Ursula had sent. "You've got to see this, Shane. Surely those two didn't come from the same litter as ours. They look like a mix of golden Lab and maybe husky."

He ushered her back into the house with a hand on her lower back. "I'm guessing somebody had more than one mama dog, or else they had one that had several boyfriends," Shane said with a chuckle. "Do you think their new babies are prettier than ours?"

"No, I do not!" Luna exclaimed as she grabbed her coat and purse. "Holly and Mutt are adorable."

Her phone rang when they were on their way out to

Shane's truck. She saw that the call was from Ursula and answered it. "Hey, looks like we both got puppies today."

"Yep, we did," Ursula said. "We're on our way to get dog food. Our pups are going to live in the barn until we can train them not to run away. Want to meet us at Dairy Queen for burgers?"

Shane opened the door for her, and she slid into the passenger seat. "We were just thinking we would eat at the Dairy Queen too. Shall we eat first and then go to the store for dog food?"

"Sounds good to me," Ursula answered. "We're on the way so we will claim a booth since we're ahead of you."

Luna ended the call and dropped her phone in her purse. "Looks like our first public date is going to be a double with Remy and Ursula."

Shane raised his eyebrows and flashed a bright smile her way. "I wouldn't care if the whole family joined us, as long as they understood that we are a couple from now on. Did I hear that one of your sisters told Ursula it wasn't a date unless she got a good-night kiss?"

"Oh, honey"—Luna grinned—"we're way past that."

———

When Luna and Shane arrived at the Dairy Queen, Ursula and Remy were already at the counter. Her older sister waved and raised an eyebrow.

Luna held up her hand with her fingers laced in Shane's. "Our first official date," she said.

"Good for you. We just ordered, and we're going to claim that booth over there by the windows," Ursula said.

"I had something more romantic in mind for our first date, but I'm not complaining," Shane whispered.

Remy paid for his and Ursula's orders and then turned around to follow her to the booth. "So y'all survived the first speed bump?"

"What we had was a breakdown of a major bridge, maybe with explosives involved. It was certainly a lot bigger than just a speed bump," Luna argued. "A speed bump is disagreeing over what to have for supper."

"Or breakfast if we're lucky." Shane chuckled.

"You got that right," Remy agreed.

"What can I help you with this afternoon?" asked Milly, who had worked behind the counter ever since back when Luna was in high school.

"Ladies first, especially since this is our first date," Shane said.

"Oh, really?" Milly asked.

"Yes, ma'am, Shane and I are officially dating," Luna answered. "I'll have a double bacon cheeseburger, fries, and an order of nachos."

"My granddaughter, Felicia, is going to be so disappointed," Milly said as she rang up the order. "She's been trying to get up the nerve to ask Shane out for weeks."

"Just make Luna's order a double, and add a couple of large sweet teas, please, ma'am," he said as he pulled out his wallet.

Milly handed Shane a couple of bills and several coins

and then winked. "If things change, you let me know and I'll tell Felicia to get over being shy and call you."

"Thank you, but I don't think things are going to change." Shane slipped an arm around Luna's waist and ushered her to the booth where Ursula and Remy waited.

Luna slid into the booth beside a big plate-glass window overlooking Main Street. "It would have been quieter and less busy in one of the back rooms."

"Oh, no!" Shane took his place right beside her. "I want everyone who parks out front or who drives by to see that I'm with you."

Luna nudged him on the shoulder. "That's sweet."

"I'm just a sweet guy," Shane teased.

"Remy thinks I'm a Christmas witch," Ursula whispered. "This morning, I asked him what he wanted for Christmas…"

"And I said that I had everything that I could ever want," Remy finished for her.

"But then, when I pressed him for ideas," Ursula continued, "he said that he had been thinking about getting a puppy from a nearby shelter and training it to be a cow dog."

"I guess I should've asked to win the lottery," Remy said, "because my wish came true within the hour."

"Can you believe that people would just toss puppies like they do?" Ursula asked.

"People can be *so* cruel," Luna answered. "I don't like it, but I'm not complaining because I got what I wanted for Christmas too, and they were free."

"Not really, darlin'," Shane said. "On Monday, we'll take them to the vet. They'll need shots and a clean bill of health. Maybe they'll even have a vaccine to cure ugly so that Mutt can grow up to be like that beautiful swan you were talking about."

"Oh, hush," Luna scolded and then kissed him on the cheek. "Not all babies are born beautiful."

"Have y'all heard if anyone else got pups dropped on their doorsteps?" Shane asked.

"Not yet," Remy answered. "Four might have been all they had, and they were just putting one out at each house."

"Our second little feller might have come from that old, abandoned house on the corner," Shane said. "It's still got curtains in the windows, so whoever was giving away puppies today wouldn't have known that the Harrison couple who used to live there died a while back, and their kids haven't found a buyer for the place yet."

"Property in Spanish Fort isn't so easy to get rid of," Remy said. "I was surprised to see a winery go in down south of us. I understand that Jake, the man who owns the business, had to buy more land than he needed to get the place that he wanted. I'm going to talk to him about leasing what he's not using to grow hay on next year."

"Think the puppies will be ready to watch over the cattle by that time?" Ursula asked.

"Maybe," Remy answered.

"Luna, what do you think about training Holly and Mutt to be fishing dogs?" Shane asked. "I could teach them to dive into the water and bring up big catfish."

Luna shook her head. "You can't do that! What if they drowned? Oh, no, those two babies are going to grow up to be our watchdogs. We might even let them sleep in the store to keep burglars out after the place is closed at night."

"Mutt could ugly them to death." Shane chuckled.

Luna air slapped him on the arm. "I told you once or twice, or maybe it was three times, not to talk about that sweet little boy that way. He was nice enough to come around to the backyard and keep Holly from whining, so he has a job to do."

Milly brought their order out on a tray and set it in the middle of the table. "I hear you're building a convenience and bait store down on the river. Is that right?"

"Yes, ma'am," Shane said.

"When you get ready to hire some help, give me a call. Felicia is tired of working at the pizza place here in town." Milly gave him another wink.

"Thanks, but I've already got my staff lined up," Shane told her.

"Keep her in mind," Milly said as she hurried back to her place behind the counter to wait on the next group that arrived.

"Looks to me like you better keep your running shoes by the front door, my friend," Remy teased Shane while he helped Ursula divide the orders.

"Hey, I've got watchdogs now," Shane told him. "They may not be ready to attack an intruder just yet, but I bet either one or both of them could trip a burglar up and then lick them so much that they'd be glad to run away from my place." He popped a chip loaded with nacho cheese and slices of jalapeño peppers into his mouth.

"I'll train them to do just that," Luna said.

═══════

On the ride home that evening, Luna thought about how her feelings had changed from that morning until then and vowed to always remember that the beginning of every day might not be perfect, but there was nearly always a lovely sunset in the evening.

"Never go to bed angry," she muttered.

"What was that?" Shane asked.

"I was repeating an old saying about never going to bed angry," she answered. "But I want us to go a step beyond that. Never let an argument fester even for a few minutes."

"I agree." Shane made a right turn, and less than half a block down the road, he pulled into the driveway of his house. "I don't ever want to be as miserable again as I was last night."

"I got drunk with Aunt Bernie, and that didn't even help," Luna admitted.

Shane opened the truck door to the sounds of howling coming from the backyard. "If I'd had some liquor in the house, I would have done the same."

Luna quickly hopped out of the truck and took off around the house in a fast jog.

"Whoa, wait just a minute," Shane said.

"What?" Luna turned. "I hear the babies crying. Do you need help unloading the new doghouse and the food?"

"No, darlin'." He raced over to where she was standing, took her in his arms, and bent her back for a true Hollywood kiss. "I'm making sure that everyone knows this is a date, including you, because tonight you have to go home and deal with your family."

For a moment, she forgot all about the new puppies or that they were probably hungry. Her thoughts went to going back and tangling up the sheets on his—no, not his anymore—their bed as soon as they finished feeding the new babies.

"You keep the pups entertained so they don't run out the gate when I bring in their doghouse and all the stuff we bought for them."

Shane's words brought her back to the present.

"Honey, don't you worry about Endora or any of my family," she told him. "After that kiss, I might not ever go home again."

"Fine by me." Shane whistled all the way back out to the truck.

While they were getting everything set up for the dogs, the sky turned that foggy shade of gray that said the forecast could be right about snow falling on the area. Luna would love a white Christmas, but the weatherman had been wrong before.

"What if it snows and they get cold?" she asked. "Do you think we should keep them in the garage?"

"I have my doubts that they are housebroken, and the

garage hasn't been puppy-proofed," Shane said. "The igloo will keep them warm, and they will cuddle up together. Their little bellies will be full, and they'll be worn out from all their romping around with the new toys we bought them. I'd still like to get our Christmas tree up tonight. After that..." He let the sentence hang in the air.

Luna gave each of the puppies a kiss on the nose and started for the house. "After that, I'll go home and remind Endora of what she said this morning, even though I'd rather go back to bed with you."

She followed him into the house but stopped just inside the door to turn and stare at the dogs for a few more minutes. "I'm hoping that our relationship will help her understand that all men aren't like Kevin and that she can trust people again. She hasn't made a single friend since we came back to Spanish Fort. I think her best friend's betrayal hurt her as much or more than her lousy ex did."

Shane took her in his arms and hugged her close to his chest. "Thank you."

Luna let the peace and comfort that she felt in his arms surround her for a full minute before she took a step back. "We need to get your tree put up, and if we don't get started, we're going to end up in bed, and what is that noise? It sounds like"—she cocked her head to one side—"almost like cows mooing."

"No, darlin'." Shane kissed her on the top of her head. "We need to put *our* tree up, and..." He frowned. "That *is* cows, and they're right outside."

Shane's phone rang, and both he and Luna jumped. He ran back to the bedroom to answer it and seconds later came out in a dead run. "That is cows we keep hearing. Remy's cattle got out and have wandered seven ways to Sunday. He and Ursula are gathering up what went south. Your folks are trying to herd what is in their yard back over to Remy's."

"And the ones we heard?" Luna asked.

"Are headed toward the river," Shane said.

"I'll help." Luna grabbed her coat.

The two of them raced out the front door just in time to see one cow throw back her head and bawl as she made her way down the path toward the river. Another one answered her cry, and she picked up her speed.

"We've got to get ahead of the lead cow and turn her around," Shane shouted. "Then the rest will follow."

Luna bypassed the cow that threw back her head and let out a cry every few feet and was close enough to see the tail end of the next heifer in the parade when she slipped and fell flat on her back in a fresh cow patty. One minute, she was trying to suck air into her deflated lungs, and the next, she was scrambling like a crawdad to get away from that lonesome cow bringing up the rear. She had just barely gotten clear when the cow picked up speed and started to run.

Luna hopped up, brushed the crap from her hands onto her jeans, and took off after the cow again.

She could almost hear Bernie telling her to invite Shane to join her in the shower, because sex in the water was the best. Then the old girl would tell her a long-winded story about how good Bubba or Tank or some other guy with a weird name was when she got drunk and went skinny-dipping with him.

"Dammit!" she heard Shane swear when she had bypassed four other cows. "You sorry heifer, why did you have to get in the water? Luna, can you turn the others around and head them back to the road, then try to get them into our backyard?"

"I'll try," she called out, "and I'll put Mutt and Holly in the garage so they don't get trampled."

"Move before both of us freeze," Shane said. "I'm not talkin' to you, Luna."

"I know," she said as she got in front of the next cow that was playing follow the leader and trying to go a few more feet into the river.

Take off your coat and flap it at her, and do some yelling. Aunt Bernie was back in her head.

Luna didn't argue but just followed directions. If all the cows got into the water, then she and Shane would have a terrible time getting them back to the house. "You stupid animal," she yelled. She started to brush a strand of hair back away from her face, then remembered what was on her hands. "Don't you know that it's too cold for you to be wading in the river? Shoo! Turn around and go back."

The cow made a beeline for the old willow tree and pushed under the dead limbs to huddle together with her sister bovines against the trunk.

"I've got you cornered now," Luna said. "I hope the

bunch of you are happy. You've ruined the night Shane and I were going to put up our tree. If you don't behave and get on up to our yard, I'm going to…" She popped her hands on her hips, shivered against the north wind blowing off the water, and noticed weeping willow branches were tangled up in their horns. "I'm going to get a grip on the limb hanging down from your horns." She tried to keep her voice calm as she approached the nearest one. "And I'm going to lead you back to my house, and the rest of you are going to follow. Do you hear me? If you don't do what I say, I'll call Aunt Bernie to come down here, and you do not want to face off with her."

The cow must've heard stories about Bernie because she lowered her head and didn't even moo one time. With trembling hands—fear and cold mixed together—Luna reached out and grabbed the makeshift rope and tugged on it.

"I meant what I said," Luna said. "I've got a phone in my pocket, and Bernie can be here in five minutes."

The cow moved forward one step.

"You have got to be as stubborn as a mule." Shane's voice cut through the darkness.

Luna glanced back to see him pushing the animal. The cantankerous cow finally bellowed loud enough to shake the ornaments off the Christmas trees on the Oklahoma side of the river and stepped out of the water onto the sandbar. Luna's cow broke loose and ran toward her. The other four took off like they'd been shot with a cattle prod, and the whole bunch of them started running back up the path.

"Get ahead of them and open the gate into the yard," Shane yelled.

Luna had never run so hard, and she was completely out of breath when she threw the gate open. Mutt and Holly used the occasion to tear out of the yard, but when they saw the cows coming at them full speed, they made a hasty retreat back into their igloo.

"All I have to do is get that lead cow to turn," Luna muttered as she stood outside the gate and flapped her coat in the wind. "My Christmas spirit is gone. I'm cold, and I still have to talk to Endora."

The lead cow came at Luna like she was going to run over her, but Luna stood her ground and kept waving her coat. At the last minute, the old gal made a hard right turn into the yard, and all the others followed her. Shane brought up the rear and slammed the gate shut.

He put his hands on his knees and panted for a few seconds before he stood up. "Remy owes us a steak dinner."

"I hope"—Luna slipped inside the gate—"that it comes from one of these."

Shane straightened up. "What are you doing?"

"I'm not carving a steak out of one of their hind ends," she answered. "I'm getting my babies out of the igloo and putting them in the garage." She weaved her way through the cattle and dropped down on her knees to coax them out.

Shane joined her and reached inside to drag Mutt out first. He handed him off to Luna and then grabbed Holly. "Let's go through the house. The way that old lead gal is looking at the gate, I'm afraid she'll barrel through it if we open it again."

When they set the puppies down in the garage, they immediately began to explore every corner. Luna pulled out her phone and called Ursula, who answered on the first ring.

"Hello," she said. "Did any come your way?"

"We've got six penned up in our backyard," Luna answered.

"We'll bring the cattle trailer down and get them," Ursula said and ended the call.

Luna slipped the phone back in her pocket and glanced over at Shane. "I had at least hoped to share a hot shower with you."

Shane began peeling off his clothes. "We can get one if we hurry. At least we'll be clean and won't smell like fishy river water." He left a trail of muddy, wet clothing all the way to the bathroom. "Come on and join me. You've got to be freezing cold. Most of the time, you were out there without a coat on."

"We were going to put up our tree tonight," she groaned.

Shane adjusted the water in the shower and then turned around to help Luna get undressed. "You've got dirt and leaves in your hair, darlin'. What happened?"

"I slipped and fell," she said as she shivered. "That old caboose cow almost ran over me."

"Holy smoke!" Shane checked her body for scrapes as he removed her clothes.

"I'm fine," she assured him. "We made a good team out there, didn't we?"

"Always." He pulled back the shower curtain and led her inside with him. The warm water felt great but not nearly as good as his naked body next to hers when he gathered her into his arms.

"What happens in the shower stays in the shower, right?" she whispered.

"Last time I checked the rule books, that's exactly what it said." He grinned.

<hr>

Luna gave him a quick kiss on the cheek on her way out the door after the cows were loaded up and the puppies returned to the yard. "We'll get the tree up sometime this week. It's still four more weeks until Christmas, so we can get that tree up."

Shane brushed a strand of hair from her face. "I understand that putting up a tree together means we're a couple."

Just that simple gesture made her wish she could spend the night, but she really needed to check on Endora—not that she was putting her before Shane but more that she could feel Endora getting antsier by the minute.

"That's exactly what it means," she told him with a nod. "How about next Sunday? We can go to church together, and then after services, the church is having a potluck in the fellowship hall. I am going to sit beside you and make sure that all the women in this area know that we are together."

"A little jealous, are you?" he teased.

"Not just a little—and with good reason," she answered.

"Santa Claus will be there for the little kids. Mama is bringing enough food to feed an army. I'll be helping in the evenings, so we'll be super busy getting ready for that and the big Paradise Christmas party that we host every year. We'll be eating leftovers until the following Tuesday when we have our own Paradise Christmas party. I'll have to be home to help with everything every waking minute until that party is over."

"Can you take one day off to make and decorate cookies with me after that? Maybe on the following Wednesday?" Shane asked. "Granny always fixed up plates with at least a dozen on each one, and we took them around to all the folks in Spanish Fort and to the nursing home in Nocona to pass out to the residents. I want to keep up that tradition."

"That is so sweet," Luna said. "I'll be here bright and early on that Wednesday morning."

"Or you could just come home with me after the party on Tuesday and spend the night," Shane suggested.

"I like that idea even better." She tiptoed, wrapped her arms around his neck, and brought his lips to hers.

Chapter 13

THE PORCH LIGHT WAS on when Luna parked her car beside Endora's that night, but the rest of the house was dark. She wasn't sure if she was disappointed or relieved that no one was still up. One part of her was glad she had been wrong about Endora being nervous. The other part wished that Endora had been up so she could tell her all about her day—like they had always done.

"Hello," Aunt Bernie said from the bottom step. "I don't have whiskey tonight, but if you want a little nip, it'll only take a minute to run out to my trailer and get a bottle."

"What are you doing sitting here in the dark?" Luna asked.

"It's too cold to wait for you on the porch," Bernie answered with half a shrug, "and I couldn't sleep until I knew you were all right. Of course, I don't sleep until after midnight anyway. It comes with the territory of not closing the bar until two o'clock."

Luna sat down beside her and draped an arm around Bernie's thin shoulders. "I'm fine, but the sisters have plans for tomorrow morning, so we should both get some sleep. You don't want to miss any gossip, so you better set an alarm."

"If I'm not here when the fun starts"—Bernie stood up—"you call me and let it ring until I answer."

"I will," Luna promised and watched her aunt slip out the front door.

Luna tiptoed up the stairs, opened the door into her bedroom, and switched on the light to find Endora sleeping in her bed. She rose up to a sitting position and rubbed the sleep from her eyes. "You are finally home."

"Why are you in my room?" Luna asked.

"I wanted to be sure you got home, and I've got some questions that I need answered. I couldn't sleep in my own bed until we talked. Being in here was like we were together," Endora said.

My gut feeling was right, Luna thought as she sat down on the edge of the bed. "What are these pressing questions?"

"Did you ever like Kevin or Krystal?" Endora asked, then covered a yawn with her hand.

"Do you want the truth or a sugarcoated lie?" Luna asked.

"I want the truth," Endora answered.

"I didn't like either of them, but Krystal was your friend, and you were dating Kevin, so I didn't say anything," Luna answered.

"Why? What was your reason?" Endora asked.

"Kevin had a wandering eye. He flirted too much with other women, especially Krystal. I don't know why he proposed to you because it was evident to me that he wasn't ready to settle down."

"He sure settled down with Krystal soon enough," Endora argued.

"The scandal at the school caused that—at least in my opinion," Luna said. "The teachers and administration were upset with him for what he did to you. He had to marry her to save face," Luna added, voicing her opinion.

"Okay," Endora said with a nod. "I can buy that, but why didn't you like Krystal? She spent a lot of time in our apartment, and you never said a word."

Luna tried to phrase her answer carefully. Endora didn't need to feel like her own sister had kept things from her. "That woman gossiped about everyone behind their backs, even her good friends at the school. You can bet anyone like that is talking about you when you're not around."

"Why didn't you tell me?" Endora asked. "Why did *you* let me get hurt?"

"You are my sister, my twin," Luna answered. "I wanted to be wrong, and when Kevin proposed, I even prayed that he would change. And I didn't *let* you get hurt. You had to have seen the signs just like I did, and you just swept them under the rug."

"Did you know about their affair before I did?" Endora asked.

Luna set the rocker in motion with her foot. "I did *not* know, but I suspected something was up from the way they made eyes at each other like they had this big secret. They were always whispering in the hallways and the teachers' lounge. I really hoped they were talking about what kind of gifts to buy for you or parties they were planning to throw for you—that kind of thing."

Endora's chin quivered, but she didn't break down and cry. "Will you tell me if you ever have thoughts like that again?"

Luna crossed her heart like she had done as a child. "I promise."

"We're twins," Endora said. "When you hurt, I do. I want us to never lose the closeness that we share, but I want you to be happy like you are right now. I realize that you are going to spend more and more time with Shane, and I respect that now. I was wrong not to trust you, but please, always act on your gut feelings. If you see him whispering to another woman, then confront him, and if I even get a whiff that he's flirting with others, I will tell you."

"I will do more than just confront him," Luna said.

"We'll do it together if that happens," Endora declared. "I'm still having trouble getting from anger to acceptance, but I want you to know that I'm here for you like you have been for me all these months. I couldn't have made it through these tough times without your support."

Luna hugged her twin sister tightly. "I love you, Sister."

"I love you right back." Endora wiggled free of the embrace. "I'm glad we cleared the air, and now I'm going to my room."

Luna walked Endora to the door. "Are we good then?"

"We definitely are," Endora said. "You know this would have been easier on both of us if our older sisters would have gotten married and settled down by now."

"Or if we'd moved away from each other like Rae and Bo?" Luna asked.

"Yes," Endora said. "Then it wouldn't feel like we are splitting one heart right down the middle."

"We'll figure out how to live apart and be grown-ups— but not tomorrow or even next week," Luna said.

"Good night," Endora said with half a smile.

"Good night." Luna stood in the doorway and watched Endora pad barefoot across the hallway. It seemed like an omen when they closed their bedroom doors at the same time.

Luna crossed the room, picked up her phone, and started to send Shane a message but then changed her mind. She tiptoed downstairs, went out the front door, and drove to his house. No, that wasn't right. She drove home.

—————

The next week flew by so fast that when Luna looked at the calendar the next Sunday morning, she could hardly believe how fast December was passing. Or that she and Shane had missed church for the second week in a row.

"I need to sneak through the back door. I should already be in the fellowship hall helping Mama and my sisters coordinate things. See you later," Luna told Shane when he snagged a good spot in the church parking lot.

He kissed her on the cheek and said, "I'll go see where Remy and your dad are. Save me a chair beside you."

"You'll have to save me one." Luna gave him one more

kiss. "I'll be helping serve dinner, so I'll be one of the last ones to sit down."

"Aha," Aunt Bernie said the moment Luna was in the room. "Did you oversleep or…"

"Bernie!" Mary Jane scolded.

"I'll just draw my own conclusions from the glow on your face," Bernie said. "Damn…I mean, dang it…I wish I was young enough to get so tired that I didn't make it to church the next morning."

Endora raised an eyebrow.

"Don't go giving me a dirty look," Luna told her sister. "I made it in time to help, and I doubt that anyone even missed me in church. They were all thinking about the dinner rather than gossiping about who was sharing hymn books."

"Amen," Ursula said. "Remy and I got here late too. I got involved with Daisy's next few entries in the journal and writing the next chapter, and Remy was working on final tests so we didn't get to bed until midnight."

This wasn't Luna's first rodeo—or maybe she should think first potluck dinner—so she set about taking lids off casserole dishes and helping arrange everything. Meats—ham, fried chicken, smothered pork chops, turkey—and dressing all on one end, casseroles next, then vegetables, breads, and desserts. She hoped that by the time everyone had gone through the line, there was a little turkey and dressing left and maybe a slice of Dolly Devlin's pecan pie. She hadn't had time for a single bite of breakfast.

Aunt Bernie poked her in the ribs with a bony elbow as

they were getting the buffet tables ready. "I heard that y'all had to wrangle half a dozen cows trying to take a swim in the Red River. Did you share a shower after all that?"

"Aunt Bernie!" Luna scolded.

Bernie fanned her face with a napkin. "I just now remembered the time that my mother let me go to church with Matty Ray Thomson."

"Oh yeah?" Luna asked as she admired the table loaded with casserole dishes.

"We went to church all right, but we didn't go inside," Bernie whispered. "We had a little of the moonshine that his grandpa made. It was hotter'n blue blazes, but not nearly as hot as the sex we had in the parking lot while we listened to the congregation sing, 'I'll Fly Away.' The memory gives me hot flashes to this day."

"That was way too much information." Luna blushed, glad that a parade of folks had begun arriving through the door from the sanctuary into the fellowship hall.

"Where's Remy and Shane?" Ursula asked.

"I figured they'd be first in line, right behind the preacher and Daddy," Endora answered. "They should already have been here, unless there was an emergency—" She stopped midsentence and clamped a hand over her mouth. "You don't think anything is wrong with the puppies, do you?"

"Not on your life," Bernie said. "I peeked out the door a few seconds ago. Your fellers are all the way to the end of the line with Joe Clay. They ain't goin' to give up a chance to eat with their womenfolk. Reminds me of a story…"

Luna held up a palm. "A story that you can tell us at home. I'm surprised that lightning didn't shoot through the rafters after what you told me a few minutes ago."

"Me and God made a deal." Bernie winked. "He can let me get old as long as I can keep all my memories."

"Y'all are not really in love if you think of dogs before boyfriends." Endora scowled at both her sisters. "What if Shane or Remy dropped right there in the sanctuary with a heart attack?"

"Don't even think like that." Luna shivered.

Ursula shook a finger at Endora. "Or speak such things out loud."

"Your boyfriends are fine," Mary Jane said. "They are just romantic like Joe Clay, and for that I'm grateful."

"So no worries," Ursula said and then turned to Dolly Devlin, who was next in line. "What can I help you with?"

"I'll have a serving of that sweet potato casserole," the short, gray-haired lady who was Bernie's friend answered.

Luna sidestepped over to Ursula's place behind the table. "Do you share recipes? I'd love to know the secret for making your pecan pies."

Dolly shook her head. "Honey, it's an old family recipe that I promised I wouldn't give out to anyone that's not kin to me."

"Can you adopt me for a day?" Luna asked.

"Nope," her husband, Walter, said from right behind her. "But..." He leaned over and whispered, "The big secret is to follow the recipe on the back of a bottle of dark corn syrup, only use all brown sugar instead of white, and then throw in two tablespoons of Jack Daniel's whiskey."

"Walter!" Dolly scolded. "You don't tell things like that in church."

Maybe Bernie should tell Dolly some of her stories, and then Walter's wouldn't seem nearly so bad, Luna thought.

"That's no worse than lyin' in church about it being an old family recipe." Walter chuckled.

"I heard all that. Now that you know the recipe, it's your job to make three for Christmas," Mary Jane told Luna.

"We'll hide one and share it later when no one else is around," Ursula whispered.

"No use in trying that," Bernie told them. "I can sniff out a pecan pie even if you lock it up in Joe Clay's gun safe."

"You wouldn't hide something like that from me, would you?" Endora asked with an innocent expression on her face. "I'm positive that pecan pie would help me get to the acceptance stage."

Luna nudged her twin with a shoulder. "You've played that card enough, Sister!"

Endora giggled, and the sound was like music in Luna's ears.

"Speaking of desserts," Ursula whispered. "Did anyone think to save a bowl of Mama's blackberry cobbler for Daddy?"

Luna said, "I hid a serving for him in the kitchen."

The buzz of dozens of conversations and bushel baskets full of gossip still sounded like a field full of bees after most folks had finished eating and were having coffee or a second glass of tea. Some folks were even lining up for seconds when Luna saw Remy, Shane, and Joe Clay finally bringing up the rear of the line. Her heart did one of those little flutters that happened every time she saw Shane—up close or even across the room.

Joe Clay raised an eyebrow at Mary Jane, and she pointed toward the kitchen.

"I saved back a bowl for you, and it's sitting on the cabinet beside the toaster."

"Thank you, darlin'," he said with a grin and then laid a hand on Remy's shoulder and one on Shane's. "I'll try to get her to make another blackberry cobbler for Christmas, but that last bowlful belongs to me."

"Aww, shucks," Shane said. "I love cobblers! But for now, it looks like these good folks left plenty for us to fill up on right here."

"And I do see a little bit of chocolate cake over there," Remy said.

"Has waiting in line built up your appetite?" Luna teased when she saw how much food was on Shane's plate.

"A man doesn't let the gas tank go empty before he fills it again," Shane teased. "It could cause a major disaster at one of those inopportune moments. Where are we sitting?"

"How about at the table over there on the south side where no one else is right now?" Luna asked as she left her post and fixed her own plate—getting the last portion of the turkey and dressing.

"Better hold on to your boyfriend," Bernie whispered as they were all sitting down.

"Why?" Luna asked.

Bernie nodded toward the two tall red-haired women coming out of the kitchen. They had their eyes glued on Remy and Shane and were coming right at the table where the sisters were all seated.

"Hello, I'm Felicia," the curvier one said. "Looks like we're the stragglers who are getting to eat last. This is my cousin, Kasey. We've been washing up the pots and pans in the kitchen with my grandmother, Milly. You might know her. She's worked at the Dairy Queen in Nocona for years."

"Yes, we know her," Mary Jane said. "Glad y'all were able to join us today. Are you going to be members of our little church?"

Felicia settled into the empty chair beside Shane. "No, ma'am. Grandma likes to come with her sister, Aunt Dolly, when she doesn't have to work on Sunday, and she talked us into coming with her."

"We don't go to church anywhere on a regular basis," Felicia said. "When we don't have to work, we usually party on Saturday and sleep in on Sunday. Grandma calls us CEO Christians. That means Christmas and Easter Only. I figure that's better than nothing."

"I see," Mary Jane said. "If you ever decide to go to church regularly, we'd love to have you join us here."

Luna wanted to jump up in the middle of the table and shout, "No!" at the top of her lungs. The way those women were sizing up Shane and Remy, she damn sure didn't want them coming to church every Sunday.

"Well, thank you, ma'am," Felicia said.

Kasey sat down on the other side of the table right beside Remy and batted her eyes at him so often that it made Luna want to strangle her and watch her turn blue.

Kasey flashed what Luna called a fake smile across the table at Mary Jane. "Grandma and Aunt Dolly are taking the second shift in the kitchen so we can eat. They told us we might meet some good-lookin', church-goin' men here, and they weren't wrong." She turned her focus back to Remy. "Grandma says that you're a professor over at the college in Gainesville. I went there for two years, but then the money ran out. I intend to go back someday, though, and get my degree in early childhood development. What do you teach? I might take your classes when I enroll again. Maybe we could talk about it over drinks some evening."

"American history," Remy answered. "I'm pretty sure it's not a required class in the field you are planning to study."

"Oh, honey," Kasey downright flirted, "I'd take that class just to hear you talk."

"Oh! My! God! I mean 'gosh' since we're in church," Felicia gasped, shifting her gaze from Luna to Endora and back again. "There's two of you that look just alike. You have to be twins."

"Yes, we are," Endora said from across the table. "I'm Endora, and Luna is my sister."

"Me and Felicia get mistaken for twins, but we're just

cousins." Kasey kept looking from one twin to the other. "I don't think I've ever seen twins that still look so much alike when they're grown women." She finally noticed Ursula. "Do you have a twin too?"

Remy slipped an arm around Ursula and gave her a hug. "This is my girlfriend, Ursula, but she's not a twin."

"But we do have another set of twins in the family, Rae and Bo, and two more sisters, Ophelia and Tertia," Ursula said.

"Pleased to meet all y'all," Kasey said and winked at Felicia. "Where did you get such unusual names?"

"We get that question a lot. My mama is a romance writer. She writes under M. J. Marsh," Luna answered.

"And all seven of my girls are named for characters in whatever book I was writing at the time they were born," Mary Jane said.

"Seven?" Kasey gasped.

"That's right," Mary Jane replied. "Three single births and then two sets of twins. Seven baby girls in just a little more than five years."

"Did you have a nanny?" Felicia asked.

"No, she did not," Ursula answered. "She raised us by herself and managed to put out three books a year and used her earnings to put my father through med school at the same time. Her superhero cape is hanging in the hall closet at the Paradise."

"That would be our home," Endora said. "It's just up the road a little way. Y'all should see it all lit up at night."

"Or better yet, we're having a Christmas open house on Tuesday night from six to ten," Joe Clay said with a smile. "Your aunt Dolly will be there. Y'all should join her. There's always lots of food and eggnog."

Felicia cut her eyes over to Shane. "Thank you for the invitation. We'll save the date and be there."

Luna laid a possessive hand on Shane's arm and then shot a dirty look across the table at Joe Clay. Why would he do something so downright stupid? She didn't need Felicia trying to slip in between them and cause problems. "Mama, it looks like you've got plenty of help," Luna said when she'd finished the last bite of her dessert.

"Oh, no!" Mary Jane shook her head. "I know what you are thinking, but you can't run off before Santa Claus comes. I want a picture of you and Shane with him. Y'all have to stand behind his chair," Mary Jane answered, "and then we're taking a photo of all the kids that are here, including Shane and Remy, in front of the Christmas tree. We'll have them printed and bring them to church next week for their parents to take home."

"But we're not all here yet," Luna argued. "The rest of the sisters won't get home until tomorrow, and we usually do the Santa pictures when we're all seven together."

"That doesn't matter. We'll do more Santa pictures when everyone is home," Joe Clay said. "Your mama loves pictures. She still has all the albums she's made since you girls were babies. Do you remember what she used to threaten you with when you were teenagers?"

"Sweet Lord!" Endora whispered.

"He is at that," Mary Jane agreed, "but I do not threaten, darlin'"—she touched Joe Clay on the cheek—"and all my girls can tell you that I deliver what I promise."

"She's a good bit like me in that area," Bernie said. She turned to Felicia and Kasey. "So you girls like to party, do you?"

"Yes, ma'am, we do," Kasey answered.

"I owned a bar for right about sixty years, and I can tell you right now, that's not the place to find a man who wants a lasting relationship." Bernie filled a fork with sweet potatoes.

"Maybe we just want a fling," Felicia said with a sideways glance and a wink at Shane.

Shane completely ignored the woman and said, "Miz Mary Jane, tell me more about the picture albums."

"It means that Mama would threaten us," Ursula explained, and then she did a perfect imitation of Mary Jane's voice. "If you don't behave, I will bring out all my albums and show them to your boyfriends." She turned toward Mary Jane and asked, "Are you going to drag them out for Remy and Shane?"

"You mean like real pictures, not digital?" Felicia asked and then shivered. "I'm glad my mama and grandma didn't keep records like that."

"Amen!" Kasey agreed.

Luna remembered those horrible pictures that had been taken when she started high school, back when her mother finally let her wear makeup. Ursula had tried to help her learn the art of putting it on, but she had pushed her sister away. The pictures that were taken all that year—holidays, spring break when the family went to Disney World—proved that she should have listened to Ursula.

Her thoughts were interrupted when a vision of baby pictures popped into her head. There she and Endora were, lying side by side on a white fur rug, each wearing nothing but a headband to hold back their wispy blond hair.

Shane leaned over and whispered softly, "I can read your mind right now. I'll show you mine if you show me yours."

"In that case"—she pointed at him—"you go first."

"Any time," he said and then went back to eating his dessert.

"Y'all excuse me," Joe Clay said as he pushed back his chair and headed for the door.

Shane followed suit. "Me too."

"And me," Remy added.

"I understand where Daddy is going, but why Shane and Remy?" Ursula asked.

Mary Jane's eyes twinkled like they did when she had a secret that she could hardly keep inside. "They passed the first test for boyfriends."

Luna was speechless for a few seconds. "Mama, you didn't!"

"Do you know something that we don't, Luna?" Ursula demanded.

"Like I said, wait and see," Mary Jane answered. "But both of y'all need to realize that it takes a confident and strong man to do what y'all's boyfriends are doing."

Luna started to say something but then she heard, "Ho!

Ho! Ho!" and Santa Claus came through the back door, followed by two elves who were well over six feet tall. Jingle bells on the curved toes of their green shoes tinkled with each step. Green tights and green tunics almost reached their knees, but instead of the traditional elf hats, they had cowboy hats perched on their heads. Little kids swarmed around them like bees around a honeypot and followed them all the way from the door to the chair where Santa took a seat, and the two elves set big green bags on either side of him.

"Good God!" Bernie piped up from the end of the table where she had been quietly—for a big change—eating her dinner. "I wish I'd known those guys would dress up like that before now. They would have made a big splash at Bernie's Place. I wish Bubba Wilson would have had a getup like that instead of that rip-away police uniform he liked to use when we did role-playing."

"You did what?" Felicia gasped.

"Hon…nee"—Bernie drew the word out—"don't tell me two hussies like you girls don't know anything about role-playing. I knew lots of barflies like y'all through the years."

"Oh, yeah, what kind is that?" Kasey growled.

"The kind that don't have very many morals in their pockets. Take it from me, girls, if you're thirsty, you better go to another watering hole other than where Remy and Shane are hanging out. The seven Simmons sisters protect theirs with more than you want to deal with," Bernie said out of the corner of her mouth. "And if they need help, I've broken up enough bar fights to know how to help them out."

"Are you threatening us, old woman?" Felicia asked.

"Aunt Bernie does not make threats," Luna said. "And she's very wise, not old."

Bernie leaned over and whispered, "I knew there was a reason you were my favorite.".

Without another word, Felicia and Kasey picked up their plates and headed back to the kitchen.

"Ho! Ho! Ho!" Santa said again as he got comfortable in the big chair in front of the Christmas tree in the corner. "Has everyone been good little boys and girls? If you have, then I might have a present for you."

"Yes!" The shouts and squeals could be heard from all over the room.

Luna and Endora had helped wrap the presents in the bags for weeks so they knew that every little child who came to the services and the potluck that day could have a gift. Santa—a.k.a. Joe Clay Carter—would give a surprise from his right side to the boys and from his left to the girls.

"I told you that Remy and Shane had passed a big test in Joe Clay's eyes." Mary Jane smiled as she stood up and motioned for her daughters to follow her. "It's time for us to set up the table with the nut, fruit, and candy sacks for the kids to take home with them."

Luna pushed back her chair and locked eyes with Shane. He tipped his cowboy hat and smiled. She whipped the phone out from the pocket of her long, denim skirt and took a quick picture of him. Nothing—not one solitary thing— that he could see in her mother's albums would ever worry her again, not after seeing her boyfriend in green tights and a cowboy hat. And she had the picture to prove it.

―――――――――

The albums didn't come out that night after everyone was back at the Paradise, but Mary Jane had printed copies of the pictures she had taken at the church and brought them out of her office to share. "Test two passed," she whispered to Luna as she passed out the photographs.

"And that was?" Luna asked.

"They were willing to take pictures in those costumes," Mary Jane answered.

"Didn't we look cute," Shane said as he looked down at his copy of the pictures she had taken at the church. "Luna, darlin', if you had one of those red-and-white costumes like girl elves have, we could both dress up when we take cookies around to all the folks. The folks in the nursing home would get a big kick out of seeing elves coming to visit. They'd love a little excitement to go with their cookies."

"If she don't want to do that, I will," Bernie said. "I might even sing and dance for the residents there. Man alive, I'm glad I'm not in their shoes. I'm glad I've got family that's willing to let me and Pepper live in their backyard."

"We wouldn't put you in a nursing home, no matter how nice it is," Mary Jane said.

"Luna's got a costume," Ursula said. "When she was six-teen, Mama bought her and Endora each one of those little red-and-white shortie things so they could be Santa's helpers and help pass out presents at the church potluck. They both whined about wearing them, but Mama threatened them with the albums. Someday, you'll get to see the pictures if Mama makes good on her word."

"I'll wear mine if you will wear the elf costume," Luna said as a picture of bedroom role-playing flashed through her head. Why did Bernie have to say that about role-playing? Now it was stuck in Luna's head.

"I'd be willing to bet that neither of you have that kind of nerve," Endora said.

"How much?" Luna asked.

"Fifty bucks," Endora answered without hesitation.

Luna stuck out her hand. "You are on."

Endora shook it. "I'm glad to take your money, but I do have one request. You have to take a selfie of yourselves in the nursing home and at least a couple of the houses where you take the cookies as proof. I don't just hand out money on your word."

"We'll take the pictures," Shane said, "and we'll use the money to buy Christmas presents for the new puppies. Speaking of those critters, I'd better be going home to feed them."

"Me too," Remy said as he stood up. "It's starting to get dark, and I've got chores."

"I'll go with you," Ursula said as she got to her feet and followed him out the back door.

Shane stood and pulled Luna up with him. "Walk me to the door?"

"Of course," she answered. "Will you tell the puppies that I'm missing them?"

When they reached the foyer, he dropped her hand and put on his coat and hat. "I wish you were coming home with me tonight. I promise I'll wake you before dawn."

"Me too, but all of us will be swamped for the next couple of days," she said as her arms snaked up around his neck. "Rae and Bo, Tertia and Ophelia will all be here before morning. They always take a couple of personal days and come home for the Christmas party and then come back a few days before the holiday." She gave him a long kiss that promised nights at his house later in the week. "We'll be cooking and working for the open house right up until we open the doors for folks to come inside on Tuesday night."

"Then cookies on Wednesday?" He held her close to his chest for another minute before stepping back.

"And a sleepover?" she asked.

"Yes, please, ma'am." He grinned, gave her a quick kiss on the lips, and left.

Luna marched back into the living room where the rest of her family was watching a Hallmark Christmas movie. She popped her hands on her hips and demanded, "Okay, Daddy, what were you thinking when you invited those two women to our party? Didn't you see how they were flirting with Remy and Shane?"

"If he hadn't invited them, I would have," Bernie said. "I've been itchin' for a good old-fashioned bar fight for a month. That would liven up any party for sure. I haven't gotten to kick the sh…crap out of anyone in a long time, but I've still got my fightin' skills."

"I saw exactly what they were doing." Joe Clay nodded the whole time he answered.

Luna crossed her arms over her chest, drew down her eyebrows, and tapped her foot on the floor. "Then why would you sabotage my and Ursula's relationships?"

"I didn't," Joe Clay replied. "What I did was make it possible for both of you to know, beyond a shadow of a doubt, that your boyfriends could take a little more heat without getting burned."

"What you saw in the church was just a little opening act for what could be coming, so bring out your boxing gloves." Bernie chuckled and put up her fists in a fighting position.

"Y'all need to know if what you think you have with Shane and Remy is worth fighting for. There will always be trials and tests in a committed relationship. Remember the preacher who came to dinner when you girls were little?" Mary Jane added.

Ursula nodded. "None of us could ever forget that wimpy little man, but we put him going really fast. By the time dinner was over, he couldn't wait to get out of here. We had a seven-sister committee meeting in my room when we found out he was coming and set up a plan to get rid of him. Endora threw a fit because Mama invited him."

Luna plopped down on the sofa. "We didn't want him to be our daddy, so we *had* to do something. That was in Endora's selective vegetarian days. She would scarf down a hamburger, but she wouldn't eat lasagna with meat in it. The preacher was real happy about that since he didn't eat anything that once had a face."

"And when Ophelia had told everyone at school that we were turning the Paradise into a place for Baptist nuns," Endora said, laughing.

"Do tell more," Bernie said.

"He scolded me when I welcomed him to Paradise," Ursula remembered. "He said that I should say 'our home.' That was when we decided that if he made it past dessert, it would be a miracle."

"Then Mama served him a glass of sweet tea to drink while we waited for the lasagna to heat up, and he said it was too strong and weak," Endora said. "And he made a play for Mama while he was redoing his tea. He said something about her perfume, and she told him that us girls had bought it for her at Walmart."

"And after that, he tried another tactic and asked Mama when she was going to stop writing and do something more spiritually profitable with her time," Ursula said.

"How did you know all that? You girls were upstairs," Mary Jane asked.

"They sent me down to eavesdrop," Endora said with a smile. "When he said that he didn't think it was proper for Joe Clay to be living here, I almost ran into the kitchen and kicked him in the knees."

"This all just proves what I was telling those hussies about you girls all standing together if one of you is threatened."

"Yep, we did," Luna said. "Remember when he got all prim and proper and told us we shouldn't be eating sugar, that neither he or his mother would ever think of eating it because it was poison for the body? Then he said that he would have to train us girls to have watered-down sweet tea on Sundays only. Then we would have to give up meat."

"I decided right then and there that I wasn't a vegetarian anymore, and I ate a big chunk of that lasagna. I didn't want to be like that sorry sucker," Endora said with a smile.

"Then Ophelia said, 'Praise the Lord,' and got in trouble for using the Lord's name in vain. So she said that we were training to be nuns," Luna remembered. "Preacher Francis asked if we were Catholic, and Luna told him that we all had different fathers. I can still see his pasty face turning even paler. He asked Mama if she'd been married five times."

"And I told him no, just the once." Mary Jane burst out laughing. "I had forgotten that whole incident. But I do remember that suddenly he had to get home to his mommy. He actually called her that. We never saw him again."

"You girls fought for what you wanted when it came to that preacher." Joe Clay laughed with Mary Jane and then dried his eyes on a napkin. "Now, let's see if you are willing to put forth some effort to save your relationships with Remy and Shane. Maybe Felicia and Kasey won't even show up, and if they do, they might bring a date, just to try to make the guys jealous."

"So you're telling me that you invited those two awful women to test me and Shane?" Luna asked.

"I think it's a wonderful idea," Endora said.

"Me too," Bernie agreed. "I can't wait for the party now. It's been years since we've had a good old catfight in the house. And you girls need to write down some of this stuff that happened when you were little girls."

"Aunt Bernie!" Mary Jane scolded.

"Well, it has been a long time," Bernie declared. "Just so you know, Luna, I'm willing to throw my fists into the fight if you need some help."

Mary Jane pointed right at Luna. "I was hoping, since you're used to pulling prepubescent boys apart in schoolyard fights, I could depend on *you* to break up a fight."

Luna shook her head. "Not me, Mama. I'll be the one on the top of the dogpile getting my licks in. Nobody messes with my sisters."

"I'll be right there with you," Endora added. "I'll get a picture of Krystal in my mind, and I'll pretend that she's the one I'm clawing at. I already feel better just thinking about it."

Luna moved across the room and sat down on the arm of Endora's chair. "As long as y'all stand back and let me at those two hussies first, we'll be just fine. Daddy, you should know that I'm ready to fight for Shane, and I know Ursula won't let anyone get between her and Remy. Even if it shuts down the party, I will do it. The rest of y'all can tag in if we can't get the job done. Nobody messes with the Simmons sisters."

Endora flipped back her long, blond hair. "You got that right."

"Damn straight!" Bernie did a fist pump.

Chapter 14

"SHANE TEXTED ME THIS morning and asked me what he should wear," Luna said as she and Ursula covered several long tables with bright red tablecloths on the day of the party. "I hope Remy doesn't show up in a tux, because I told Shane that jeans and boots were fine."

"I told Remy he had to wear the elf costume," Ursula said in a low voice.

"Did you really?" Luna gasped.

Ursula's eyes twinkled. "Yep, but he told me he wouldn't do it unless I borrowed your little red outfit."

"I heard that," Bernie said, not two feet behind them. "You haven't lived until you play dress-up with a sexy guy. I remember when me and Bobby Joe…"

"I thought it was Bubba Wilson," Luna corrected her.

"That was for my sixtieth birthday. Me and Bobby Joe had a good time in an old Volkswagen Bug when I was in my thirties. We pretended we were Bonnie and Clyde," Bernie said. "We didn't rob any banks, but we took a Sunday road trip through the countryside and wasted a few shotgun shells shootin' up in the air. Enjoy all the fun while you can. You'll get old someday. Gravity will get your boobs, your ass…butt… Dang it! This learning not to say bad words is a b.i.t.c.h." She spelled out the word, and then after a long sigh, she headed back to the kitchen.

"Do you think all her stories are real?" Ursula whispered.

"After drinking with her the other night, I wouldn't doubt anything she says," Luna replied in a low voice, "but if she's willing to tell all that, just think about the really good ones that she keeps secret. Do you think we'll be able to tell shocking stories when we are her age?" She positioned a poinsettia in the middle of the table and then added a candle in a quart jar on either side.

"I just wonder how much of her DNA Mama got," Ursula whispered.

"I'm sure it was watered down by the time it got to her." Luna shivered at the idea of her mother telling stories like Bernie just did. "Changing the subject here. What were we talking about? Oh, I remember, elf costumes. You can borrow my little red outfit anytime you want, except for tomorrow. I'll wear it to deliver cookies if the weather permits."

"Endora has one just like it. I'll just borrow hers," Ursula said.

Endora breezed through the room with a floral centerpiece in her hands. "I have what?"

"Her ears sure haven't gotten dull with age and disappointments," Luna said. "I swear, she could hear a rat chewing cheese out in the barn in the middle of a tornado."

"Oh, hush," Endora fussed. "Being the baby of seven older sisters, I had to develop good eavesdropping skills."

"We were talking about borrowing your Santa's helper costume, maybe for a little role-playing with Remy before he gives back the elf outfit," Ursula answered.

"You may not!" Endora declared. "That outfit is still pure. It hasn't been in a man's bedroom."

Luna took the basket of Christmas flowers from Endora and headed toward the foyer with it. "I know where this goes, but back to the costume—is it going to remain a Santa helper virgin until it has to be thrown out, or do you have plans for it?"

"That would be my business." Endora glared at Luna. "There are some things about me that not even my twin sister or any of my other sisters need to know."

Luna laid her hand over her heart. "I'm hurt. I thought we shared everything."

"Yeah, like the fact that you were sleeping with Shane for weeks before I even knew you were dating," Endora shot back.

"Am I missing something? Who's sleeping with who?" Ophelia covered a yawn with her hand as she came out of the kitchen where the rest of the sisters were helping Mary Jane. "That drive just about whooped me yesterday."

"Just a twin-sister fight," Ursula answered.

"And I don't have a boyfriend to be sleeping with," Endora answered. "But Luna does, and she's been sleeping with Shane for weeks now, and she didn't even tell me. I'm her twin and she's supposed to share things with me."

"You go first," Luna said. "Who have you been role-playing with in that little red-and-white costume in your closet?"

"I don't want to get in the middle of that story," Ophelia said, "but I would like to know what y'all got Mama and Daddy for Christmas."

"I haven't been shopping yet," Ursula answered. "Why don't we all get together and go shopping when we're all back home. Maybe on the twenty-third?"

"Works for me," Ophelia said. "I'll be here on the twentieth if possible. Rae and Bo plan to get here about then, but Tertia's school lets out before so she'll get home early."

"We'll tell everyone not to make plans for that day, and we'll make it a sister day," Ursula said.

"Is Mama invited?" Luna asked.

"Nope," Ophelia answered. "We will be shopping for her and Daddy, and besides, after all this holiday stuff, they'll need a little time to relax and enjoy some peace and quiet without all of us underfoot. I've got an idea for something that we could all go in together to get them, but I'm not saying a word about it until we are away from the house."

Luna laid a hand on Ophelia's shoulder. "Why can't we have a meeting up in Ursula's room like we did when we were kids?"

"Because Mama might hear, and if y'all agree, I want it to be a big surprise," Ophelia answered. "I need coffee. We can talk to the other sisters about this later today."

Ursula looped her arm through Ophelia's. "I could use a hot chocolate."

"Me too. You want to take a break, Luna?" Endora asked.

"I'm good." Luna headed for the foyer.

"Hey." Shane knocked on the front door and then poked his head inside. "Y'all need any help?"

"Sure, we do," Joe Clay answered as he came out of the kitchen. "We never turn down help in this house. I just came inside for a minute to get warm and was on my way back outside to check on the brisket. I can do that without any help, but you and Remy can bring down the card tables and chairs from the attic for Mary Jane. I'll be back by the time he gets here and show y'all where they are."

Shane removed his coat and hung it on the rack inside the door, then opened his arms and took a step toward Luna.

She walked right into them, laid her head on his chest, and for a few seconds just enjoyed being so close to him. "I've missed you."

"Me too," he said and brushed a soft kiss across her lips.

Joe Clay and Remy came inside the house at the same time, and Joe Clay motioned for the two guys to follow him up the stairs. They had barely reached the top of the stairs when Bernie and Endora came through the foyer with table-cloths piled high in their hands.

"No boys upstairs." Endora frowned.

"No, darlin', that would be *men*," Bernie told her. "You girls aren't little girls anymore. You are *women*."

"Thank you," Luna mouthed across the room at her aunt.

―――――

Luna's bed was piled with discarded outfits that evening when she finally decided to wear a simple black dress that skimmed her knees and accent it with a ruby necklace and matching earrings. She had tried on Ursula's pretty green-velvet dress and cape, but it didn't fit her right. She picked out a red satin dress that she'd worn to a faculty party the year before, but she didn't like the way it looked when she saw her reflection in the mirror.

She was trying to decide whether to take off the black dress and add it to the pile when Endora peeked into the room without knocking. She was dressed in a black dress—only hers was sleeveless—and had chosen to wear a necklace that matched the one Luna was wearing. Big, bouncing blond curls floated on her shoulders just like Luna's, and she was wearing black high heels identical to Luna's.

"I guess we are still twins, even though things are changing," Endora said. "Do you think Shane will get us mixed up?"

"Not a chance, but if they show up, there's a good possibility that Kasey and Felicia might," Luna answered.

"Want to have some fun if they dare to flirt with Shane and Remy?" Endora asked.

"Definitely." Luna nodded and decided that the black dress was a sign. "Remember when we used to fool the teachers and kids at school?"

"Those were the good old days, and I'm grateful for them. If you hadn't taken that final algebra test for me in high school, I probably wouldn't have graduated."

"And you helped me write my research paper for the senior English final," Luna said as she led the way out of the room.

"Good memories," Endora agreed, "but I bet that Mama

would have grounded us forever if she'd found out what we were doing."

"Like you said about your red Santa helper outfit." Luna stopped at the bottom of the stairs. "Some things you just don't share."

"You got that right, Sister," Endora agreed.

Bernie met them in the foyer where she had insisted on being the greeter for the evening. "Y'all look beautiful this evening, but it's sure enough going to be hard for folks to tell you apart."

Luna gave Bernie a sideways hug. "You look pretty amazing yourself. That hot-pink jumpsuit is really festive."

"Oh, honey, it's at least twenty years old, but I drag it out for parties still. Mama always said a redhead shouldn't wear pink, but I ignore that old rule." Bernie beamed. "Remember now, if you need any help with those hussies, you just holler right loud."

"They probably got the message that you gave them at the potluck and won't even have the nerve to show up," Endora said, "but we appreciate your offer."

"Pepper is sleeping in the office," Bernie whispered. "He's little but ferocious, so he can bite their ankles if I just sic him on them."

Luna scanned the living room, but Shane wasn't among the early birds.

"He's not here yet," Bernie told her, "but I hear a car door slamming."

Luna smoothed the front of her dress and made sure that

her necklace was hanging just right. She knew the sound of Shane's boots on the porch so well that she was sure the next guests were not him.

Bernie opened the door and smiled at Dolly and Walter. "Come right in," she said. "We're so glad you could come out tonight. Let me take your coats."

"Endora and I can do that," Luna said and reached out for Dolly's coat. They carried them into her mother's office and hung them on the clothes racks with several others.

"If you can help Aunt Bernie, I'm going to help serve at the food table," Endora said.

"I've got this," Luna agreed.

Bernie stepped to the door and called out. "He's here! I heard a truck and peeked out the door."

"You're more excited than I am," Luna teased.

Bernie nodded. "I probably am, but I love it when my prophecies turn out to be right. I'm going to give y'all a second or two alone and check on Pepper. Bless his little heart, he's being a good boy tonight."

Luna opened the door just as Shane knocked. He just stood there staring at her for several seconds before he finally said, "You are gorgeous."

"You clean up pretty well yourself, Mr. O'Toole." She motioned him inside with a flick of her wrist.

He stepped inside the door, pointed up at the mistletoe, and then drew Luna into his arms for a kiss that jacked up the temperature in the house twenty degrees.

"Hey, move over." Dennison Andrews came into the

house without knocking and said, "You kids move over and let us show you how it's done." He pulled his wife, Wanda, into his arms and planted a kiss on her lips.

When the kiss ended, she patted him on the cheek. "I can see that there's mistletoe hanging from almost every doorway, but Denny, darlin', if I catch you standing around under that stuff with another woman, you will be sleeping on the couch until Valentine's Day."

"What if some good-lookin' woman grabs me and pulls me over there under it? That wouldn't be my fault, would it?" Dennison teased.

"Any kissing goes on with any woman but me," Wanda said, "and, honey, I will consider it *your* fault. I smell smoked brisket, and I'm starving, so let's go let these two lovebirds have another minute or two of privacy."

"Yes, ma'am." Dennison winked at Shane and ushered his wife into the living area with his arm around her waist.

"Does that business of not kissing another woman go for me too? I'm asking for me and Remy both." Shane asked as he backed Luna up under another bunch of mistletoe hanging in the doorway into the office and kissed her until they were both breathless.

She was still panting when the door opened—again without anyone knocking—and Felicia and Kasey breezed into the foyer. Luna glanced around the foyer for Endora or any of her sisters, but none of them were in sight. So much for any help she would get if one of those women even looked cross-eyed at Shane.

"Welcome to the Paradise," she said in a tone that could have frozen ice on the devil's spiked little tail. "Can I take your jackets?"

"After I looked up your mother on the internet, I figured you'd have a butler or, at the very least, a hired coat lady in a uniform. From what I found out, she could buy a whole country if she wanted to," Felicia said as she removed her velvet jacket.

"She could if she thought it was important," Bernie said. "You girls be nice now and remember what I told you at the potluck dinner."

Luna refrained from rolling her eyes, but it took every bit of her effort. "All of us do whatever needs done here tonight. Wander around all you want, and please, feel free to have something to eat. Daddy has been smoking brisket all day, and we've all been cooking sides and desserts for the past couple of days."

"Will there be many sexy guys here?" Kasey removed her long coat to reveal a red velvet dress that was cut up to her hip on one side and had a V-neck that went almost to her belly button in the front. Her red hair was twisted up into a bundle of curls that was held in place with a small tiara set just right.

"Don't know about sexy, but I bet you can find someone to kiss you under the mistletoe," Luna answered and thought of Old Man Versey and smiled at the visual of him cornering either one of those women for a kiss.

"What's so funny?" Felicia asked.

"Nothing," Luna answered. "I was admiring your lovely little crown."

"I got it when I was crowned football queen over in Henrietta four years ago," Kasey said. "I don't get to wear it often."

Felicia fluffed her red hair over one shoulder. "I was a candidate for queen that night too, but Kasey got the crown. We were both seniors."

"That means you are what—twenty-two years old?" Luna asked.

"That's right. Old enough to know better but too old to care." Felicia laughed at her own joke. "That means we should know better than to flirt with men who are already taken, but you never know when we might cause a man to see that younger and prettier is better."

"Are you talking to me?" Luna asked.

"Take it any way you want," Kasey answered for her. "Where's the bar? You do have an open bar, right? I mean, this is an old brothel, so surely you don't have a party without liquor."

Shane moved over a little closer and drew Luna to his side with an arm around her waist.

Felicia pointed up at several bunches of mistletoe hanging in the doorways and even dangling from the ceiling. "We won't need much booze to have a good time with all this hanging around." She took a step toward Shane and moistened her lips.

"I wouldn't try that," Luna hissed.

"Meow!" Kasey said and held up fingers that had been polished in bright red like cat claws. "We're just testing the waters right now but, honey, the night is young. Now point me to the bar."

"We don't have a bar. We are serving eggnog, punch, and wine, but no hard liquor tonight," Luna said through gritted teeth, "and the upstairs is off-limits."

"We got dressed up and shaved our legs for this," Kasey growled.

Felicia looped her arm into her cousin's. "We're here and we will have a good time. If all else fails, I've got half a bottle of Jim Beam in the car. We can sneak out there and get a little taste every now and then. We might as well have some food and find us some cowboys to flirt with. Who knows? Maybe we'll even sneak a kiss or two with this sexy guy when his bossy lady isn't looking."

"I don't think so," Shane said. "I'm in a very committed relationship with this lady."

"But me and Kasey could be twice as much fun with no strings attached." Felicia batted her long, fake lashes at him, and when more people arrived, they moved on into the living room.

"Are you sure the upstairs is off-limits?" Shane asked. "I might need a place to hide."

"Darlin', you don't need to hide," Luna told him. "I'll protect you."

Bernie came out of the office and popped her hands on her hips. "I'm dying my hair stove-pipe black next week. I don't want to be a redhead anymore. I gave those two fair warning. I might have to take matters in my own hands if they don't listen."

Sassy the cat came down the stairs like the regal queen she thought she was and sat down on the bottom step.

"I'll see you later, darlin'." Shane gave Luna a kiss on the cheek. "I'm going to see if Joe Clay needs any help carving up the brisket."

Resisting the urge to throw Felicia's and Kasey's coats on the floor and stomp on them a few times with her spiked high heels was not an easy task for Luna, but she managed to hang them up with only a dirty look toward each of them.

"You okay in here?" Endora asked as she peeked inside the door. "You look like you just chewed up some railroad spikes and spit out staples."

"That's one of Grandma Marsh's old sayings, and I'm not okay," Luna answered and then went on to tell her twin about Felicia's and Kasey's rudeness and what they'd said about kissing Shane.

"Well, it looks to me like they're about to get what they deserve," Endora whispered.

"What are you going to do?" Luna asked, glad to see some spunk back in her twin but more than a little worried where it might lead. The price of getting even with those two women wouldn't be worth ruining the Christmas party for everyone.

"Whatever she does, I'll back her up on the play," Bernie said as she brought another jacket into the room. "I've been around some pretty wild women, but I've never seen any-thing like those two."

"Sister, don't you worry about a thing. I'll take care of them." Endora patted Luna on the back. "Nobody messes with the Simmons sisters, and most especially not with my twin. Aunt Bernie, you can leave this one to me. Those two won't be staying until the party is over."

"If they haul you off to jail, I'll come bail you out." Bernie tipped up her chin and set her lips in a firm line.

Endora's eyes began to sparkle like they had before the Kevin/Krystal catastrophe. "And, Aunt Bernie, if I'm in jail, you'll probably be with me."

"Yep, but…" Bernie agreed as she leaned forward and whispered, "I've got a bottle of Jameson in my purse, so we'll have a party in the cell."

Luna wasn't sure what would happen, but after a few min-utes, she figured that Endora had just given the two women a good tongue-lashing. Something must have woken Pepper, because he shot past her legs, growling and barking like a pit bull. When he saw Sassy, he took off after her like he would a squirrel. Instead of tearing up the stairs, she ran under the credenza in the foyer. Her tail was fluffed out like she had just stepped on a bare Christmas tree wire, and Pepper looked like a punk rocker with all the hair on his back standing straight up.

Luna started toward the animals about the same time that Felicia and Kasey came out of the bathroom, and Endora started for the living room with a tray of full eggnog cups. Everything seemed to be moving in slow motion. From the smug look on Felicia's face, she had just said something catty to Endora, and Kasey laughed about it. Endora glanced across the foyer and sent Luna a sly wink, then fell forward.

The tray went flying, but Endora didn't go down with it. Felicia and Kasey did not have that kind of good luck. Felicia landed face up with Kasey right beside her—their legs and arms tangled up together. Sassy chose that moment to dash out from under the credenza. Pepper was right behind her, growling and biting at her tail. They stopped long enough to lick eggnog off the two women's bodies, but that didn't last long. Both Felicia and Kasey slapped at the animals and tried to get up but kept slipping and falling in the eggnog. The cat and dog jumped from one woman to the other like they were playing on a trampoline, stopping every second or two to lap up some more of the eggnog that was all over their dresses and faces.

When they got tired of that game, Pepper took up the chase again and howled like he was hot on the trail of a hundred-pound wild hog. Sassy turned on him and did one of those loud, guttural meows that said she would fight the dog to the death, and then the two of them met in the middle of the foyer and touched noses. After that, Sassy pranced off to the kitchen with her tail pointed at the ceiling.

Kasey's tiara had bounced across the floor, hit the credenza leg, and rolled back to land in the tray that was now filled with spilled eggnog. Pepper turned around, marched down the steps, and promptly hiked his leg on the tiara.

Kasey and Felicia both looked totally bewildered when they finally stood up.

"You know where the bathroom is since you just came from there," Luna said.

"Bless him, his little heart is beating a mile a minute. Poor little darlin' did his part, so he gets two treats tonight." Bernie lowered her voice and whispered. "Well done, Endora. You deserve a crown for that performance."

"Hey, it wasn't all me even if I did have a lot of fun causing it." Endora laughed with her. "You and Luna turned Sassy and Pepper lose."

"Nope, that much was an accident," Luna admitted.

"Well, then." Endora looked up at the ceiling. "Thank you, Lord, for the accident. Sassy and Pepper helped those two catty women roll around enough that they've almost cleaned up what eggnog got on the floor." The ground-floor bathroom door always creaked, so when Kasey threw it open, Luna, Endora, and Bernie all turned around.

"You bitch! You did that on purpose," Kasey growled as she headed right toward Luna, stopping right in front of her face.

Bernie wedged herself in between them and glared at the woman. "Girlie, that is enough out of you and your cousin. Now would be a good time for you to leave."

Felicia glared at Endora. "You deliberately ran into us with that tray of eggnog and spilled it all over us. Our dresses are ruined so bad that we can't take them back to the store tomorrow and get our money back."

"The least you could do is offer to reimburse us for them." Kasey looked from one twin to the other and back again. "Which one of you tripped us anyway?"

"Neither one," Bernie answered. "Your own smart-ass attitudes did that for you. Karma is the *real* bitch."

Luna opened the front door for them. "Y'all have a good night now. But wait, did you get your tiara?"

"Throw it in the trash," Kasey snapped. "After what that dog did on it, I don't even want it anymore." She stormed out the door with Felicia right behind her.

"Told you I'd fix it," Endora whispered. "But I can't believe that Sassy and Pepper actually did that nose bump."

"I had a talk with both of them and told them that we could use a little help tonight." Bernie scooped Pepper up in her arms. "I'm taking this boy out to the trailer. Don't let anything exciting happen while I'm gone. I'm thankful that none of that happened in the living room. I don't think anyone even knew what was going on in here."

"I've always said that cats know what we're saying," Endora said. "And I swear, Felicia tried to trip me on purpose, probably thinking I was you and that I'd spill it all on myself. We can talk about all this later. You and Shane need to make the rounds and visit with everyone."

"See you after the party, or..." Luna raised an eyebrow.

"Or in the morning." Endora finished the sentence for her sister. "I'm trying but trusting is still somewhere off in the foggy future."

Bernie started out the front door but turned around and shot a wink over at Endora. "Don't be stumbling around and falling into people."

"Wouldn't dream of it." Endora smiled.

Luna started toward the kitchen and met Shane coming toward her. He pointed up to a sprig of mistletoe over her head. She barely had time to moisten her lips before his mouth closed over hers in a long kiss.

Everything about the incident with Kasey and Felicia disappeared as the heat filled Luna's body and visions of Shane lying beside her in his bed popped into her head.

The mood was broken when Mary Jane and Tertia came out of the living room and headed toward the kitchen.

"Don't let us disturb you," Tertia said with a grin. "We just have to go refill the brisket platters."

"Y'all make a gorgeous couple," Mary Jane said. "We'll need pictures before the evening is over."

"I'm just reflecting a little of the light from your beautiful daughter," Shane said. "And, Miz Mary Jane, you really should stick a little closer to Joe Clay. As lovely as you are, he needs to be sure everyone here knows that you are his sweetheart."

Mary Jane flashed another smile. "Shane O'Toole, you must've kissed the Blarney Stone before you came to the party tonight. Rest assured, though. I've got seven daughters who would never let anyone come between me and their daddy. You can bet they're all keeping a close watch on both me and Joe Clay tonight."

"Yes, we are," Luna said seriously.

"Y'all go mingle among the folks, and we'll take those pictures later this evening," Mary Jane said.

Shane laced his fingers with Luna's, and they walked into

the living room together. The huge house had never seen so many people, not even back when the place was a brothel.

In her mother's books, Miz Raven always put up a Christmas tree. She threw a party just for the girls on that night, and no customers on Christmas or Easter was a hard and fast rule. Luna wondered if that was fact or fiction.

Shane nudged her on the shoulder. "What are you thinking about? You haven't even blinked in several seconds."

"I'm sorry," she whispered as she locked her arm into his. "I was picturing the Paradise back in the brothel days. Did they decorate it up like this? They wouldn't have had lights everywhere like we do, but from Mama's book, they did have a tree. I'm sorry. That's not fair to you. I should be thinking about how lucky I am to have such a sexy guy beside me."

"Honey, you can think about whatever you want, as long as I get to stand beside you," Shane said.

"And that is just one of the many reasons I've fallen in love with you," Luna whispered.

―――――――

Ursula eased down on the sofa facing the fireplace and propped her bare feet on the coffee table. "The party was great this year, but we were so busy helping take care of everything that we didn't even get one dance. Matter of fact, I didn't even get to dance with Daddy, and I think he and Mama only managed to have part of one."

Remy plopped down beside her and draped an arm around her shoulders. "Do you have the energy to dance?"

"No, but..." She cocked her ear to one side. "What are those pups barking about?"

"I hope it's not..." Remy started and then jumped up off the sofa. "They're on the back porch."

Ursula glanced at the time—two o'clock in the morning. A vision of chasing cows flashed through her mind. She would ruin her party dress if she had to go help chase down cows again.

Remy was already at the back door when she stood up and unfastened the side zipper on her long, black fitted dress, letting it fall to the floor. "Did the cows..."

"No," Remy said with a sigh. "I have no idea how those pups got out. I'll go put them back."

"I'll help," Ursula said on her way down the hall. "I just need to get into some jeans."

The puppies barked at Remy frantically and circled him, herding him toward the barn, where he discovered that his young cow was getting ready to give birth to her calf.

Remy dropped down on his knees and hugged both dogs. "Looks like you two won't need much training after all."

Ursula sat down on a pile of loose hay and leaned back on a bale. "We should give them names if we're going to keep them."

Remy lay back in the hay, and Ursula cuddled up next to him. The two pups curled up at their feet, put their paws over their noses, and went to sleep. "How about Chance and Shadow?"

"From the old movie *Homeward Bound*?" Ursula asked.

"I watched that movie over and over when I was a little girl. That's where Sassy got her name."

"Then our puppies have names," Remy said. "I have to stay here and make sure this young cow doesn't need any help. I'd rather not have to call for the vet, but I will if the birth doesn't go easy. But you can go back to the house and get some rest."

"Let me just rest here with you for a few minutes. I'm too tired to even move right now." Ursula covered a yawn with her hand and moved even closer so she could lay her head on his shoulder.

"Living with a professor slash rancher is tough," Remy said.

"Sharing life with an author is worse," she answered as her eyes fluttered shut.

Sunshine streamed through the window in the barn door when Ursula opened her eyes. She rolled over and reached out to wrap her arm around Remy and then realized that she wasn't in her bed. She sat up to the aroma of coffee and the smell of hay. She noticed movement across the barn and saw Remy coming out of the tack room with a mug in each hand.

"Good mornin'," he said cheerfully. "Looks like we fell asleep. Grandpa kept an old electric percolator out here. Don't know how old the coffee is, but it will wake us up enough to get to the house and make some good stuff."

"Mornin'." She reached for the cup he held out to her. "What time is it?"

"Ten o'clock," Remy answered. "I've got a surprise for

you, so take a couple of sips to help get your eyes open and then I'll show it to you."

Ursula hurriedly took two sips of the worst coffee she had ever drunk and stood up. "Aunt Bernie and Mama both say that there's good in everything, so I'll just say that stuff tastes awful, but it is hot, and it did wake me up. Now where is this surprise, and where are our puppies?"

"The puppies dug out under the door to the corral, so we might as well let them roam free. Right now, they're romping around in the pasture between the barn and fence." Remy poured out the rest of his coffee on the ground and took her hand in his.

"Where are we going?" she asked.

"Not far," he answered and led her across the barn floor. "We've got a new baby calf in a stall back there—born in a manger of sorts."

"We've got a new calf?" Ursula picked up the pace and practically ran to the stall. "Oh, Remy, look at him. He's perfect."

"Yes, he is," Remy said. "From those broad shoulders and his size, he could make us a fine breeder bull someday."

"Merry Christmas to us," Ursula whispered, "and, darlin', days like this make living with a professor slash rancher wonderful."

"We could go home, have a hot shower together, and then make some breakfast," he suggested.

"Or we could go home, have shower sex, then maybe bed sex, and then have breakfast." She smiled up at him.

"I like your idea better," he said with a grin.

Chapter 15

Luna awoke before daylight the next morning to find Shane propped up on an elbow and smiling. The dreamy look in his emerald-green eyes didn't leave any doubt that he was thinking about the night before—just like she was.

"Good morning," she whispered. "Are you having second thoughts about seeing me the first thing in the morning for the rest of our lives?"

Shane leaned over and brushed a sweet kiss across her lips. "You're always beautiful to me, whether it's with mussed-up hair or in a fancy dress like you wore last night. But, darlin', what I like best is waking up with you right here beside me and getting to look my fill of you."

She rolled over closer to him and cuddled up next to his side. "For an ex-Army Ranger, you sure are romantic, Shane O'Toole."

"Darlin', that comes from my Irish genes, but I'm not shooting you a line. I'm telling the absolute truth," he told her.

She snuggled down even closer to him. "Having you beside me every time I woke up last night was…" She hesitated and sat straight up in bed when she heard the puppies whining and scratching at the back door.

"Evidently our new babies don't like snow," he told her. "They wanted to come inside the house when I put their food and fresh water out on the porch this morning, but we shouldn't let them start doing that. They're going to be big dogs."

"It's snowing?" She threw back the covers, grabbed the white shirt he'd worn to the party the night before, and shoved her arms down into the sleeves as she jogged over to the window that looked out into the backyard. The new doghouse had several inches on the top of it, and the puppies were chasing each other in the snow.

Shane got out of bed and pulled on a pair of camouflage pajama pants and an army-green T-shirt. "I noticed that the ground was covered when I put food out for the pups."

Luna continued to stare out the window. The wind blew the falling snow into miniature tornadoes out there on the road. "We might get to have a white Christmas, Shane."

He crossed the room, wrapped his arms around her waist, and buried his face in her hair. "It could all melt before Christmas. But I think we have to rethink our costumes to deliver our cookies this afternoon."

"Why would you say that?" Luna asked.

"I'm not getting in and out of the truck and wading through snow in elf shoes and tights." He chuckled. "The weather report says we could get from four inches to a foot by evening."

"We could wear Santa hats, and I could lace some jingle bells together into a necklace for us to hang around our necks," she suggested as she turned around and laid her head on Shane's chest. "Everyone's expecting us to have costumes on."

"That sounds like fun," Shane agreed. "I would have given anything in this world for a morning like this when I was on a mission in the sandbox or in some hot, sweaty jungle."

"How did you guys celebrate Christmas when you were in those places?" she asked.

"Wherever I was, Granny always managed to get a box to me with homemade baked goods and presents in it. Granny always told me to share with everyone. Even with that, it was tough to keep our spirits up."

"I can't imagine being away from family during the holidays. All of us sisters have always gotten to come home for Christmas, no matter where we were. I believe it would break Mama's heart if we didn't make it in for the holidays," she said.

For the first time, she wondered how her mother would feel if all seven of her daughters settled down in the town where they were living right then, and she only got to see them once a year. What if she never got to spend more than a few days at Christmas with her grandchildren?

Luna didn't want her children to grow up not knowing their Nana and Poppa at the Paradise, or all their cousins, for that matter. Once or twice a year wasn't enough for them to all get together.

Shane rested his chin on the top of her head. "If I made it back to Texas at all, it was usually after the first of the year.

I was stationed with guys who had families, and I felt like they deserved to be home with their kids on Christmas Day a lot more than I needed to be here in Spanish Fort."

"Did y'all always spend the holiday with your Granny and Grandpa O'Toole when you were a little boy?" she asked. "Surely, our paths must have crossed at church or somewhere. This is a ghost town, for goodness' sake. Everyone knows everyone, and yet I don't remember seeing you until last summer when you came home from the service."

"No, when I was a little boy, we spent Christmas Eve with them, Christmas at home, and then New Year's with my mama's folks down in south Texas on the coast," he answered. "I loved being close to the ocean, but I liked this place better. The Red River kind of stole my heart even when I was just a toddler. I hope someday when we have kids that they love this little community as much as I do."

"Kids? You're already thinking that far into the future?" Luna was ready to move in with Shane before long, but...

There are no buts in real love. A line from one of her mother's books came back to her.

"Yes, I am," Shane admitted. "Aren't you?"

"I didn't think guys had thoughts like that." She avoided his question.

"I don't know about all guys," Shane said, "but I do. I want a big family. Growing up with no siblings and no cousins..." He paused for a long moment. "Let's just say, I want our kids to grow up in a family like you have."

"What is a big family to you?"

"As big as you want, but at least four kids," he answered.

Whew! she thought as she mentally wiped her forehead. *I didn't think we'd be having a heavy conversation like this for several more months.*

"You're awfully quiet," he said. "Is all this talk about kids this early in our relationship scaring you?"

"No, but we've only been dating a few months, and..." She had to be honest with him, no matter what.

"We're talking about the future here, darlin', not tomorrow," he assured her. "I just want you to know that I'm serious about our relationship and where it's heading."

"I'm not running anywhere," Luna said, "and I'm just as serious as you are, but what if I only want two kids, or what if we really want a son, and we have seven girls like Mama did?"

"You'll be the one doin' the birthin'." Shane chuckled. "I don't care if we have two or a dozen. I just don't want my kids to be raised alone like I was. I had love and happiness, but I want our children to have that plus brothers and/or sisters and, honey, I can teach girls to fish as well as boys so it's okay if we have seven girls. I taught you to like fishing, didn't I?"

"Yes, you did, and yes, you can," she agreed.

"Good, then we've got that settled," he said as he took her hand and led her out of the bedroom. "If we don't get away from that bed over there, we can forget about making cookies."

"We could go by the bakery and buy cookies," she

suggested. "But then, where's the fun in that? The bed will be there tonight. I hope the snow sticks around until all my sisters get home for Christmas. We always looked forward to building a real snowman while the decorations were still up."

"What do you and your sisters have planned while they're home?" he asked as he switched on the kitchen light.

"We will spend the twenty-third doing our Christmas shopping. We'll be at the mall in Wichita Falls. It'll be hectic, but we'll get through it."

Shane let go of her hand and took bacon and eggs from the refrigerator. "I haven't done my shopping either. We've been so busy with planning the new store and subcontracting out the individual jobs that..."

She set the oven temperature at the right degree to cook the bacon. "That what?"

"That I haven't bought anything for you," he said. "Do you have a list made for what you want Santa to bring you?"

"Yes, but there's only one thing on it," she told him.

"And that is?" Shane closed the door.

"I want *you* for Christmas," she answered.

He crossed the room in a few long strides and wrapped her up in his arms again. "You've got *me* for more than one day."

"I've got you and snow and puppies," she said. "My life is good."

"You never cease to amaze me, and that reminds me of an old country song that my Granny loved. She and Grandpa used to dance around the kitchen floor when it came on the radio." He pulled his phone from his pocket and hit the screen a couple of times. Then he laid it on the counter and held out a hand. "May I have this dance, Miz Luna?"

She recognized "Amazed" by Lonestar the moment the song started. She put her hand in his and let him lead her around the kitchen floor in a slow country dance. He sang along with the lyrics that talked about never being so close to anyone. Dancing with him in the kitchen with her hair a mess, no makeup, and wearing only his shirt proved that this was where she belonged forever.

Shane came into the house with snow on his shoulder and on the brim of his black cowboy hat. "Everything is loaded up. Got our necklaces and Santa hats ready?"

Luna jammed her feet down into a pair of cowboy boots she'd had since she was in high school and tucked the legs of her jeans down into them. She hung a necklace of jingle bells around his neck and handed him a Santa hat. "You might want to just tuck this into your pocket and put it on when we get there." She shoved her red-and-white hat in her coat pocket and pulled the hood up on her coat. The bells around her neck jingled with each step she took across the floor.

"Do you think the puppies will be all right until we get home? What if the snow blocks the door into their doghouse?" Her hood wasn't much help when the wind blew the fine powder against her face.

"They will be fine," Shane assured her. "Those igloo

things are built to keep them warm in the winter and cool in the summer. Let's get you inside the warm truck."

"If it gets up over the doorway into their little house, I'm bringing them into the garage so at least they'll be dry."

"Yes, ma'am!" Shane scooped her up in his arms and carried her to the truck.

"I *can* walk in the snow," she protested.

"What if you fell?" He opened the door with one hand and settled her into the passenger's seat. "Your sisters would hate me forever for not taking care of you properly, and besides, this snow is moving out in the next hour. What we've got now is pretty much what we'll have."

"Well, we couldn't have that now, could we?" Luna said. "Endora *might* be a handful, especially after last night when she found her spunk again."

"What happened, other than some eggnog getting spilled?"

"You knew about that?"

Shane slammed the door shut and in just a few seconds slid behind the wheel. "I heard Ursula say something about it to Remy."

"Well," Luna said, "let me entertain you on the way to the nursing home."

———————

Shane was still laughing when they reached the outskirts of Nocona. "I wondered what happened to Fanny and Kitty."

"Felicia and Kasey," Luna corrected him. "But it bodes well for you that you can't even remember their names."

"Darlin', the only name that matters to me is Luna Simmons," Shane said as he made a right turn and drove east.

"Where do you keep that Blarney Stone hid?" Luna teased.

"Right here." He tapped his chest. "But what you call blarney, I call truth."

"Then thank you for that lovely compliment," she said. "I haven't been to the nursing home since Endora and I were in elementary school. The music teacher brought us here to sing Christmas carols to the residents."

"I haven't been in fifteen years," Shane said as he turned into the parking lot. "I was home on Christmas Eve, so I drove Granny to deliver her cookies. I didn't know if the same folks would be working here as back then, so I made a call yesterday to be sure we could visit today."

Luna unfastened her seat belt, opened the door, and slid out of the seat. "I can help carry a couple of boxes inside. The snow has just about stopped."

"Weather update is now saying that another snowstorm is on the way, and that one is going to dump a foot on us. I hope it doesn't play havoc with your sisters getting home," Shane said. "Don't bother with the boxes. The lady I talked to said that she had a cart we could use."

A lady with short gray hair and a round face hurried over to open the door for them. She motioned toward the stainless-steel cart with three shelves over to the left. "I figured it was about time you would be getting here, so I brought that out of the kitchen for you to use. I'm Hilda Jones, and this is a very sweet thing you are doing."

"I'm Luna Simmons," Luna said.

"I'm Shane, and my Granny O'Toole used to bring cookies every year."

"I remember her very well. She was such a darlin' lady. The residents will love the treats, but what they'll love even more is the little bit of company," Hilda said. "Violet, our head nurse, will want to explain things to you before you start passing the cookies out. Some of the folks can't have sugar."

"Granny always brought some for those folks, so we made some without sugar," Shane said and then pushed the cart out into the white fog.

"We have sugar-free chocolate chip and snickerdoodle cookies," Luna said.

Hilda patted her on the shoulder. "That's fantastic. I hear Shane is going to build a convenience store in Spanish Fort. That could be the start of bringing that little community back to life. While he brings in the boxes, I'll go get Nurse Violet."

"Thank you," Luna said.

Shane pushed the cart back inside, whipped off his cowboy hat, set it on a box on the bottom shelf, and then removed his coat and hung it on a rack inside the door.

Luna threw back the hood on her coat, pulled out her Santa hat, and jerked it down over her blond hair. "Your turn," she told Shane.

He wiggled to make the bells around his neck jingle as he jammed his red-and-white hat on his head. "I'm ready to go. Are you?"

"I'm ready, but…" She lowered her voice. "Promise me that when we're old, even if we're in a place like this"—she paused—"that when it snows, you'll take me out in it."

"I promise, *but* we won't be in a nursing home," he said. "I predict that we will have a long, long happy life together, and then one night, we will kiss each other good night and go to heaven together. Before that, we are going to sit on our back porch and watch our great-grandkids play with Holly and Mutt's puppies' descendants and teach all the kids to fish. But, sweetheart, if you leave this world first, please wait a few hours in front of the pearly gates. I'll be right behind you in just a little while, and we can go in together."

Luna removed her coat and hung it on a rack by the piano. "Oh, yeah? How do you know that we will pass away together?"

"It's hereditary in my family," he explained as he hung his camouflage jacket beside her coat. "Granny died one day and Grandpa the next. The doctor said a heart attack got him, but I always figured that he died of a *broken* heart, and that's what I'll do if you aren't in my life."

"That has to be the most romantic thing you've said yet," she said. "But if you go first, please wait for me. Our journey won't end with our last breath on this earth, but we'll take it right on through eternity."

"Hello." A tall nurse with gray streaks in her dark hair came from behind the counter. "I'm Violet. I remember when your grandparents used to come to visit the residents during the holidays. It's nice of you to come visit today like they did. To make things easy for folks who might be coming to see relatives and friends, we've got a sheet on each door. I'll show you what I'm talking about."

Violet's long stride beat both Shane and Luna to the first room on the left. "The elementary students from Prairie Valley made color sheets for each of the residents and we added their names at the bottom. If it's a Santa picture like these two, then the residents can have sugar." She pointed across the hallway. "If it's a Christmas tree, like that one, then please give them the sugar-free. I'd suggest you start with this room right here and go to the end, then come back up the other side. Some of our residents can be pretty spicy, and some are withdrawn, but they'll all love company."

"When we finish here, do the doors on the other wing have pictures on each door?" Shane asked.

"That end"—Violet motioned to the hallway across from the lobby and dining area—"has patients that have lost their cognitive abilities. But some of our residents on this wing don't have family at all, and some have relatives who live far away and can't come see them but a couple of times a year. Visitors mean a lot to them, especially during the holidays."

"We're glad we can help," Shane said as he opened the box on top of the cart, knocked on the doorjamb, and poked his head inside. "*Ho! Ho! Ho!* Has Vernon Dalmont been a good boy this year?"

Vernon's brown eyes glittered. "Oh. My. Goodness! Yes, I have. Come in and have a seat. Aren't you Ira O'Toole's boy?"

"I'm his grandson," Shane said. "My name is Shane, and this is my girlfriend, Luna Simmons."

"You look just like your daddy." Vernon pointed to an arrangement of pictures on the wall. "Look at those, son. That's me and your grandpa when we were in Vietnam together. We met at boot camp, and when we got back, I was his best man at his wedding. That's him and the love of his life, Fiona, and me over there on the end."

The lyrics of that country song "In Color" came to Luna's mind as she stared at the pictures with Shane. Right there in front of them was some of Shane's heritage.

With the help of a cane, Vernon got up out of his recliner and pointed to another photograph. "There's me and your grandpa on a little fishin' trip down the Red River with your daddy. I'll never forget that day."

"Where did you live before you came here?" Shane set the cookies on the table beside Vernon's chair.

"Over around Blossom, Texas," Vernon answered, "but I always loved this area. I didn't ever have a family, so when I got too old to take care of myself, I came here. Your grandpa was already gone, but I feel close to him. We stayed friends all through the years. Are these cookies like the ones Fiona made?"

"Same recipe," Shane said with a smile.

"Then I'll hoard them and won't share with any of the

ladies who come in here to flirt with me." He winked at Luna. "I don't see a ring on your hand. Do I need to give Shane some pointers?"

"No, sir." Luna grinned. "He's doing very well on his own."

"Simmons? Kin to the woman who bought the Paradise?" Vernon asked.

"That's my mother," Luna answered.

"The ladies in here read her books and then bring them to me. She's an excellent writer, but the best ones are the stories about the ladies who lived in the Paradise when it was a brothel. Now, that was a piece of history for sure." Vernon eased down into his recliner again. "Where's my manners? You kids take a load off and sit down over there on the love seat."

"We can't today," Shane said. "We've got a bunch more cookies to deliver, but maybe we'll come back and visit again another day. I'd love to hear stories about my grandpa and my daddy. Or better yet, when spring comes, I could steal you for a day. We could go fishing on the Red River again. I'm starting up a guide service."

Vernon gave him a nod. "Anytime, son. I'll be right here, and that fishing trip would be better than winnin' the lottery. Y'all have a merry Christmas, now. You've sure made mine brighter with your visit, son. Don't wait too long to come back to see me. Doc says this nasty thing growing in my head might send me on for an up-close visit with Saint Peter before summer. I've made my peace with it, because I'll get to spend time with Ira and Fiona when that day comes around."

"I'm so sorry," Shane and Luna said at the same time.

"Don't worry," Vernon said with a broad smile. "I've had a full life, and I'm happy to go when the good Lord calls my name, but I would like one more trip down the Red River before I go so I can tell Ira all about it."

"We'll make it happen as soon as it gets warm enough," Shane promised.

"And until then, we'll come visit," Luna promised around the lump in her throat.

"I'll look forward to it." Vernon waved goodbye.

"Did you remember him coming to visit your grandpa?" Luna asked as they pushed the cart down the hall to the next room.

Shane shook his head. "No, but I kind of remember Grandpa talking about his best friend, Vernon, and that same picture of Granny and Grandpa on their wedding day with the best man and maid of honor is still setting on the dresser in their old bedroom. Dolly was always her best friend, so that's who she asked to stand up with her at the wedding."

"It's so sad that he doesn't have family. I can't imagine getting old with no one around." Luna checked the next room to find a picture of a Christmas tree on the door with Virgie Ellis's name on the bottom. She picked up a plate of sugar-free cookies, knocked on the open door, and peeked inside. The room was decorated to the hilt, with green garland looped around the walls and multicolored twinkly lights around the window. A small tree covered in what looked like a thousand ornaments sat in the corner.

"Hello, come right in." Virgie motioned with her hand. "Are you a new nurse?"

"Ho! Ho! Ho!" Shane said in a booming voice. "Has Virgie been a good girl this year?"

Virgie nodded but didn't try to get up out of her rocking chair. She was dressed in a red sweat suit with Rudolph on the front of the shirt. Her short, thin hair was as red as her outfit, and the gray roots testified to the fact that it was not natural.

"Honey, Santa Claus ain't as pretty as you, and God would know I was lyin' through my teeth if I ever claimed to be a good girl." Virgie pointed toward the plate of cookies in Luna's hand. "But I'll tell a little white one and say that I've been an angel all year if that's cookies your pretty wife is bringing me."

"I'm not—" Luna started.

"She is beautiful, isn't she?" Shane butted in. "We just wanted to stop by and wish you a Merry Christmas and leave a few cookies for you."

"Y'all could just leave them all with me and stay a while," Virgie suggested. "I would give them out for you. The woman in the next room down is an old biddy who tries to make time with my Vernon, and everyone in this place knows I've claimed him for my own. Her name is Gladys, and that don't even go together as good as Vernon and Virgie, now does it?"

"That does sound cute," Luna said as she set the cookies on the dresser and headed toward the door.

Virgie tilted her head to the side in a flirtatious gesture.

"Do you have any special brownies in one of them boxes? If you do, give them to Gladys. That hussy thinks she's the queen around here—all prissy and dressing up in fancy clothes just to go to lunch in the dining room. I'd like to see her do something stupid."

"Sorry, ma'am," Shane said. "We've just got plain old cookies. You have a Merry Christmas."

"You, too, darlin'." She waved. "And if you ever decide to divorce your wife, you come on back around. Us older women make good lovers."

"I *will* remember that." Shane nodded and escaped out into the hallway.

"Am I going to have to ban you from visiting this place?" Luna teased. "Why did you butt in when I was about to explain that we weren't married?"

Shane kissed her on the forehead. "Honey, I've only got eyes for you, I promise. But we're never going to get all these cookies passed out if we don't keep moving. Virgie is lonely, and if she'd thought we weren't married—yet—she would have tried to convince me to fall down on my knees and propose right there. The nursing home staff has enough drama to deal with without that. When I ask you to marry me, it won't be in a nursing home."

Luna tiptoed and kissed him on the cheek. "You are so right."

Luna looked up at the picture on the door of the next room and saw that it was decorated with a Christmas tree and the name Gladys was printed at the bottom. She brought out a plate of sugar-free cookies and peeked inside. "Hello, Gladys. I'm Luna Simmons here to wish you a Merry Christmas and bring you some cookies."

The decorations in Virgie's room paled in comparison to what was in Gladys's room. Gold tinsel laced with glittery, fake diamonds was draped around the room and circled the window, the mirror above the dresser, and even the door into the bathroom. The tree that stopped just short of the ceiling was decorated totally in gold ornaments, and even the shiny white ribbons twirled and floating down on four sides of the tree had little gold Christmas trees printed on them.

"Come right in here." Gladys motioned. "If I'd known I was having company, I would have gotten dressed up."

"You look gorgeous," Luna said.

"I wore this old thing last year." Gladys smoothed the front of her gold lamé pantsuit with her veined hands. "You should come back and visit us on New Year's Eve. I'm going to outshine that hussy Virgie for sure. I ordered me a red dress that's split up to my hootie-hoot in the front and a pair of red velvet slippers to match it. I'm going to dance the last dance of the year with Vernon, and if we're lucky, I'll talk him into coming back to my room for some cuddling."

"We'll be having our own family party out at the Paradise that night, but if we weren't, I'd love to join you," Luna said. "You have a Merry Christmas now."

"You too, sweetheart, and thank you for the cookies." Gladys waved. "When you get down to Virgie's room, don't you believe a word she says about me."

Luna bit back a giggle. "Yes, ma'am."

She wasn't really sure what she had thought the elderly folks might be like in the nursing home, but she had surely never thought about them being gossips, much less octogenarians flirting with each other. These old folks were so funny that she wouldn't mind coming back to see them when she had more time to sit and really visit. That made her think about what Shane had said about not wanting to live without her by his side. If they ever did have to live in a place like this, she vowed that they would share a room and have a king-sized bed brought in. And if another woman made eyes at him, there would be a worse catfight in the hallway than the one at the Paradise Christmas party.

Chapter 16

"WELL, LOOK WHO'S COME dragging in at dark," Endora teased when Luna and Shane came into the house that evening. "You and Ursula live the closest, and you are the last ones to get here."

"Hey now, I had to wade through a foot of snow to help feed the cows before I could come over here," Ursula argued and immediately thought of the chapter she was writing about Daisy making snow ice cream for the ladies who lived in the Paradise back then.

"I heard that you caused this beautiful mess, Luna," Bo said.

"How did I do that?" Luna protested as she removed her coat and hung it up.

"When y'all had that couple of inches earlier, you said you wanted enough for us to build a snowman when we all got home," Ursula reminded her sister.

"Well, darlin', you got your wish," Tertia told her. "The five-hour trip home took Rae and me seven hours. Rae is cranky because she hates driving so slow."

"I'm not cranky," Rae protested. "I'm aggravated, but building a snowman after supper will make me feel all better."

"Shane, do I hear you out there?" Joe Clay called out from the living room. "Come on in here. Remy and I are watching a ball game on television until supper is ready."

Shane kissed Luna on the cheek. "Do you need me to help with something?"

"I believe all nine women can put supper on the table," she answered.

"Then I'm going to go watch the game."

For a full minute, Luna just stood in the middle of the kitchen and enjoyed the hustle and bustle of all her sisters being home. After visiting Vernon, she would never take a single moment when the family was all together like this for granted.

Ursula got down a big stack of plates and started setting the table. "Are we really going to drive all the way to Wichita Falls in this weather tomorrow? We could just go as far as Nocona and do our shopping in the stores there."

"Nope," Ophelia said. "We'd have to go in and out of stores all day. We can go to the enclosed mall in Wichita Falls, and besides, Rae can drive for us. She's used to maneuvering a vehicle in more snow than this."

"Yes, I am, and yes, I will, and I agree with Ophelia. We can get a lot more done at the mall than in Nocona," Rae agreed.

"I don't remember ever building a snowman in the dark," Tertia said.

"Me either," Ophelia said.

"With all our Christmas lights lit up, it's as bright as day out there," Mary Jane said, "and a snowman will add to all the decorations. Remy and Joe Clay have said that they'll help us. And I will take a picture of all nine of you kids around…"

"Mr. Frosty," all seven girls singsonged at once.

"That's right." Mary Jane beamed. "I thought y'all were too old to remember what we called the first snowman we built here at the Paradise."

"We were so excited to see enough snow to build a real one that we will never forget that memory," Luna said.

Ursula smiled at the visual that popped into her head. Daisy, Miz Raven, and the seven girls had all had snow ice cream, and Daisy had entertained them all with stories about when she got thrown in jail for marching for women's rights.

"What's so funny?" Luna asked.

"I don't want to bore you with a funny scene in the story I'm writing," Ursula said.

"If it's funny, we want to hear about it," Luna protested.

"We've talked about Daisy, but I was thinking about the snow ice cream they made and how in the chapter I'm writing now, she's got most of the women in the area up in arms about women's rights and they're meeting right here in the Paradise to discuss what they're going to do. In her diary, it's snowing the night of the meeting, and some of them have to walk a good way to get here."

Endora did a fist pump. "Yay for Daisy."

"Amen!" Bernie said from the end of the table. "If I'd been alive then, that woman would have been my hero."

"Holy smoke!" Mary Jane gasped. "That's even better than the stories I wrote about this place."

"She had been jailed in New York for marching for women's rights, so she wasn't taking any more crap from anyone," Ursula told them. "Pretty soon she had the whole town in an uproar. Jack was so embarrassed that he begged her to come back home, but she wasn't having any of it. She was enjoying her freedom and her new friends too much. She didn't divorce Jack, and she didn't serve any clients at the brothel, but she cleaned and cooked for room and board and used the living room for her headquarters for her women's rights organizing. She even fomented a strike among the town's women."

"Bravo." Bernie clapped her hands.

"Wives refused to cook meals or clean houses until their husbands showed them some respect. In the end, they even moved out of their homes and took the children with them and lived for weeks in the churches around the county, leaving the men on their own to take care of themselves. Women who worked in brothels, the preachers' wives, and all the women in the whole area camped out with them and stood together for their rights. Can't you just imagine them setting up camps and sleeping on pews?" Ursula asked.

"Did they accomplish anything?" Bernie asked.

"The tide turned at some point because Remy is here today. Jack was relentless in his courting of Daisy, and he eventually started lobbying the men to give the women their rights. He turned out to be a good guy, so Daisy went back to live with Jack and had children with him," Ursula answered. "According to what she wrote, all women are strong and they should always empower each other no matter what their profession," she went on, "and she says there's nothing with more power than a castiron skillet."

Luna finished her job and started filling glasses with ice. "Mama, when I get married, I want you to buy me a cast-iron skillet for my wedding gift."

"She won't have to." Bernie's tone was so serious that all the women whipped around to stare at her. "I will buy a whole set of them for each of you. That way, you'll have a small one for little infractions, a bigger one for when your husband does stupid things, and a really large one for cheaters or beaters."

Endora started the applause, and the others joined in. "The memory we are making tonight will be about cast-iron skillets and snowmen."

"I heard something about snowmen," Shane said as he, Joe Clay, and Remy came into the kitchen. "What's the biggest snowman you've ever built?"

"We had a couple of snows in Dallas, but we had to rake up all the snow in the backyard to build one that wasn't much bigger than our Barbie dolls," Luna answered.

Shane chuckled. "I remember building one about that size and then letting G.I. Joe tear it down."

"Well, there is enough snow out there now to build one that would intimidate Barbie and G.I. Joe," Joe Clay said.

Ursula glanced around at her family, then locked gazes

with Remy. Life didn't get any better than the love flowing among all of them in the kitchen that night.

———

Ursula was mesmerized by the blanket of pure white before her while everyone was choosing up sides and rushing out to start working on a snowman. She and Remy were supposed to be helping Shane and Luna make the base for Mr. Frosty, but before the yard was messed up, she wanted one more visual memory of the way everything looked that evening all covered in white as far as her eyes could see.

"We should go help." Remy slipped an arm around her shoulders.

She waved her hand to take in everything around them. "It's so beautiful," she whispered. "The Christmas lights are making the snow sparkle like diamond dust is lying on top of it. It's a shame we have to mess it all up."

"It's like life." Remy pulled on his gloves.

"How's that?"

"You can't have both." Remy grabbed her hand and pulled her out into the yard. "Gotta choose. The snow will melt in a few days, but the snowman will be here for a lot longer, and you can have the memories of making him with all of us."

"I'll take the memories." Ursula let go of his hand and rushed out in the yard to help Luna and Shane roll up the first big ball of snow. The further they got with the chore, the more it looked square rather than round.

"What do we do?" Ursula asked in a frustrated tone. "Mr. Frosty is looking like SpongeBob SquarePants."

"We can shape it after we make it as big as y'all want it to be," Remy answered. "That's just a matter of chipping away some corners and then patting more snow in where it's needed to make it perfectly round."

"Just like a relationship," Ursula muttered.

"What was that?" Luna asked.

Ursula repeated what she had said and then added, "You chip away the rough edges and use love to round it out."

"You got that right," Luna said. "Can you believe how fast the past month has gone by?"

"Time flies when you are having fun," Bernie said from behind them. "That's going to be a helluva—heck of a...big just don't cut it—big snowman."

"Yes, it is," Tertia answered from the other side of the yard where she was rolling up another ball.

"Thank goodness we've got three big, strong men to help us put him together." Ophelia and Endora finished making Mr. Frosty's head. "I'm going inside to find something to use for his eyes and nose."

"And to get him a scarf," Endora yelled.

"Bo and I'll break off a couple of branches from the mesquite trees to use for his arms," Rae said.

Luna and Ursula watched Shane and Remy remove snow from some areas of the roll they had made and pack it into others, and in no time, they had made a perfectly round ball.

"He's going to be a big one, but just look at what we've done to the pretty yard," Luna muttered.

"It's worth it," Ursula said. "Look at the expression on Mama's face and think about the pictures she'll take for our albums. She's happiest when we are all home and she can take photographic memories. I wonder how often she gets the albums down and goes through them."

"Thinking about kids, both past and future," Luna whispered, "have you and Remy talked about children?"

Ursula nodded and took a step closer to her sister. "He was raised alone, so he wants more than one, less than a dozen."

"How did you feel when he brought up having children so soon into your relationship?" Luna asked.

"Like I had found the right man," Ursula told her. "I'm ready to settle down, and being a full-time author will let me stay home with the children. You could do the same. Take them to the store with you until they are old enough to go to school."

"I've thought of that already," Luna whispered. "Does it ever bother you that—"

Ursula held up a hand and shook her head. "I know things are moving fast for me and Remy, but I'm okay with that. Mama said for me to listen to my heart, and it's telling me that everything is good."

"Thank you." Luna gave her sister a quick hug. "I needed to hear that."

"You are so welcome."

In seconds, all five of the other sisters had gathered around them for a group hug. "I don't know why we're doing this, but it sure feels right," Tertia said.

"We are celebrating falling in love," Ursula told them and noticed that Mary Jane was taking a picture of them.

Then she whipped around and took several shots of the three guys circled around the snowman. They checked it from all angles and reworked the bottom so that it had a bowl-shaped depression in the center for the middle section. Then together they lifted Frosty's rotund belly onto the base—with a fair amount of grunting and groaning—and worked on smoothing up the round parts and making an indention in the top for the snowman's head.

"I would never have never thought to do that," Ursula said.

"Me either," Luna agreed, "but it's sure making him more solid."

"And I've got the pictures to prove that you girls worked together without arguing," Mary Jane said.

"It's my influence that made that possible," Bernie teased. "I'll ask the universe to keep y'all safe on your shopping trip, and use my powers to keep y'all from arguing all day."

"Now, you are asking for the impossible," Mary Jane said.

"You girls might want to rethink that trip," Joe Clay said from a few feet away. "The weatherman is calling for freezing rain to settle on all this snow. The roads are going to be terrible."

"We could all load up in the old van tonight and go

to that hotel over there beside the shopping mall," Ophelia suggested. "We'll get a couple of bottles of wine on the way and have a slumber party. Maybe we can get a couple of adjoining rooms."

Tertia raised her hand. "I'm game for that. Even Rae shouldn't be driving over there on black ice, and we need really need to get some shopping done."

"I could do it," Rae agreed, "but I'd need a bottle of whiskey instead of a glass of wine when we got to the hotel."

"I think that's a great idea." Bernie put in her two cents. "I'd go with you, but the hotel probably doesn't allow dogs. Pepper would pout if I left him alone all night."

"I could use my veteran's discount and get some rooms lined up if all y'all are serious," Ophelia offered.

"It's already eight o'clock," Joe Clay said. "It'll take y'all two hours to pack and another hour to drive over to Wichita Falls."

"All we have to do is throw some pajamas, a change of clothes, and our toothbrushes in a tote bag," Ursula said. "We can do that in five minutes and be at the hotel no later than ten o'clock."

Ophelia made the call and then gave them all a thumbs-up sign. "We're good to go, and I even got two adjoining suites."

"I'll worry about y'all out in this kind of weather," Mary Jane fussed. "Why don't you wait until the roads are clear?"

Ursula threw an arm around her mother's shoulders. "Not a one of us has done our Christmas shopping, Mama. You've got the normal three presents under the tree for each of us, and there's none from us to each other or to you and Daddy."

"Well, far be it from us to keep you from buying a present for each other or for me," Joe Clay joked. "Let's finish up this snowman and let your mama take a few pictures. Then I'll get the old van out of the barn, and Rae can drive. She's used to slick roads."

"I promise I'll get them there and back safely, Mama. I live in the coldest part of Oklahoma, and I'm out on patrol at night in worse weather than this," Rae assured her mother.

Mary Jane covered her ears with her hands. "I really don't want to hear about that."

"Then let's don't talk about it but know that I've been trained to drive in any kind of weather so trust me to get all these sisters of mine to and from Wichita Falls safely." Rae handed her mother the two branches she and Bo had snapped off the nearest mesquite tree. "Would you put Mr. Frosty's arms where they belong?"

Ursula could almost read her mother's mind. All seven of her girls would be in the same vehicle after dark during bad weather. She thought about offering to stay behind and send a shopping list with the other six. Lord only knew that she'd rather spend the night snuggled down in a warm bed with Remy than to go to Wichita Falls that night. There would be masses and masses of folks doing last-minute gift buying tomorrow at the mall. She could very well imagine them milling around in hundreds—maybe thousands—trying to figure out what to buy their Great Aunt Gert or Grandpa Willie.

Remy startled her when he gave her a sideways hug, and she jumped away from him. When she realized what she had done, she took a step forward and wrapped her arms around his neck. "I'm sorry. I was psyching myself out about how to deal with all the people in the mall tomorrow. I should stay home and let the others go when I feel like this."

Remy chuckled. "How long has it been since all of you girls spent a night together outside the Paradise?"

Ursula tried to think of the last time she and her sisters had even met up outside the Paradise, but nothing came to mind. "Never, except when we were little girls and had to go to my father's place for a night or two," she finally answered.

"I really think that you all ought to make this a Christmas event. Maybe even make it happen a couple of times yearly," Remy said. "If I had brothers, I would want to go to a ball game with them once in a while, just to reconnect and catch up. Life can get in the way so fast, darlin'. Why do you think your mama is so adamant about her pictures?"

"We get together on holidays at the Paradise," Ursula argued.

"It's not the same," Remy said. "You should go with them. Either text me or else remember all the funny things that happen and tell me about them when you get home tomorrow evening."

Luna walked up just at that moment and put a gloved hand over her mouth to stifle laughter. "Like how Endora can't hold her liquor. One glass of wine and she's ready to pole dance."

"I am not!" Endora declared right behind her. "That's Tertia and Bo. I'm the good sister."

"Yes, you are—good at not remembering what you did the night before," Luna teased.

"See, you are already having fun," Shane said, stepping up next to Luna and Ursula.

Mary Jane whistled so loud that it seemed to rattle the limbs of the trees even worse than the wind. "Gather around our snowman. Ursula, Endora, Luna, Shane, and Remy on the right. All the rest of you on the left, and Aunt Bernie in front of Frosty. Don't split and run until I raise my hand. I'll take several pictures, so I'll be sure and get a good one."

"And after they all take off, would you like for me to take one of you and Joe Clay?" Shane asked.

"Yes," Joe Clay answered for his wife. "We'd like that. This is the biggest Mr. Frosty that we have ever built here in Spanish Fort."

"In that case, let's make it a really special one." Ursula jogged toward the house and brought out a floppy old hat that her mother wore when she gardened, and a box marked EXTRA DECORATIONS on the side. She snapped off a couple of twigs from a nearby mesquite tree. "Daddy, would you take that old, beat-up cowboy hat off him."

"What are you doing?" Mary Jane asked.

"We're making a snow lady instead of a snow man. Seems right fitting since this is the Paradise where seven sisters were raised." Bernie clapped her hands.

"And where Daisy fought for women's rights. She would

be so proud of us." Ursula draped garland around the crown of her mother's floppy gardening hat and let the streamers hang down the snowman's backside. "Here, Daddy, put this on Miz Frosty. None of us is tall enough."

Joe Clay set the hat on the now snowwoman's head. "What now?"

Bernie handed him a couple of small twigs. "Put these where her ears would be, and then you can hang an ornament on each for her earrings." She reached into the box and brought out a bibbed apron with tie strings at the neck and waist. "Ursula, you are the tallest woman here, so you can do the honors with this."

Luna strung a few ornaments on a ribbon and attached them to the lady snowperson's branch used for an arm. "This is her bracelet."

Ursula dug around in the box and handed Remy a long string of garland made of red wooden beads. "Can you put this around her neck for a necklace?"

"Sure thing." Remy reached up, removed the hat, and handed it to Ursula. He positioned the beads just right and then reset the hat.

Bernie clapped her hands and laughed out loud. "That is the grandest thing I have ever seen, and I love it. Daisy and the women from the Paradise couldn't have done a better job."

"Mr. Frosty would be flirting with this lovely lady."

"I hereby christen Miz Frosty with her own name. She is now Raven, after the first madam here at the Paradise."

Bernie bent forward at the waist. "I bow to Madam Raven."

"We have made precious memories tonight," Mary Jane said. "But if y'all are going to make it to that hotel before midnight, you'd better line up for your pictures."

"Yes, ma'am," Ursula said. "It's not every day we get to take pictures with Madam Raven."

Shane grabbed Luna's hand and pulled her over to stand beside her twin, who was reaching up to hold Raven's twiggy hand. In just a couple of minutes, the photos were taken, and all the sisters made a mad dash for the house except for Ursula. She and Remy drove away in his truck so she could pack, but she was back in record time and hustling the other six to hurry up.

Ursula stopped in Luna's room to find her staring out the balcony doors.

"I don't want to leave Shane," she whispered.

"I don't want to leave Remy either, but we are going to do this." Ursula dumped out a tote bag and filled it with pajamas, underwear, and a clean change of clothing. "You need to do this. We need to do this. We are going to do this."

"Who are you preaching at?" Luna asked. "Me or you?"

"Both of us," Ursula said.

"Did I tell you about Vernon, the old guy at the nursing home?" Luna asked and then went on to tell her sister his story.

"All the more reason for us to go on this trip. Family means everything. Go get your toothbrush and whatever else you need from the bathroom," Ursula said.

"You ready?" Endora asked from the doorway.

"She will be in a minute." Ursula pointed toward the door.

"Are you dragging your feet because you would rather stay here and spend the night with Shane?" Endora asked. "Do you realize that all seven of us have never done anything like this together before?"

"Yes, she does, and so do I," Ursula answered.

"And we didn't even plan it," Endora said. "Remember back when we were little and we would all sneak into your room and strategize our next moves—whether it was talking Mama into letting us stay home instead of going to spend a weekend with our father or figuring out how to get her and Joe Clay together?"

"Do you miss going to see our father?" Ursula asked.

Endora shook her head. "I was so little when he and Mama divorced that I didn't really get to know him, and our stepmother never liked us being underfoot anyway. I always felt like she was constantly afraid we would leave a fingerprint on one of her priceless things."

"Did you feel the strain and awkwardness when we had to go there?" Ursula asked.

Endora followed her sister. "Worse than awkward. If it hadn't been for y'all, it would have been even more miserable, and it's probably the reason we all have trust issues."

"But we have a great dad in Joe Clay and shouldn't have trouble trusting," Ursula argued.

"But there's men like our father and my ex floating around out there too," Endora reminded her. "But let's go enjoy spending time together and not think about those ugly things."

"What ugly things?" Bo asked as she and Rae peeked into the room.

"Men who can't be trusted, but we're not going to talk about that," Endora answered. "We're going to focus on our first ever sisters' night out."

"We've had sisters' nights ever since we moved into the Paradise," Rae told her. "I remember one of the firsts was when we decided to play matchmaker with Mama and Joe Clay."

Luna came from the bathroom, picked up her packed tote bag, and started down the stairs with three of her sisters right behind her. "That was in the Paradise, so it doesn't count as an official night out with just us seven sisters."

"What are y'all talking about?" Ophelia asked from the foyer.

Luna didn't even slow down but went straight toward the kitchen with all six of them behind her now. "We'll talk about it in the van. Daddy already has it pulled up to the back door. Where's Mama?"

"She said to tell all y'all to have a good time," Joe Clay answered, "and that she was going to have a long bath and then read for a while."

"No hugs or warnings about not picking anyone up on the side of the road." Luna started to open the back door.

"I'm here to hug each of you and tell you not to pick up strangers or drink that wine you talked about while you are driving." He gave each of them a quick hug. "Ophelia, it's your job to call or text when you are in the hotel and remember that you are not to pop the corks on those bottles of wine until you get in your rooms. Now, get on out of here, and let me and the boys watch a good old western on television."

"Thanks, Daddy." Ursula gave him a second hug and then stepped outside to find Remy waiting beside the old blue van that Joe Clay had bought twenty years ago so he could haul the whole family to church and to sporting events the girls were involved in.

When she got close enough, Remy opened the panel door on the side and then opened his arms. She walked into them and wrapped her arms around his neck while five of her sisters got into their seats.

"Text me when you get settled into your room, and if the party gets wild, you could send some pictures," Remy said.

Endora leaned out the door and said, "What happens at the hotel stays at the hotel."

"Yes, ma'am." Remy grinned, gave Ursula one more hug and a sweet kiss on the lips.

Shane jogged over to the van, leaned in, and planted a long, lingering kiss on Luna's lips. "If you want, you can bring all your presents over to our house tomorrow night to wrap them. There are rolls and rolls of Christmas paper out in the garage. Granny always bought a bunch at the after Christmas sales."

"I'll be there as soon as we get back," she promised. "How good are you at wrapping?"

"All thumbs, but I can talk to you while you do the work, and I'm sure the puppies will be glad to see you." He took a step away from her and headed for the house. He rounded the van and then whispered something in Ursula's ear before he slid the door shut.

"What did he say?" Luna asked.

"He said to take good care of you, that you were precious to him," Ursula answered.

"Ahhh," Rae said as she settled into the driver's seat. "That's so sweet, but let's leave all the boyfriend business behind and just focus on *us* tonight and tomorrow."

"Can't do it," Ursula told her. "I'm in love and I don't intend to ever leave it behind."

"Me too," Luna declared.

"The oldest and the youngest," Bo said with a long sigh. "Doesn't seem fair that they are probably going to be the first to get married, but life is life, and we don't get to control all of it. If we could, I'd already have a contract and be nominated for a CMA award."

"I agree that life is not fair," Endora said, "but the toughest experiences teach us who we can depend on."

Ophelia gave her a fist pump. "Amen to that, baby sister."

"Okay, this wagon train is about to leave the Paradise. Everyone buckled up?" Rae asked.

"We're ready," Luna answered.

Rae put the vehicle in gear and headed down the lane. "Rule number one!" she called out as she came to a sliding stop. "What happens at the hotel or what is said at the hotel stays there. That means our two sisters who are in love can't tell their fellers."

"Why?" Luna asked.

"Because once we get into that second bottle of wine, we might tell some secrets like what we've bought for presents, or other heavier things, that we do not want ever spread around," Rae answered.

"Does anyone else have any other rules?" Luna asked when Rae made a right-hand turn onto a still-slick road and headed south.

"That's the important one," Rae said, "but if y'all think of any more, we'll make a list. I'm sure if we do this every year, we will have a whole bunch of them after this initial year."

As usual, Daisy came to Ursula's mind. She didn't have family in Texas, but she had a family of women—both in the Paradise and in the community—who became her sisters.

Chapter 17

THE ROAD FROM SPANISH Fort to Nocona still hadn't been cleared, so the going was slow, but Ursula didn't mind. She was reminded of all the years when her folks would load all seven girls in the same van and drive them all the way to Wichita Falls just to look at the lights. That night, the houses were sparse, but they all looked inviting. Some just had a Christmas tree displayed in a window. Others were decorated almost as much as the Paradise.

"What's everyone thinking about?" Rae asked as she slowed down to a snail's pace to make the next curve in the road.

"That if we have to go at this speed the whole trip over to Wichita Falls, we'll probably get there about the time the mall opens in the morning," Luna said.

"I made a phone call before we left home," Ursula said. "Once we hit Nocona, the highway has been cleaned off, but I was thinking about how Mama and Joe Clay always took us to see the lights when we were all still living at home."

"And then Daddy would take us all to that little café on the edge of town for burgers, fries, and milk shakes," Tertia added.

"He said it was for all eight of his girls," Ophelia said and then pointed to a house that they were passing. "Look at that house with all the cutout ornaments in the yard."

Suddenly, Rae slammed on the brakes and the van went into a spin.

I knew I shouldn't have come on this trip, Ursula thought as the van spun around like it was attached to a giant merry-go-round. Her eyes tried to adjust to different pictures flying by the window of a herd of deer, bare tree limbs, and lights going past in warp speed.

Somewhere in the melee, she heard Bo cuss and Tertia saying something about Jesus being sweet. Ursula expected her life to flash in front of her eyes, but it didn't. All she got was instant clarity. She knew that if she came through this unhurt, she was going to fall into Remy's arms, tell him she how much she loved him, and that she was throwing away her birth control pills.

Then everything was suddenly so still and quiet that Ursula wondered if they had all died. She even looked up to see if there was a bright light she should be going toward. Tears began to roll down her cheeks.

Luna sobbed. "I know we aren't supposed to talk boyfriends, but I love Shane. No, that's not right. I'm in love with him."

"Why are you"—Ursula had to work to catch a breath—"crying?"

"Because that just made me realize how sad Mama and Daddy would be if we had all died and that I might never get to be a mother." Luna wept even harder.

"Are we dead?" Endora whispered.

Ursula looked around at all her sisters to find that all their faces were pale—even Ophelia, the big bad soldier, and Rae, the equally as bad policewoman. "Is everyone all right? Do we need to call Daddy or go to the emergency room and get checked out?"

"I think I'm alive," Endora answered. "I can talk and hear Luna crying, and I don't see blood."

"Same here," Luna sniffled.

"Well, now," Rae said in a breathy tone, "that was scary as hell. Anyone want to do it again?"

"Not just no," Ursula panted, "but hell no!"

"I bet that herd of deer is giving thanks that you had good brakes," Bo said from the front passenger seat. "It's a miracle they all got across the road without even that last little fawn getting bumped."

"I saw the first one jump over the fence, but I thought they'd stay back." Tertia's voice quivered.

Rae took a deep breath and let it out in a loud whoosh. "There was nothing I could do but brake."

"Are we going back home?" Luna asked.

"The van is pointed toward Nocona, so my vote is that we go on," Rae answered, "and that we don't tell Mama about this—not ever."

"We're only a couple of miles from the outskirts of Nocona, and the roads are supposed to be better from there on over to Wichita Falls," Ursula added from the back of the van. "My vote is that we go on, and I agree about not telling Mama. Seems to be an omen that we got stopped in the right lane with the nose of this old van going south, but Lord, I'm glad I wasn't driving."

Rae took her hands from the steering wheel and shook them. "Okay then, that takes part of the tension out of my body, but the adrenaline rush is going to stick around until morning." She put her hands back on the wheel and eased down the road. "What were we talking about before I literally saw the deer in the headlights?"

"Seeing the lights." Luna's voice came out high and squeaky. "And I mean the Christmas lights, not that bright, white light that beckons us toward the pearly gates."

"I'm going to change the subject," Ursula said. "I don't want to talk about lights anymore. When we stop at the convenience store in Nocona, I'll spring for the wine. I'm buying a bottle of blackberry. What do the rest of you want?"

"Anything red," Rae answered. "And lots of it after what we just went through. For a minute there, I felt the van begin to lean a little, and I thought it would roll over for sure."

"Zinfandel," Endora replied in a still shaky voice.

"I'm a cheap date," Ophelia said. "I like Boone's Farm Strawberry Hill."

Tertia had taken a notepad from her purse. "I've got blackberry, zinfandel, chardonnay, which takes care of white, and Strawberry Hill. Think that's enough? I thought I was okay, but my handwriting is pretty bad right now."

"After our brush with death, we might ought to add a six-pack of beer," Ursula answered.

"Or maybe we should just wait until we get to the nearest liquor store to buy our wine and add a bottle of Jameson to the order?" Bo said, "And I'll spring for that. I like good whiskey better than wine anyway, and I need a good stiff drink tonight. I'll probably have nightmares. I got something while we were spinning—whether it was a vision or just a wake-up call—but I got a clear message that I need to give up chasing a dream in Nashville that isn't going to happen."

"Me too," Ophelia said. "Fate or the universe or angels from heaven told me I had made the right decision."

"Who else got a message?" Luna asked.

All four of her other sisters raised a still trembling hand, including Rae. "But I don't want to talk about it right now," she said. "I just want to ease on down to Nocona and pray that the roads are better. Then we'll get some booze and hunker down in our rooms for the night. We won't even need to drive over to the mall tomorrow morning since the hotel is in the same parking lot."

Ursula noticed that Rae was now gripping the steering wheel so tightly that her knuckles turned white, and she drove the last few miles so slowly that a wagon and set of mules could have gotten them there faster. As soon as they passed the WELCOME TO NOCONA sign, the roads began to be less slick. They were still slushy, and with the drop in temperature in the next few hours, they would be greasy again by morning. Hopefully, if the sun came out, the ice would melt by the time they started home.

Ursula was still in the flight-or-fight mode from the

adrenaline rush when Rae turned down Main Street and headed west. She figured everyone else in the van felt the same way and thought that talking might help so she said, "I'm starting Christmas shopping in July next year."

"And miss all this fun?" Rae asked.

"Oh, I'll go with all y'all, but I'll have my presents bought and wrapped and ready to put under the tree," Ursula declared. "I brought my list, but my brain is so rattled right now that I might not be able to think straight for days."

"Mine too, but I'm hoping in a few weeks, this will just be a funny inside joke that we all share," Endora said. "Being twins, the two of us got a double dose back there, because we each also felt the same fear the other one did."

"Double joy and sorrows," Luna whispered. "But I got to admit, my thoughts are on my relationship with Shane. I want to spend the rest of my life with him, and one little pothole in the road when we were spinning around could have flipped the van out into a ditch. All of us could have been hurt, or worse, and my dream of working beside Shane for the next fifty or sixty years would have been gone in the snap of my fingers."

"I feel the same way," Ursula whispered around the lump in her throat.

———————

Ursula sent her mother a text and then one to Remy telling them they had arrived while Ophelia got them checked into the hotel. She got a thumbs-up emoji back from her mother and a smiley face blowing kisses to her from Remy with a short message saying that he had begun to worry about her.

She almost sent back an "I love you" but decided that should be said face-to-face, not with a text.

"Okay, sisters," Ophelia said, "we're on the third floor and the elevator is right around the corner, unless some of you feel the need for a little exercise and want to take the stairs."

Ursula didn't answer but just followed the signs to the elevator and pushed the button. "Think we can all get in at once, or should some of us wait?"

"We can all fit in," Endora answered.

When the doors opened, Ursula stepped inside and went back to the far corner. It was crowded but the doors closed, and there were no creaks or groans when the elevator made its way to the third floor.

"Rooms 301 to 323." Ophelia pointed to the sign at the end of the short elevator hallway. "It looks like our rooms are close by. Here's the second key, Luna. Open the connecting door when you get inside."

Luna slid her key down the slot, opened the door, and found two queen-sized beds and a sofa bed. "Six beds, seven women."

"You and I can bunk together." Endora dropped her tote bag on the sofa and opened the connecting door. "Whoever doesn't snore can stay in our room."

"That would be me," Bo said.

Rae raised her hand. "And me. I guess the two sets of twins are going to take this room, then."

"I'm good with Tertia and Ursula," Ophelia called out from the other room. "I brought my earplugs. By the way does Remy know that you snore, Ursula?"

"Remy says that *old p*eople snore but that I purr," Ursula answered. "I'm getting out of these jeans and putting on a pair of pajama pants, then I'll play bartender so we can get this party started."

"I bet he has earplugs hidden under the bed," Ophelia said. "I bought my first ones when I was in basic training, and the women I bunked with were not old by any stretch of the word. They were all about my age, but they could raise the roof off the barracks when they fell asleep." She kicked off her boots, pulled off her jeans, and removed her sweater and bra. Then she took a pair of sweatpants with ARMY written down the side of the leg and an olive drab T-shirt out of her tote bag and put them on. "I'm ready for a glass of Strawberry Hill," she said as she climbed up in the middle of one of the beds.

"Give me a minute," Ursula said as she finished getting into Betty Boop Christmas pajamas. Then she unwrapped one of the plastic glasses the hotel provided and poured it full of wine for Ophelia.

Luna wasn't at all surprised when she and Endora pulled out matching nightshirts with Rudolph printed on the front of each one. They would be twins even when they were both old and wrinkled. That part of who they were would never change.

"Now that I've got wine and we are safely away from slick roads and deer-in-the-headlights scenarios, let's talk about Mama and Daddy's Christmas present," Ophelia said.

Luna would rather that they help her with some ideas for a unique gift she could give Shane, but she pointed to the bottle of Jameson and nodded toward Ursula. Tonight was all about being with her sisters, even though it would be downright impossible not to think about Shane.

Ursula poured her three fingers of Jameson. "That enough for a starter?"

"That's probably enough for a finisher." Luna smiled and carried it over to sit beside Ophelia on the bed. "I can't hold my liquor as well as our military sister, and Aunt Bernie can back me up on that."

"I hear a story," Bo said. "I wonder if we get a few more drinks in you if you won't be able to keep your mouth shut about how Shane is in bed."

"As much as I love you all," Luna said, "that ain't goin' to happen. I'd pass out before I'd tell those kinds of secrets. We were talking about ideas for Mama and Daddy. What have y'all come up with?"

Ophelia raised her glass. "First, a toast to being sisters."

"Hear! Hear!" Endora held up her glass of blackberry wine. "And a toast to living through a near-death experience. Now, start spitballing ideas for gifts."

Ophelia nodded. "Mine is that we all chip in together and send them on a Caribbean cruise. I found one out of Galveston in March that's on sale, and it's got all kinds of benefits like a drink card and some cash to spend on the ship. I've already booked it, but if all y'all want to help out, we can give it to them together."

"Count me in," Luna said. "They have everything they need, and if they need or want anything more, they go buy it right then."

"Me too," the other five sisters chimed in.

"But we'll need to buy them something small so they'll each have seven gifts under the tree," Endora said. "I thought about getting Mama some bath oil and going to that T-shirt place and having Daddy made a funny one about living through seven daughters."

"Great idea," Luna said.

"Now, on to the next item," Ophelia said. "This is hush-hush until after Christmas Day because…" She paused. "Well"—she took a drink of her wine—"I don't want my announcement to be the big thing and make Mama's favorite holiday not as important."

"You are getting married?" Ursula asked.

"Good lord, no!" Ophelia gasped.

"Are you pregnant?" Luna felt just a little jealous.

"Again, no!" Ophelia almost choked on a sip of wine. "Now my news doesn't seem to be so big."

"Spit it out," Bo said.

"I got an early out," Ophelia said. "I'm home for good. My things are in a moving van on the way even as we speak."

"Thank God!" Endora said with a long sigh. "Luna and Ursula are already spending more time with Shane and Remy than they do at home. That would leave me all by myself in the Paradise with Aunt Bernie"—she rolled her blue eyes toward the ceiling—"when Mama and Daddy go on their cruise, and just the thought of rattling around in that big old place, alone even for a week, is depressing."

Ophelia raised an eyebrow. "Not as much as having to be the only one around with Aunt Bernie, I bet."

"Hey, girl." Endora shot her a dose of stink eye. "You're going to be next in line for Aunt Bernie to try to get married off."

"Not me." Ophelia's shudders were visible. "I'm not ready for that."

Home! Luna thought. Here lately when she thought of that word or even pictured it in her mind, it was Shane's house, not the Paradise.

By midafternoon the next day, Ursula had all her shopping done and had sent a group text to all her sisters telling them that she was sitting on a bench at the exit closest to where Rae had parked the van. As each one arrived, she handed off the Magic Marker that she carried in her purse. "I'm filling Mama's role today," she said.

"Thank goodness you remembered," Endora said as she sat down on the end of the bench and wrote her name on every one of her bags. "We would have had a mess if all seven of us had to figure out what belonged to who."

"Hey, are y'all's feet hurting as bad as mine?" Tertia asked when she took the marker from Endora and wrote her name on her bags.

Luna answered. "I meant it when I said I'm going to start

shopping in July next year. This fighting crowds and trying to find presents for everyone this late in the game is not fun."

"What's not fun?" Bo asked, just walking up.

Luna repeated what she had said.

"I'm going to do the same thing." Endora covered a yawn with her hand. "But I do want us to do the hotel-and-wine thing a couple of times a year. Maybe we'll do it just before all the holiday parties, and we can bring Mama with us. We could all shop for our pretty outfits for the Paradise party."

"We can't leave Aunt Bernie at home," Luna said. "She'll be the life of the party."

"We could get one of those rent-by-the-night houses close to the mall if they come with us," Ursula suggested.

"I'd like that." Rae sank down on an adjoining bench and stretched her legs out. "How are we ever going to get all these bags in the back of the van?"

"We'll cram them in." Luna answered.

"I'm done!" Ophelia announced when she sank down on the bench beside Tertia.

"With one little bag?" Ursula asked. "Where's the rest of your purchases?"

"Right here, and look, I already put my name on it." Ophelia held up a brown bag the size of a grocery sack. "My gifts are small this year."

"Great things come in small packages," Bo said right behind her, "so don't expect great things from me." She took the marker from Tertia and sat down on a long bench in front of Luna and Endora.

"Or from me." Rae said with a nod. "If we do this again, we might need to hook Daddy's flatbed trailer up to the back of the van just to get all our stuff home. Has anyone heard anything about the weather and the roads?"

"Slick roads all the way home," Bo answered. "Everything from here to the Louisiana border got a sleet storm while we were drinking and giggling in the hotel room last night. You still driving us home, Rae?"

"Yes, I am," she said. "I sure don't want to trust any of y'all to get us and all these presents home in one piece."

"You're not getting any arguments from me," Luna said. "Just get me home…" She paused when she thought of that word again.

"Just get you home what? You didn't finish your sentence," Rae said as she marked her bags.

"Safe," Luna finished.

"I promise I will," Rae said. "I wouldn't want to deal with Shane if I didn't. I'll walk over to the hotel lot and drive the van up to the curb so we can load up and be on the way."

"You wouldn't want to deal with Mama if you didn't," Endora warned.

Luna stood to the side and watched all her sisters load their bags into the back of the van, and then she added hers wherever she could cram them in. One of her favorite memories from childhood was when her mother brought all of them to this same mall and let them buy Christmas gifts for each other. They weren't allowed to spend more than five dollars on each present, so there was lots of junk jewelry, fingernail polish, and lotions in their bags. When they got home, they all rushed to their rooms to wrap all the presents.

I want that for my kids, Luna thought. *I want a big family so there will be lots of presents under the tree. Even if they don't cost a lot, unwrapping them is the fun part, and the love behind all of it is what is important.*

She was still thinking about that when she got into the van and fastened her seat belt. Maybe she and Shane *would* have four or five children.

He hasn't even proposed to you or asked you to move in with him. Aunt Bernie's voice popped into her head.

Rae twisted her long, black hair up into a messy bun and held it there with a hair clamp. "Mama called a few minutes ago and said for us not to eat on the way home. She's made a pot of potato chowder and some hot rolls, and there's a pan of warm gingerbread with lemon sauce for dessert."

Luna had just finished doing the same thing with her blond hair when her phone pinged. She dragged it up out of her purse to find a text from Shane: Mary Jane has invited me to have supper with y'all tonight. I'll be there when you get home.

She sent one back: On our way. Missed you.

She would tell him later that she was on the same page as he was now about having a big family and that home wasn't really the Paradise anymore, but it was the place he kept calling *our h*ouse.

"I will not miss trying to tame my curly hair into a bun every morning," Ophelia said.

"I hear you," Tertia said, "but I've always been more than a little envious that you got the red hair, and mine is just mousy brown."

"All right." Rae put the van in gear. "This wagon train is headed home. Pray there's no deer crossing the roads or any other animals for that matter. Unless y'all want to stop and pick up any more puppies someone might put out on the side of the road."

"No. More. Animals." Ursula punctuated each word by poking her forefinger at Rae.

Luna leaned her head back and closed her eyes. The conversation between her sisters went from one subject to another, and at first, she added a word or two but didn't say them out loud. Her mind was on presents under the tree for five or six little blond and the excitement there would be on Christmas morning.

One minute, she was dreaming about Shane helping her gather up all the wrapping paper to cram into a big garbage bag before they went to the Paradise for Christmas dinner, and the next, she visualized the kids trying to decide which toy they could take with them to Nana and Poppa's house and wondering whether their cousins had gotten the same thing that they had.

Then suddenly Rae braked, and it was déjà vu all over again. Luna's body pulled against the seat belt to keep her from flying out over Rae's shoulder through the windshield. Then the van came to a long, sliding stop with tires squealing on the pavement, and Luna felt like a rag doll being tossed backward.

"What in the…" she squealed in a voice that she didn't even recognize as her own.

"Some idiot…" Rae's voice was even higher than Luna's.

"Stopped right in front of us, shoved a box out from the back seat. He didn't even get out of the car or make sure that the box was safely off the road, and then he took off so fast that the car fishtailed all over the road," Ursula finished for her sister.

"Dear God!" Bo gasped. "What if there's a baby in that box? We could have run over it."

Endora slung the door open on her side of the van and hopped out. "If there's a baby out there, I'm rescuing it."

Rae rolled down the window and yelled. "Don't you pick that thing up. It could be a bomb or some kind of poison."

"You watch too many cop shows," Luna said as she slid the panel door open on her side of the vehicle and went to help her twin. "It's probably just trash or maybe a practical joke with a couple of fresh cow patties in it."

"I am a cop, and…" Rae put the van in park, unfastened her seat belt, and opened the door. The road was still icy enough that she slid most of the way to the box, but she beat both Luna and Endora. "Don't touch it, and don't open it until I—"

"It's okay," Endora said. "I hear baby kittens in there, not a bomb ticking."

"It could be an audio tape of some kind to—" Rae argued.

"I don't think *that's* a bomb." Luna pointed at a little paw sticking out a hole in the side of the box. "Looks to me like some hard-hearted person tossed out kittens with the idea that a semi would run over them. It's a good thing whoever did this is long gone, or else he would have to deal with all seven of us."

"I hope whoever is that cruel gets to sit on a barbed-wire fence in the middle of hell for all eternity," Endora declared as she opened the top of the box and looked inside to see two little orange and white kittens. "These are mine. Y'all got puppies, and I'm allergic to them, so these are mine."

"Twins," Rae said. "Look, they have identical markings."

Luna picked both of them up, turned them over, and said, "They're both girls, so they might really be identical twins." She put them back into the box and handed it to Endora. "They're all yours. I hope Sassy doesn't hate them, though."

"If she does, I'll keep them in my room." Endora cradled the box in her arms and headed back to the van. "We should get this vehicle off the road before we get rear-ended."

"Kittens?" Bo asked when Endora was back in her seat with the box in her lap.

She removed the lid from the box and smiled. "Yes, and I've already laid claim to both of them."

Luna wouldn't have cared if there had been a dozen kittens in the box. To see her sister's bright smile and to hear the fire in her voice when she condemned the people who had tossed them out was a true Christmas miracle. She had thought her feisty twin had been replaced by a moody one that was headed for a bitter old spinsterhood and would never be the same again. Had she known that a couple of orange and white kittens would help bring Endora out of the doldrums, she would have gone to the shelter months ago and rescued a couple.

"Guess I didn't get my wish about no more animals on the road," Rae said as she eased back into the traffic.

"Why do people do this to innocent little kittens?" Endora fussed. "There are shelters everywhere for unwanted baby animals, and it's Christmas. Folks are looking for puppies and kittens to give their kids for the holiday."

Ophelia leaned up over the seat and reached into the box to take one of the kittens out. "You've already claimed them, but I can be their aunty since I'm going to be living in the house."

"I don't mind sharing," Endora told her.

Aunty. Luna bit back a smile.

Heaven help whoever had the first baby in the family. The little child would come into the world with six aunties, and possibly—given enough time—as many uncles. There would be no way the kid could avoid being spoiled rotten with love.

And that's not even thinking about all the love Mary Jane and Joe Clay will shower him or her with. Aunt Bernie's voice was back.

"What is making your eyes twinkle?" Endora asked. "Don't even ask if you can have one of my kittens or try to play the twin card by saying you should get one since we're twins."

"I've got puppies," Luna told her, "and they might not get along with kittens. I was thinking about the next generation of family and the fact that we'll be aunties for real then."

"Are you pregnant?" Endora gasped.

"Nope, but I want to be—not right now, but before long," Luna answered. "My biological clock is ticking and reminding me that I'm twenty-seven. Yours should be doing the same, Ursula. And the rest of you might be hearing a like noise."

"Shh," Ophelia told her. "I'm only two years younger than Ursula, and I don't even have a boyfriend in sight. You"—she pointed toward Luna—"are four years younger than me and you're in a really good relationship. But, honey, you and Ursula have probably nabbed the only good men in or around this area. Besides, what guy is going to be interested in an ex-soldier with unruly red hair? I will most likely have to be satisfied to be everyone's favorite aunty."

"Hey, wait a minute," Tertia fussed. "You can't be the favorite. I've claimed that crown already."

"It's Christmas," Luna said. "Miracles happen."

The proof was right there in the way that Endora was looking at those two little balls of fur.

Chapter 18

"THIS LIVING ROOM LOOKS like you bought out all the stores in the mall," Shane said when they had brought in all Luna's shopping bags from the truck and lined them up against the wall in his house. There was barely a trail from the Christmas tree to the sofa.

Luna plopped down on the sofa, removed her boots, and wiggled her toes. "Imagine seven times this many at the Paradise. After we get the presents all wrapped, we'll be taking most of them down there tomorrow to go under Mama's tree."

"Most of them?" Shane sat down on the other end of the sofa and put her feet in his lap.

"We'll leave the puppies' presents and the ones we bought each other here under our tree," she answered. "This is what Christmas looks like when you have a big family. You sure you're up for this kind of thing?"

He picked up one of her feet and started massaging it. "Oh, yeah, I am. I can't wait to be a husband and a father."

"That goes beyond wonderful," she groaned. "You've got until midnight to stop."

"This massage parlor closes at nine," he joked, "and then it turns into a gift-wrapping shop."

"If you insist," she said with a long sigh, "but the gift-wrapping could wait until morning."

"I don't think so," Shane told her. "I promised Joe Clay and Mary Jane I would have you home in time to help with the Christmas Day baking tomorrow morning. A lemon chess pie was mentioned, so I plan on getting you home by midmorning."

She closed her eyes and wondered when the right time would be to tell him that she was in love with him. He hadn't actually said the words yet. He'd hinted at them after that big argument they had had. She tried to remember his exact words, but the general idea was that he didn't want them to be over, and he wanted to be a part of her family someday.

How would he feel if she took the initiative and said it first? Should she wait until just the right moment, and if so, when would that be? Maybe Christmas morning? That way, it would always be a special memory.

"What are you thinking about so hard that it's causing wrinkles on your forehead?" he asked.

"Whether to tell you that I've fallen in love with you right now or wait to make it a special thing," she answered honestly.

He stopped rubbing her foot, stood up, and scooped her up into his arms. Then he sat back down with her still in his lap. "I've been waiting for you to say that for weeks. When and where doesn't mean as much to me as just hearing you say the words. I think I've been in love with you from the first time I met you. You and Endora were moving into the house on the last day of May. There were dark clouds in the sky that day, and Joe Clay called me to come help move a bunch of furniture into the barn. He introduced me to you and Endora, and it was love at first sight."

"Why me and not Endora? She and I are identical," Luna asked.

"But you aren't really identical," Shane said. "Your eyes sparkle more than hers. And you have a tiny freckle between your right eye and your hairline."

"I love you, Shane O'Toole," she whispered.

"I love you, Luna Simmons." He stopped massaging her foot, stretched out beside her on the sofa, and kissed her on the cheek.

"Do you think our kisses will always be hot even when we are eighty years old?" she asked.

"Even hotter," Shane answered, "because I intend to tell you that I love you every single day until we're as old as Bernie."

"And after that?" she asked.

"Three times a day, so if I forget one, then you'll still hear it," he said with a grin.

"Are we planning to live until we are in our eighties, then?" she asked.

"Maybe even longer. I figure it will take me that long to prove to you just how much I love you," Shane answered. "Any years after that will just be a bonus. Why did you decide to tell me tonight?"

She told him about the near wreck and the sudden stop

on the way home when they found the kittens. "If there had been a vehicle coming from either direction when Rae braked to keep from hitting the deer, it could have been a far different story. If there had been a semi behind us when she stopped so suddenly to keep from running over that box with the kittens, the truck couldn't have stopped, and it would have rear-ended us. For a few moments after we came to a stop, we all wondered if we had died. I didn't see a bright light, but I did see your face and you looked so sad. Then today while we were in the mall, all I could think of was you and the fact that I hadn't told you how I felt."

Shane buried his face in her hair. "I'm glad I didn't know about what happened, but I agree that we shouldn't ever put off what we have to say to each other." He stood up with her still in his arms and carried her down the hallway.

"We have presents to wrap," she muttered.

"They can wait," he whispered.

———

"And that's the last one," Luna said the next afternoon when she had wrapped pretty paper around the last matching Christmas aprons—one for each of her sisters, one for Bernie, and one for her mother. They were all printed with a Christmas tree that stretched from the bottom to the top of the bib. "At least it's the last one that I'm wrapping here. Your presents are at home, and I'll give them to you on Christmas Eve when we have our private celebration right here."

Shane gathered up all the bits and pieces of scrap paper

and put them into a trash bag. "I've decided what I want for Christmas, but I don't think you can buy it at the mall."

Luna's heart fell. She had found a wooden sign to hang in their new store with O'TOOLE written on it in eight-by-ten pictures of different kinds of fishing equipment. The O was a bobber out in the water. The T was a fancy lure. Then there were two more bobbers, a red one and a green one, which seemed fitting for Christmas. The L was a hook, and the E was a lure standing vertically with three hooks on the side. In a jewelry store, she had bought him a necklace with Saint Andrew on it—the patron saint of fishermen. And then in another store, she'd found a key chain that looked like a fishing lure that was engraved with, "You are the greatest catch of my life."

And now he was saying that he wanted something that couldn't be bought at the mall. At this late date, she wasn't sure she could find what he had in mind.

"I want you to move in with me," he said. "You don't have to make up your mind right now, and it can be anytime you feel like it, but before the store is finished, please. I want us to walk out to the store together the morning of our grand opening. From this house where we live—together."

"I can do that," she said without hesitation, "but I want to wait to make it an official moving in until after Christmas is over."

"Before you go back to school?" he asked.

"The day after Christmas," she answered.

"That's the best present in the whole world." He grabbed

her hand, placed it on his shoulder, put an arm around her waist, and danced around the living room with her.

All the fancy places in the whole world couldn't have been better than where they were right then. She had told him she loved him in *their* house. She would be moving in with him in less than a week—into *their* house. And someday soon, they would probably come to *their* house for a honeymoon. Why go anywhere else? They could make beautiful memories right there in Spanish Fort as well as they could make them in any honeymoon haven in the world.

Chapter 19

"IT SOUNDS LIKE WE are breaking glass with every step," Ursula said on the way to the barn to do the morning chores. "But look at that beautiful sunrise. The sun looks like a sliver of an orange coming up out there, giving some form to all the bare trees."

"It's almost as pretty as you are." Remy eased the barn door open and let Ursula go inside first. "I ordered that sunrise and all the snow so you would have a wonderful Christmas morning."

"You are one romantic cowboy," Ursula said.

Both yellow puppies ran across the floor, tumbling over each other the whole way. She sat down on the barn floor with her back against a bale of hay, and the puppies wiggled and bit at each other's tails as they climbed all over her lap.

"You are like worms in hot ashes," she said, laughing.

"They're telling you that they're glad they don't have to live outside in the cold but have a nice dry barn to explore and sleep in." Remy hefted a bag of cattle feed onto his shoulder and headed toward the barn door that led out into the corral.

Ursula could easily imagine his biceps straining the fabric

of his chambray shirt under his work coat. He held the bag of feed steady with one hand and opened the door with the other, and in a few minutes, he returned with an empty bag.

"Mama has always said that the Paradise has magical charms," she muttered.

"What did you say?" Remy picked up an ax and headed back out to the corral.

"We'll talk about it when you get back," Ursula answered.

"Then I'll hurry," he said with a grin.

She was so engrossed with the puppies and her own thoughts that she didn't realize he had returned until he sat down beside her. "The cows say Merry Christmas."

"The puppies say the same thing even though they pouted a little because we forgot to buy presents for them," she teased.

"We'll make up for it on their birthday, which I'm declaring is November twenty-first," Remy said.

"Why that day?" Ursula asked. "Don't you think they're a little older than that?"

"Probably, but we are going to celebrate that day because it was the first day that *you c*ame back into my life, and that's as special as my birthday and Christmas rolled into one," Remy answered.

Ursula set the puppies to the side and moved over closer to him. "That is so sweet. That day seems like years ago instead of only a few weeks. I feel like I've known you forever."

"You *have* known me since we were in junior high school," he reminded her.

"I guess I have." She cupped his face in her gloved hands and drew it down for a kiss that seemed to jack the temperature in the barn up by several degrees.

When the kiss ended, he moved even closer to her. "Now what were you saying about magic?"

"Mama says that the Paradise has magical powers," Ursula answered. "I always thought she was saying that for herself because Daddy came into her life there."

"Have you changed your mind?" Remy asked.

"Yes, I have. I believe that coming home"—she searched for the right word—"that this place is home. We follow our own broken roads, kind of like that old song by Rascal Flatts, but…" She hesitated.

"The song says something about blessing the broken road that led me home to you, right?" Remy said as the puppies ran off to chase after a field mouse.

"That's right. Mama also reminds us that everything happens for a reason and in the right time," Ursula said. "Looking back at our stories, I believe it."

He stood up and pulled her to her feet. "So do I, and I'm so glad that this is our right time, darlin'. When will it be the right time for you to move in with me?"

He slipped an arm around her shoulders, and together they crossed the barn. When he opened the door, a blast of bitter cold wind hit them both in the face, and Ursula pulled her scarf up over her nose. Both puppies ran out onto the snow, but they didn't waste any time at all scrambling for a foothold and scooting right back into the barn.

Ursula wondered what kind of stir moving in with Remy would cause in the family. After all, she'd only been dating him—if she could even call it that—a few weeks.

Time is just numbers on a clock and dates on a calendar, Aunt Bernie's voice scolded. *The heart knows no time or dates, and your mother told you to follow your heart.*

"I'm already practically living with you," she answered.

"But it's not official," he said as they started toward the house. "I've loved you most of my life, and I want you to spend the rest of whatever days I've got on this earth with me, so I'm asking you…will you move all your things across the fence and live with me?"

"Yes," she said, "but are you talking about right now or six months down the road?"

"Yesterday would be ideal," he answered, "but the timing is up to you."

"This afternoon is soon enough," she answered. "After Christmas dinner, I'll pack up what's left of my things over at the Paradise and move over here. I'll have plenty of help since all my sisters are home. But can we, please, drive over and not have to haul everything over the fence?"

Was she being too eager? What if living together didn't work out? How much flak was she about to get from her sisters? Questions bombarded her mind, and the answer that came to her was that she should simply follow her heart and not worry about what others thought.

"Of course we can," Remy answered.

The sun was a big orange ball sitting all pretty in a

pale-blue sky with no clouds in sight when they reached the house.

"This is the best Christmas ever." Ursula peeled off her gloves, tucked them into her coat pocket, and hung it on the back of a kitchen chair. Then she unwound her scarf from around her neck and draped it over her coat. She kicked off her boots and set them on the rug beside the back door.

"Yes, it is, and every year that we are together will get just a little bit better," Remy said. "We should make an album for every year like your mama does, so we can enjoy looking back at all the memories we are going to make."

"I would love that," Ursula said. "But this morning, do we want coffee or hot chocolate while we open our presents?"

"Hot chocolate," he answered. "We can make it together. I'll get down the mugs."

The word *together* played over and over to a country tune in Ursula's mind. That summed up everything between her and Remy. They had separate lives in that he taught classes at the college, and she had her writing, but they shared everything else, from feeding cattle to working beside one another in the kitchen.

Just like Mama and Daddy, she thought.

"What are you thinking about?" Remy asked. "You're smiling like you've got a secret. Want to share it with me?"

"The word 'together,'" she said as she poured milk into the mugs and then added the hot chocolate mix. "Neither of us had very good role models with our biological fathers, but you had a grandpa and I have Daddy."

"We were really pretty lucky, weren't we?" Remy asked.

"It's like you can read my mind," Ursula replied.

Remy put the mugs in the microwave and set the timer for two minutes. "Soul mates can do that." He slipped his arms around her waist and pulled her close to him. "You've been a little distracted lately. I've got to admit, I was a little worried until you said you'd move in with me. I thought maybe you were going to tell me that we should slow our wagons down."

Ursula shook her head. "It's not that at all. I've saved the news until today, and I'll tell you the rest of it when we open our presents to each other."

Remy kissed her on the forehead. "Then I want to go first so I can hear what you've got to say."

The microwave timer dinged, and she took the two mugs out, added a few miniature marshmallows, and put them on a tray. "Of course, you can go first because I'm dying to tell you the news. I just found out yesterday, and it hasn't been easy keeping a secret from you."

"Are you pregnant?" He picked up the tray and led the way out of the kitchen.

"No, I'm not." That was the second time someone had asked her that same question in less than a week. Could it be an omen that she might be before long?

"I'm a little disappointed," Remy said with a hint of a sigh. "If you were, I would want to go to the courthouse as soon as it opens tomorrow morning. I do *not* want my son or daughter to grow up without a father."

"I won't argue with you on that issue," she said as she sat down on the floor in front of the tree, "but let's give ourselves and the families a little time to get used to us living together before I spring wedding planning on Mama."

"Honey, I'm sure she's already thinking about plans for you and for Luna," Remy said with a chuckle.

Ursula picked up three presents and handed them to Remy. "She's probably been planning weddings for all seven of us for years. I wouldn't be surprised if she hasn't already picked out colors, dresses, and floral arrangements."

"Do you have a problem with that?" Remy asked.

"Not one bit," Ursula replied. "I trust Mama's planning."

"Which one do I open first?" he asked.

"That one." She pointed toward what looked like a shirt box. "If you don't open it soon, I'm going to blurt out my news."

No one in the whole world could open a present more slowly and more carefully than Remy did. When he finished, there wasn't a single tear in the paper. "Why do I have three presents?"

"Because that's how many baby Jesus had—gold, frankincense, and myrrh—so each of us girls have always had three things to unwrap on Christmas morning," she answered. "But that didn't have anything to do with what Santa left for us and still doesn't. We each get one gift that's unwrapped and under the tree on Christmas morning from Santa. We used to put out cookies and milk for him, but after we were grown and away from home, Mama told us that he liked a can of beer and pretzels better."

"I would imagine that Joe Clay would like the latter much better." Remy chuckled. "But I've seen him put away his fair share of your mama's homemade cookies with a big glass of milk," he said as he eased the top off the box. "What is this?" He pulled a piece of copy paper from the box and glanced over at Ursula.

"Read it," she said. "My book has sold after a stiff bidding war, and that's a copy of the dedication page. The deadline for me to have it finished is the first day of March. My agent is negotiating the deal, and the publisher wants me to sign for two more books, making it the first of a three-book series. The advance is more than I made in my best year of teaching."

Remy read the words on the paper, laid it aside, and grabbed her in a fierce hug. "You dedicated it to me. Darlin', this is the best gift ever."

"I could have never started writing without your help," Ursula said past the lump in her throat.

"Will you sign a first-edition copy for me and maybe one for my mama?" Remy asked.

"Definitely," she said. "Now open the other two."

The second one held two plane tickets to Wyoming that were dated during his spring break in March. "I can't believe you did this."

"I can't wait!" she said with a smile.

The third one contained copies of plane tickets for his

mom and Alan from Wyoming to Texas over Mother's Day weekend.

"You are amazing," he said when he saw the note attached from his mother.

"I didn't think it was fair for me to get to spend the day with my mama and you to *not* get to see your mother on that particular holiday. Also, it would have been the first Mother's Day that you wouldn't get to be with her," Ursula told him.

"You've outdone yourself, and 'thank you' seems so little. I agree with you. This is the best Christmas ever. I can't wait for you to meet my mama and stepdad and for them to come back to Texas in May." Remy pulled her close to him in a hug and then strung kisses all over her face, with a thank-you between each one.

Finally, he scooted over a few inches and picked up one small box from under the tree. "I didn't know about the three-present rule, so you only get one this year. I'll try to do better next year."

"I've got three presents already," she told him. "I've got you, puppies, and the promise of a future with you. So this is my Santa present. I forgot to leave cookies and milk out for him, though."

"What I had last night beats cookies and milk and even beer and pretzels." He chuckled and wiggled his dark eyebrows.

She didn't follow his example but tore at the paper with the gusto of a hungry puppy. She opened a long, thin box to find another lovely red velvet one. When she snapped it open, there was a gorgeous white-gold bracelet with several charms already attached to it.

"I noticed that when you wear jewelry, it's silver or white gold," he said, "so I had this made up to match your other pieces."

"I love it," she whispered.

"That first little circle with a 21 etched on it is for the day when you came home to the Paradise, and the topaz up in the corner is for November. The heart with the tiny little diamond in the middle is for the first time we kissed, the little pumpkin with an emerald on the stem is for our first Thanksgiving together, and the tiny book with the black stone on the cover is to remind you of Daisy and the story you told me about her cast-iron skillet. The last charm is a Christmas tree with a ruby on the top, and it, of course, is for today. I plan to add charms to it through the years until there's no more room and then we'll start a new one," Remy explained.

"I do believe this is a lot more than one gift. To me, it will be like Mama's albums—a reminder of all the wonderful times we've shared on this journey through life that we're taking together." She handed it to him and held out her arm. "Would you, please, put it on for me?"

"I will fasten it around your wrist every time you want to wear it for the rest of our lives," he said as he fastened the bracelet around her wrist.

"Remy Baxter, are you proposing to me?" she asked.

"Not today, but be ready, because it's coming," he answered.

"When you do, can I have a little engagement ring to go on my bracelet?" she asked.

"Yes, my darlin', you can."

Mary Jane was just taking a huge pan of biscuits from the oven when Ursula and Remy came through the back door that morning. "Merry Christmas," she singsonged.

"Merry Christmas to all y'all," Ursula and Remy said at the same time.

"Luna and Shane should be here…" Joe Clay said and then cocked an ear toward the front door. "That's them coming in. Now, we're all here."

"Merry Christmas," Luna yelled from the foyer. "I smell bacon and coffee and hot biscuits. Did you make the Christmas breakfast casserole, Mama?"

"Of course I did," Mary Jane answered.

Ursula met Luna halfway across the foyer floor and held up her arm. "Look what Remy gave me." Her other sisters gathered around and listened while she explained the reason for each fancy little charm.

"That is so romantic," Tertia said with a long sigh.

"It's gorgeous," Luna said and touched her new necklace. Two entwined hearts with an emerald in the middle hung from the gold chain. "Shane says these are our hearts that are forever meshed together, and the emerald is for May—the month that we met right here at the Paradise."

"Let's all gather up in the living room around the Christmas tree and have a moment of silence to count our blessings before we have breakfast and open gifts," Endora said.

"After that moment, do we tell everyone what we feel like is our blessing, kind of like what we do at Thanksgiving when we tell something we are thankful for?" Rae asked.

"That's right, but being thankful for something and counting it as a blessing is two different things." Endora led the way into the living room and sat down on the sofa. "I'll even go first. My blessing this year is my family and my two kittens. I didn't realize and probably wouldn't have believed how much emotional support pets could help." She glanced over at the Christmas tree where Misty and Poppy, two little orange fur balls, were tucked up against Sassy's belly and she was giving them a bath. Pepper stood right behind Sassy, guarding them as if he were the size of a pit bull.

Bernie sat down beside Endora. "I could just say 'ditto,' but I count the fact that Pepper is getting along with Sassy as a blessing too."

"Mama Sassy and Poppa Pepper only seem to get along when the babies are concerned," Remy said. "When the kittens are off somewhere else, they still spit at each other."

"But they're nice in front of the children," Bernie said, "and that might be the very beginning of them learning to get along. What would you consider your blessing, Remy?"

"Everything that has happened the past few weeks," he answered and kissed Ursula on the cheek.

"My blessing is Remy, and…" Ursula paused before blurting out the rest of her news. "I'm moving in with him this afternoon."

"Well, halle-damn-lujah," Bernie squealed. "Don't fuss at me for cussin', Mary Jane. This is a big ole blessing for sure. When can we start talking about grandbabies?"

"Not today," Ursula answered, "but we do want a big family in the next few years."

"Well, I was going to wait until later to make my announcement," Luna said, "but since Ursula stole my thunder, I'm announcing the same thing. I'm moving in with Shane tomorrow morning. We'll help get Ursula settled, and then all of you can help me move. And the top of my blessing list is Shane."

"This is really the season of miracles," Bernie said with a sigh. "And once again, you are both welcome, my prophecies have come true. If any of the other five of you need help, just come to your aunt Bernie. I'm the guru of good relationships."

"Having three of my daughters come home to Spanish Fort is a dream come true"—Mary Jane beamed—"and that's my Christmas blessing."

"Make that four," Ophelia said. "I got an early out, and the papers are all signed. I'm not leaving after Christmas."

"Miracles, nothing!" Bernie gasped. "This is pure old magic. Pepper and I are both happy about all these blessings. I'll get busy finding you a boyfriend real soon, darlin'."

"Oh, no!" Ophelia gasped. "I need to settle in before—"

"Hey." Ursula raised a palm. "Don't argue with Aunt Bernie. That's like fighting city hall. It won't do a bit of good."

"But I…" Ophelia stammered.

"No amount of talking will help, but when in doubt about anything, she's always glad to share a bottle of Jameson with you, and it helps solve a lot of problems," Luna said.

"This is one awesome Christmas," Joe Clay declared. "My blessing is that I have had seven daughters and an amazing wife to share my life with for the past twenty years."

Tertia nudged Ursula with an elbow. "By next year, I bet all of the last three of us will be back in Spanish Fort. I am bullfrog green with envy right now. Do you think there might be a few more good men in this area?"

"Aunt Bernie will kick every mesquite bush in Montague County looking for the right five," Ursula said with a smile. "And, Tertia, I really, really hope that all of you will come home to stay. To have us all close by would mean so much to Mama, and"—she paused long enough to wipe a tear from her eye—"to me. I've missed us being together like this."

"I think we all have," Tertia said. "We've spread our wings and had our adventures, and now it's time to come back to put down roots."

Bo held up her hand. "I would like to say that I've been blessed with a record contract, but I haven't. I'm giving my dream until the end of next summer, and if nothing happens, I'm coming home. So my blessing this year is that I've got family who will support me no matter what I do."

"Amen," Tertia said. "What Bo said. Only I'm coming home to stay in time for Mother's Day."

"Ditto to what Bo said, only I'm not ready to throw in the towel with my job just yet," Rae added.

"Okay," Mary Jane said. "Let's go have breakfast before I start crying. Let me add a few more blessings to my list. That would be Joe Clay, my wonderful girls, and Aunt Bernie."

Ursula slipped her hand into Remy's and gave it a gentle squeeze. "Merry Christmas one more time. I love you," she whispered.

"Your love for me is the biggest blessing I will ever have, and I will never take it for granted. Merry Christmas to you, darlin'!" He leaned over and kissed her on the cheek.

The End

Read on for a peek at the next book in Carolyn Brown's
Sisters in Paradise series, *Sisters in Paradise*

Chapter 1

BOSSY. NOSY. SASSY.

Look up any one of those words in a dictionary or on the internet, and Ophelia Simmons was sure that her Great-Aunt Mary Bernadette's picture would be right there beside it.

Aunt Bernie, as everyone called her, was pint-sized. She was living proof that dynamite came in small packages and it didn't take old age settling in for her to speak whatever was on her mind. She had owned a bar in Oklahoma for more than fifty years, and everyone who came into Bernie's Place had to follow the rules posted on the wall right above the bar or else she would toss them out on their ear—or a lower part of their anatomy if need be.

"I told you so." Bernie smiled as she slid into the passenger seat of Ophelia's pickup truck and fastened the seat belt.

Ophelia grabbed a pair of sunglasses from the console and put them on. "You told me so about what?"

"Remember back at Christmas when I said that Ursula and Luna would be married before summer was over? Well, my prophecy is coming true," Bernie answered. "I've worked my magic on those two, and now it's time for me to use my powers on you and your sister. Tertia should be home tomorrow and my new prediction is that I'll have both of you in serious relationships in no time."

"Hey now!" Ophelia started the engine and drove down the lane to the main road. "Luna was already secretly dating Shane when you moved here, so you can't take credit for that."

Bernie crossed her arms over her chest. "You can think whatever you want. I know that it was my meddling that put Ursula and Luna right where they are today, and I do *not* intend to stop working my magic until I'm either dead or I have all you girls back here in Spanish Fort, settled down, and either in a serious relationship or married. The universe has told me that is why I'm here, and I don't argue with the universe."

"Why?" Ophelia was not worried about her Aunt Bernie dying anytime soon. Heaven was *not* ready for the likes of her, and the devil didn't want her for fear she would try to take over his domain and shove him out for good.

"Why am I not dead? Or why am I determined to get all seven of you sisters settled?" Bernie asked.

"The latter one," Ophelia answered.

"I owe your mama that much," Bernie said. "She's named after me and so are you. Mary Bernadette." She poked a finger toward her heart. "Mary Jane," she said glancing in the rearview mirror back at the Paradise, then pointing across the console at Ophelia. "Mary Ophelia. So y'all are special to me. Plus, she has taken me in and lets me be a part of her family. I didn't know what I would do after I sold my bar, but your mama invited me to come on down to Spanish Fort and live with her. I thought about it a few days and decided I didn't want to be a burden." She stopped for a breath.

"You are not a burden," Ophelia argued.

"Thank you, darlin', but I was thinking about the day that you girls all came home and wanted your own rooms again, and besides I'm no spring chicken—those stairs would have killed me when I got older. So, I bought my travel trailer and moved into the backyard."

Ophelia had heard the story before, just like so many others that Aunt Bernie told and retold. "Why are you determined that Tertia and I be your next projects?" she asked.

"You will both be here. It's not so easy to work on Bo and Rae when one of them is in the Oklahoma Panhandle and the other one is in Nashville, but they'll both come home soon," Bernie answered. "First, I'll fix you and Tertia up, and then it will be Bo and Rae's turn."

Ophelia started to say something then realized the turn to the winery was right in front of her. She braked hard enough to make Aunt Bernie use cuss words that could have cracked the front windshield. Gravel flew up around them and all the black birds that had been sitting on the barbed wire fence took to the sky in a blur. If Ophelia had been fluent in bird squawking, she was fairly sure that their swear words would have riveled Aunt Bernie's.

"That sign should be bigger," she gasped.

Bernie laid a hand on her heart. "Girl, you about gave me a heart attack. The deal I made with the universe is that I would not die until I accomplish my mission for your mama. If you kill me before that time comes, then you're going to be in for a helluva lot of bad luck."

"Sorry about that," Ophelia said. She turned right at the sign pointing her back to the winery. "I think I'll drag my feet in this relationship business just so you'll stay around for many more years. Maybe I'll even be the last one to settle down."

"That's not playing fair," Bernie declared. "And besides you are thirty-one years old. Your biological clock has already started ticking." Bernie cocked her head to one side. "I do believe I can hear it ticking off the seconds."

"All's fair in love and war," Ophelia reminded her as she pulled into a parking space in front of the winery.

Bernie shook her bony index finger across the console at Ophelia for the second time that morning. "Yes, it is, and I don't lose at either one."

Ophelia motioned toward the building in front of them and changed the subject. "This is not what I expected."

"Seems like an omen to me." Bernie pointed at the sign: *Brennan Winery* in a flourishing script with shamrocks and bunches of grapes circling the lettering. "That looks downright romantic, doesn't it?"

"A sign doesn't mean anything," Ophelia argued.

"It does today," Bernie said as she unfastened her seat belt, opened the door, and got out of the truck.

Another word that could be added to Bernie's long list was spry. The septuagenarian was halfway across the parking lot when Ophelia caught up with her. "We don't have to jog, Aunt Bernie," she said.

"I'm in a hurry to take a look inside…" She stopped and pointed to a sign tacked up beside the door that said HELP WANTED in big bold letters and under that in smaller type was: *Must apply in person. No online applications. Full-time work with benefits.*

"There's your answer to what you are going to do now that school is out," she said. "I just found you a job."

The bell above the door must have been hooked up to something because she and Bernie had only been inside a couple of minutes when a man entered the room from the back. His curly blond hair touched his shirt collar, and mossy green eyes rimmed with thick lashes twinkled behind his round, wire-rimmed glasses.

"Good mornin'." His deep Texas drawl was downright swoonworthy. "I'm Jake Donegal, the owner of this little winery. What can I do for you lovely ladies?"

Acknowledgments

As always, I have many people to thank for this book. First, my readers for asking for it. Then Deb Werksman and all the folks at Sourcebooks for giving me the opportunity to write about the sisters. My gratitude to Folio Management for representing me and to my agent, Erin Niumata, who has been on this journey with me for more than twenty-five years. Thanks to my family and to Mr. B, my husband and soul mate, who has stood beside me through all the ups and downs of living with an author.

About the Author

Carolyn Brown is a *New York Times, USA Today, Wall Street Journal, Publishers Weekly,* and #1 Amazon and #1 *Washington Post* bestselling author. She is the author of more than 125 works of fiction. She's a recipient of the Bookseller's Best Award, Montlake Romance's prestigious Montlake Diamond Award, and a three-time recipient of the National Reader's Choice Award. Brown has been published for more than twenty-five years, and her books have been translated into twenty-one foreign languages and have sold more than ten million copies worldwide.

When she's not writing, she likes to take road trips with her husband, Mr. B, and her family, and she plots out new stories as they travel.

Website: carolynbrownbooks.com
Facebook: CarolynBrownBooks
Instagram: @carolynbrownbooks
Twitter: @thecarolynbrown

Also by Carolyn Brown